The HIDEAWAY

BOOKS BY NORMA CURTIS

The Drowned Village

Striking a Balance
The Last Place You Look
Living It Up, Living It Down

NORMA CURTIS

The
HIDEAWAY

bookouture

Published by Bookouture in 2022

An imprint of Storyfire Ltd.
Carmelite House
50 Victoria Embankment
London EC4Y 0DZ

www.bookouture.com

ISBN: 978-1-80314-027-8
eBook ISBN: 978-1-80314-026-1

This book is a work of fiction. Names, characters, businesses, organizations, places and events other than those clearly in the public domain, are either the product of the author's imagination or are used fictitiously. Any resemblance to actual persons, living or dead, events or locales is entirely coincidental.

For Paul and Joe, with love

1

HEDI

PRESENT DAY

Ninety-three-year-old Hedi was sitting in the parlour in a strip of late afternoon sunlight, gripping her husband Harry's hand, keeping tight hold of him to save him slipping away. The sunshine was lighting up the tapestry sofa, the pale blue carpet, her halo of white hair and Harry's hand, tanned and speckled and veined, as it lay in hers.

'You must let me call the doctor,' she said, emotion tightening her throat.

Harry's faded green eyes were warm and steady. He smiled faintly and shook his head. Talking was an effort that took breath and energy. He spoke to her with his gaze, now.

She stroked his hair. It still had a few strands of copper amongst the grey, like the memories of the young man he had been. 'Don't you leave me, Harry,' she warned him sternly. *Don't you leef me, Herry.* After all these years, her accent still betrayed her.

Hedi felt a lurch of panic deep in her guts. She couldn't bear it. But she would bear it, all the same. And when he'd gone, she would follow him. That was her one consolation, that their separation would be mercifully brief. 'Can I get you anything, my darling?' she asked him.

His gaze moved from hers for a moment, towards the window where the sun shone in. His eyelashes glowed golden as he blinked. When he looked at her again, his expression was wistful.

'What is it?' she asked him. 'You want to be nearer to the window, is that it? See the view?'

He took a deep breath. She could see the steady pulse beat in his neck, under that soft skin above his collarbone, and she wanted to kiss it in gratitude for keeping on going.

'Hedi, my girl,' he said, his voice suddenly strong. 'Call Maggie.'

Hedi looked at him in surprise. She would do anything for him, but she hesitated, trying to read him and understand his intentions. 'You want that I call her now? After all these years?'

'Yes. Right now.'

He sounded like his old self and for a moment she was reassured enough to argue with him. 'Okay, but first you must eat.'

He took his hand out of hers and flicked it at her as if he was swatting away a fly. There was no mistaking what *that* meant.

'As you wish.' She pressed her lips tightly together in disapproval and got to her feet to look for the red leather address book. They used to keep it by the phone, but as most of the entries had an X crossed through the names, it had been put away in the bookcase somewhere, squashed in with old books, too many for them to read again at this time in their lives. What was the point of them? She didn't know why they kept them, and now she was getting irritable about it. 'All these books!' It was better to be cross with the books than with him.

The address book wasn't very big, which made the search difficult. She looked along the spines, hands on hips. *Why now, all of a sudden?* 'It's no use, Harry, I...' she started to say, and at the same time she saw it. *Oh. There.*

Hedi flicked through the address book. She hadn't listed their daughter under Lewis, she was under Maggie. There were many different addresses for her, running to two pages, but just one phone number, written neatly and with careful deliberation, underlined.

Hedi went to sit next to Harry again and showed him the page. 'Look,' she said, showing him. 'I found it.'

'Good,' he whispered.

'I don't know what you expect me to tell her. I will just tell her that you want to say hello, I guess.' Seeing Harry wince, she corrected herself and patted his knee. 'That *we* want to say hello.'

Hedi never consciously thought about her daughter these days, but it didn't stop her from worrying about her on a daily basis, with a deep sense of regret.

She and Harry had failed as parents, Hedi knew that. They'd only had one stab at parenthood, and they'd made a mess of it, spoiling this little miracle that had turned up in their lives to delight them after they'd long given up hope.

As a child, Maggie had been a constant source of wonder. They had doted on her, and told her how wonderful she was, and she *was* wonderful, that was the thing. Everyone said so. Her teachers loved her, she was made a prefect and head girl; you see, they weren't biased. Harry bought her a green enamelled prefect's badge with *Perfect* on it, and she'd enjoyed the joke even though she *was* perfect, and she knew it.

'I don't know,' Hedi said to Harry now as if she had spoken this thought aloud. 'Nobody's perfect.'

They'd just done a fine job of pretending.

The rift had started with an argument over lunch. Maggie had said she wasn't hungry.

Maggie refusing the food that was in front of her brought out something dark and uneasy in Hedi. But Maggie had stood her ground and defended herself angrily.

'You don't know what I've been through! You don't know what it's like to suffer!'

When Hedi had slapped Maggie on that unforgivable day, in her head she had been slamming the door on her past. But oh, that sound of palm against cheek was like the crack of a whip; she could still hear it now. Maggie had packed her bags and left, taking their granddaughter who had inherited Harry's copper hair. She'd never been back. Of course, what Hedi had done to her only daughter was unforgivable, she understood that perfectly well. However, to apologise was to explain, and she had kept her secret for so long that she knew she couldn't reveal it now.

'I'll call her, but you must speak to her.' She picked up the phone and keyed in the number with great deliberation and a certain amount of dread.

And then Maggie answered. *That voice!* It was as distinctive as her face in Hedi's memory.

Hedi's eyes rimmed with tears that flared in the sunlight. The tears were the relief of a mother finding her lost child again. 'Maggie, it's Hedi.' She thought of adding, *your mother*, for clarity, but how many Hedis were there? 'Harry wants to talk to you. Here, Harry, you take it.'

'Hello, my darling,' Harry said, pressing the phone against his face. 'Me? I'm fine.'

He closed his eyes and smiled. 'It's good to hear you. Tell me, how are you?'

Hedi took a deep breath and stood up, smoothing her dress. She felt anxious. She wanted to talk to Maggie, too, and she hoped she could find the right words, but even now some things came out wrong, or too abruptly, as if her tongue had a malicious life of its own.

She went to the window and looked down at the street. *So many cars!* All strung together and pulling slowly up the road.

And beyond the cars, the Heath, lost from sight under the canopy of trees.

'He sounds a good man,' Harry was saying. 'You hold on to him. And Thea? The little one? Is she with you in New York?'

Hedi sharply turned back into the room to look at him. Harry was nodding, and his eyes met hers, excited and energised by the conversation.

'Of course not,' he said quickly to his daughter, and he smiled gently. 'She's all grown up now, I realise that. I'm a fool. Time flies. But you're happy, that's the main thing.'

Hedi nodded in agreement, feeling relief. Wasn't that all they'd wanted for her, that she was happy?

She smiled as she watched Harry light up with joy. In her heart she wondered if that was all it was, after all, not a physical illness but just a deep longing to be with family again.

But suddenly his tone changed. 'Of course, I understand,' he was saying to his daughter. 'You must go. I know you're busy.' His animated face settled back into solemn folds again. His voice softened. He said, very deliberately, 'Goodbye, Maggie.' He dropped the phone as if his strength had suddenly left him, and he rested his head back.

Hedi felt as if her heart was being crushed. The phone call had not been a hello, after all. It had been a goodbye. She stared at him, wide-eyed with fear.

Harry closed his eyes and nodded off to sleep. He started snoring gently. Hedi tiptoed away to the kitchen and stood by the sink, burying her face in her hands. *We've lived too long already*, she thought desperately in the dark of her warm palms. *We've outstayed our welcome.*

She straightened up and pulled herself together. What was she doing here when she could be sitting next to him? For all that the afternoon seemed bleak, she knew that there was a worse time to come when she would look back at this moment and think: *Harry was still here then, it wasn't so bad after all.*

She sat on the sofa next to him, moved his limp hand onto her knee and listened fondly to his snoring. Once upon a time it had irritated her. On her honeymoon, sent crazy by lack of sleep, she accused him of keeping it a secret from her just so she'd marry him. The 'cures' they'd tried over the years! She had taped a rubber ball into his pyjama jacket so as to make it too uncomfortable for him to lie on his back. He had bought some kind of appliance, like a gumshield, to bring his jaw forward and open up his airways. They had spent a fortune on a mound of pillows, good ones, Hungarian goose down, which cost as much as the bed, to prop Harry up and keep his tongue forward. Nothing worked, and then miraculously, in her old age Hedi had gone deaf and what a blessing that turned out to be! She took her hearing aids out every night and sometimes even in the daytime if he was talking politics. He enjoyed his monologues a great deal, but Hedi had a fear of politics, with good reason.

She chuckled to herself. All these years, his snoring hadn't changed, it was one of the constants of their marriage, but other things changed, that was the way it was.

While she was thinking these things, the Earth moved on, turning the windows away from the eye of the sun so that she awoke and found herself sitting next to Harry in shadow, slumped comfortably against his shoulder. She wiped the corner of her mouth and straightened up.

She had been asleep, she realised.

Her gaze rested on the little red leather address book. It looked purple in the gloom. Outside in the dusk, she could hear children laughing.

It was the most sorrowful time of day for her, twilight, and it always had been; it was inexplicably sad in a way that the night was not. Night-time was romantic, lights twinkling on water, striped reflections rippling in the tide.

Quietness. The children had gone home.

She looked sharply at Harry. He wasn't snoring anymore,

and he looked very peaceful, his jaw open, his hand resting on her knee, heavy and cool.

Her breath caught in her throat. She felt her stomach tense in a swift jerk of fear, followed by a profound, resigned weight which settled on her. She sighed, reminded herself to breathe. He'd left her, just like that, gone in the quietness of dusk.

She leant against him and rubbed her cheek gently against the cool cotton of his shirt for comfort.

2

HEDI

Next morning, after the undertakers had gone, Hedi put an apron over her black dress and automatically started straightening up the Sunday supplements on the little mahogany table. Harry liked to browse through them during the week.

What was she doing it for? Like all those books, the supplements were never going to be read.

She fetched a recycling bag from the kitchen and put them in it. *There.*

Hedi knew that she had to tell Maggie about Harry and at the same time say her own goodbyes. She was dreading it, because the important thing was not to make Maggie feel guilty or in any way responsible for cutting off Harry's call.

She sat on the sofa with the phone on her lap, considering her words carefully.

It would have made no difference, she would assure Maggie, whether she had carried on the conversation for another hour or the rest of the day, because Harry would have left at the end of it either way. It was what he had been hanging on for, to say goodbye to his daughter.

And once it was over, as his old self would have said, *job done.*

Hedi decided she would lie and tell Maggie the end had been sudden and unexpected.

She wouldn't tell her she had been waiting for it for ten years at least, in the low-level way of the long-married. Once they turned eighty, and had a cough or a cold, or some memory lapse that involved the keys disappearing and turning up in some odd and unexpected place, they would look silently but speculatively at each other and wonder: *Is this the beginning of the end?*

At least he'd gone first, and she was glad about that, not for the selfish reasons of being the last one standing but because being left was so much more painful than being the one to leave. And she had saved him from dying alone. That was her consolation.

All things considered, it was far better that she followed after him. She wasn't afraid. They saw death differently. Harry saw the hell. His experiences as a young soldier had marked him for life, changed his DNA, which was to be expected. But Hedi saw death as a refuge.

She pinched her lower lip between her thumb and forefinger and picked up the address book. At least Maggie had company over there in New York. *He sounds a good man*, Harry had said. She hadn't asked him who, but Harry had an instinct for these things, and she was glad Maggie had someone there to look after her. She picked up the phone, her mouth suddenly dry, and called Maggie's number.

'Yup?' Maggie asked abruptly.

'You're busy,' Hedi said. She could hear the television in the background.

'I'm always busy. But,' Maggie conceded, 'I can talk.'

All of a sudden, Hedi found that she couldn't get the words out. She felt as if they were clogging her throat and suffocating her.

'What is it? Is it Harry?' Maggie asked.

'He's gone,' Hedi whispered.

'Oh.' Maggie sounded shocked. 'So that's what that call was all about. I knew he couldn't be just ringing for a chat after all these years. Why on earth didn't he tell me he was ill? Why didn't *you* tell me?'

'Who knows these things – when a person is going to go?' Hedi replied defensively. 'Nobody knows, even the doctors don't know, don't let them tell you otherwise.' This too was a lie; the dying person understands perfectly well that he can leave this life at a time of his own choosing.

She heard the sharpness in her own voice and regretted it. 'I'm so sorry, my darling,' she said. 'I wish things had been different.'

'Is that an apology?' Maggie gave a dry laugh. 'Ha! You never apologise.'

Hedi closed her eyes, hating herself. 'It's true. One of my many failings.'

All the way across the ocean, in New York, to the background sound of the television, she listened to her daughter sniffing back tears. She wanted to take her in her arms and comfort her.

'I'm not crying because I'm upset,' Maggie said after a moment.

'Oh,' Hedi replied. 'That's good.' *Thet's goot*, she heard herself say. 'Harry wouldn't want you to be. The funeral is next Wednesday, at two. Come and stay. I've booked a car to take us to the crematorium. It will be good to have you here. You will come, won't you?'

Maggie didn't respond.

Long moments passed, and Hedi held tight on to the phone, waiting, hearing the television in the background, listening, feeling her heart fluttering nervously behind her ribs.

'The thing is,' Maggie said, her voice breaking, 'if you want the truth, I just assumed you and he had passed away a long time ago. You've been dead to me for years, and I've come to terms with that. What's the point in me coming to his funeral now?'

It hurt, and the feeling was so intense it took Hedi's breath away. It was like the slamming of a coffin lid, the heartless matter-of-fact way she said it. 'Please, Maggie...' she began, and realised she was listening to silence. 'Hello?'

Too late. She'd gone. Hedi stared at the phone.

There were no second chances, no going back to Maggie's childhood and starting again from scratch.

Hedi rubbed her face vigorously with her apron. *So. That was that.*

She went to stand in front of the wall of bookshelves. Getting rid of those books was a good place to start, because it needed no thought at all – she would get rid of the lot of them in one fell swoop. That was the easy bit.

There were other possessions that would prove more difficult to let go, and she would leave them until last. She kept them in an old tan-leather suitcase, her watches, and her tin bowl and metal spoon, their special photograph, and Harry's letter from Colonel Gonin: well-read and worn along the creases. There was a red lipstick, the colour of which was as bright now as the day it changed her life. *What a day that had been!* They were things which bore testament to the past. These she would put her mind to later. In the meantime, she would box up the books and get someone to take them away. *Crazy! So many books!*

She went to fetch the leaflet from the council on how to arrange collections – it was stuck to the fridge with a magnet of St Paul's Cathedral. She picked up the phone again. She had a lot to do. *I'm coming, Harry my boy.*

The sooner she got started, the sooner she could join him.

3

THEA

Thea was driving west with the window open, heading towards the coast along a road lit up with sunshine, her copper hair tied back, the breeze in her face. It was one of those days that looked as good as it felt.

She loved her job as a school secretary – she had an office to herself and five weeks holiday in the summer.

Adam was the other reason she was here. He was the tall, tanned art teacher who had a way of looking at things intently: flowers, the sky, buildings... and her.

Yesterday afternoon, on the last day of term, he'd come into the office as she was tidying up. He had a smear of yellow paint on his jawline. She went to wipe it off, her fingers lingering near his mouth, when he said perfectly seriously and out of the blue, 'Let's get married this summer, have a baby.'

Then, in a strange, out-of-body experience, she seemed to take a step back. It was as if she was watching herself through the wrong end of a telescope, completely objectively, going through the motions of an unsatisfactory lie but she couldn't stop herself. She had a problem with commitment.

'I'm going away for the summer, Adam. Sorry! Should have mentioned it before now.'

Adam had raised his dark eyebrows and scratched the back of his neck. His eyes searched hers, puzzled and hurt. 'Where to?'

She put the dust cover over the school computer. 'I'm not sure, yet. The coast. That's all I know.'

'Ah. Going where your spirit takes you.'

'Yeah. That's it,' she agreed.

So last night she'd left her flat in London, had a good night's sleep in a Premier Inn, a full English breakfast which was included in the price of the room, and no clear plans, other than to follow her strong compulsion to keep driving. Adam would have the whole summer to forget her.

For a moment she imagined the way he'd seen her, or as she hoped he had, as a confident, independent woman with no ties.

The feeling of disassociation came over her again and she was suddenly tearful.

Or as someone who has finally lost her mind.

An hour into her journey, Thea was heading along a narrow country road through deep countryside when she was halted by a set of temporary traffic lights glowing red. *Why?* There was no other traffic on the road but her. Impatient to arrive at her unknown destination she tapped her fingers on the steering wheel. Somehow, she still had a flake of yellow paint under her fingernail. She waited for the lights to change.

As Thea took deep breaths to calm her frustration because this wasn't the first set of roadworks she'd come across, she noticed a crooked To Let sign half-hidden in the buttercups and long grass of the verge. It was home-made: rough black lettering on a piece of wooden board with an arrow pointing to a right-hand turn. The name on the sign was The Hideaway.

The name grabbed her.

She would have missed the sign if it hadn't been for the roadworks, but she hadn't, so when the lights changed Thea decided to satisfy her curiosity and take a look.

She turned right and drove a short way down a bumpy, potholed dirt track, past a small, dark wood, and there it was, a small white cottage at the edge of a field. The grass growing wild around it was threaded with purple foxgloves. It looked as if the cottage had gradually settled into the earth, becoming part of it.

Thea parked up on the track and waded through the long grass. A red door, paint peeling, faced across the meadow. It was locked. In the window was a small, yellowing note which looked as if it had been there for some time. She cupped her hands around her eyes and inside she saw a bedroom with a clawfoot bath and to the left, a kitchen area. She dusted her hands together and walked around the side of the cottage.

A wooden outhouse, a kind of lean-to, had been tacked onto it and the peeling door was ajar. She switched the light on. Spiders scurried into corners. The ceiling was festooned with cobwebs, and the fly-speckled light bulb cast a dim yellow circle of light over the lavatory.

I mean, seriously, she thought, switching the light off and wiping her hands on her jeans with a shudder. *Who in their right mind would rent this place?*

She closed the outhouse door and looked at the surroundings. The wildflower meadow, she guessed, was once a garden. It sloped down gently, and some distance away, a backdrop of trees grew thickly on a hill.

Intrigued, she walked down the field and to her delight she found it bordered an estuary. Even better, a silvering wooden jetty, roughly constructed, jutted out into the glittering water.

Thea stepped onto the jetty cautiously, testing it. It felt solid enough. There were gaps between the planks large enough to get her heels caught in, so she took her shoes off and walked to the end and looked across the water, hands on hips. She gave a shiver of pleasure.

Directly across the water, at the base of the tree-covered hill, was a white hotel with cars tucked away to one side. People were eating at wooden tables in the shade of blue umbrellas by the water's edge.

Holidaymakers.

She'd always liked that word, as if a holiday wasn't something you undertook, it was something you constructed for yourself.

The estuary was dazzling in the midday light. This was a view a person would never get bored with, she thought, no matter how long they lived here. To the left of the hotel a wooden bridge stretched across from one side of the water to the other. From where she was standing, the river wound its way out of sight in both directions.

That hotel bar would be my local, she thought. She looked down through the gaps in the planks. The sunshine illuminated green weeds undulating in the current. *On evenings when I'm feeling too lazy to walk, I'll just carry a glass of wine down here and watch the sun setting over the river.*

Thea stood there for some time, mesmerised, memorising the scene, the breeze playing with her hair, until at last she turned and made her way back along the jetty, wading through the long, sweet grass, stirring the scent of blossom with each stride, disturbing insects and grass seeds. Imagining the place was hers.

She stopped a little way back from the house and took her phone out of the back pocket of her jeans and switched it on to take photographs. It looked so beautiful with the bright green grass, the purple foxgloves, the red door, the dark woods behind it, and then, just as she'd got it into perfect focus, she changed her mind and tucked her phone away again. There was some-

thing intensely real and unforgettable about this place. She
didn't want to diminish it. She walked all the way around the
building. At the back, shaded by the woods, was the window of
another bedroom. She trailed her hand along the rough white-
washed walls and back on the doorstep she stepped onto the
stone threshold and put her palms flat against the red door. The
wood was warm in the sunlight.

Mine.

She wasn't avaricious by nature, but she wanted to possess
it, greedily. It felt old, and yet solid, decades of DNA imprinting
the place. There was value in age.

It felt like home, like someplace she'd already known and
finally come back to: this cottage, this grass, that view. But it had
another quality that attracted her, and it was to do with the
neglect, the cobwebs, the dust. It felt unloved, and she could
relate to that.

She sat on the doorstep cross-legged, resting her arms on her
knees, looking out at the view beyond the meadow and feeling a
low-level thrill of excitement.

What am I doing?

She'd got sidetracked. She'd started out on this journey
intending to look for a beach. She wondered – awful thought –
if she was turning into her mother, falling wildly in love with
dreams.

But as she sat on the doorstep watching a bumblebee
wriggle comically into a flower, she realised she was perfectly
happy, like the happiness of dreams. The dream had rekindled
enjoyment in her for the first time in days. And everyone knew
that fresh air was good for the soul.

This place is good for the soul, she thought stubbornly. *The
Hideaway.* If she could stay here a month to think and sort
herself out, that would do it. But she was getting ahead of
herself. Firstly, she had to find out whether she could afford it.

Can't hurt to ask, she thought, getting to her feet. She was just making an enquiry, just out of curiosity. *Why not?*

In the window the yellowing paper with the fading phone number on it looked as if it had been there for a long time. She keyed it into her mobile and realised there was no signal. *Great.* Walking back down the meadow with the phone in front of her, she was looking for a bar. She got one by the jetty and tried again. The phone rang and went to voicemail.

'Oh, yeah, hi, I've just seen your sign saying that The Hideaway is for rent. My name is Thea Lewis. I would be grateful if you could call me back. Thanks. Bye.'

Now what?

Voices drifted to her from the white hotel on the other side of the river. She sat on the edge of the jetty, rolled up her jeans, took her shoes off, dangled her feet in the chilled water and waited for the phone to ring.

4

HEDI

Hedi took a deep breath, stood up while holding her black jewellery box and looked around. *What a mess.* She had created chaos out of order – the room looked as if it had been ransacked. It was going to take a long time to sort things out if she carried on in this unmethodical manner. And it wasn't just her history that she was sorting out, either, it was Harry's, too.

There was some jewellery in a little box which could go to a charity shop. She would be buried wearing her gold wedding ring.

She thought about the Hungarian man who had sold it to her, a shifty, take-it-or-leave-it type. He had watched her as she weighed it doubtfully in the palm of her hand. It felt like nothing.

'But it's so thin! Won't it wear away?' she had asked him.

'It will last as long as your marriage,' he'd mocked.

And so it had proved. She held out her hand now to look at it. The ring was as shiny as new on her wrinkled hand and though her blue veins were prominent, her nails looked good.

Maybe Maggie's little girl would wear it eventually.

Little girl! Listen to her! She was as bad as Harry.

Thea would be a woman now, a woman in her thirties.

Her attention came back to the task in hand. She looked in dismay at the papers, books, old purses containing currency that was no longer legal tender, pens that didn't work, writing pads containing appointments written in a shorthand that she could no longer decipher.

She had made a start on clearing the books, but they were very heavy to carry down the stairs and she had only been able to carry three or four at a time.

She went to the wardrobe to fetch the small tan-leather suitcase. She sat on the bed and opened it to console herself. There they were, her treasures, the few things that meant something, the material things. Anything else that she had accumulated along the way – compassion, pragmatism, stoicism, love, the qualities that Harry had loved in her, these things would die with her.

She felt grief for her own hidden self.

There's no one left who knows me.

And she had only herself to blame.

Later that day she took the last of the bin bags down and she stood on the doorstep holding down the skirt of her black cotton dress. Her muscles were aching and her knees hurt. All morning, she had struggled to carry them down the stairs and now she was watching the men from the council toss them into the back of their truck as if they were nothing.

She didn't feel much of anything, watching the men. Certainly, she had no regrets. '*Beggage,*' she said aloud.

There. They threw the last bag in, closed up the truck, got into the cab and drove down the hill. Her first job was done.

She turned to go back inside and was startled by her neighbour, Joy, who was watching her from the shady hall they shared, her arms folded over a grey blouse, a barricade of condemnation.

In all her life, Hedi had never known a person so misnamed as Joy. Her parents must have given her the name out of irony, or spite.

Joy wore her grey hair in a sharp, no-nonsense, jaw-length bob held out of her eyes by hair grips. She spoke like a school-teacher, all commands and reprimands, and Hedi had had enough of that kind of attitude to last her for a lifetime.

'I heard a lot of noise,' Joy said. 'Comings and goings.' It was a statement tinged with disapproval.

Hedi raised her chin. 'Is that so?'

Harry had introduced her to that phrase as a way of taking the heat out of arguments. You could use it very effectively in any circumstances in which someone was spoiling for a fight. 'Is that so' acknowledged their statement while at the same time neither agreeing nor disagreeing. It was, said Harry, who had been a keen rugby player in his younger days, like being passed the ball in a game and then dropping it and walking away, avoiding the chase and the scrum.

Hedi had argued that Harry's analogy was very poor indeed in her view, because as a rugby player, the try and the scrum were surely what the game was all about.

'Is that so?' Harry had replied.

So there they were, Hedi standing in the open doorway at the top of the steps with the wind blowing her hair and Joy blocking the hallway, squinting in the daylight and planning a fresh gambit by the looks of things. She seemed to be expecting an apology for the noise or, at the very least, an explanation for the comings and goings.

'I wondered if you were moving,' Joy said. It sounded like an accusation.

'Moving?'

'Now that Harry's... gone.'

'Moving?' Hedi said. 'No, I'm not moving, but actually as a matter of fact I am intending to go away.'

'Oh.' Joy was momentarily perplexed. 'You mean on holiday? Anywhere nice?'

Hedi raised her fine eyebrows and thought about it for a moment. 'I hope so,' she replied. Wherever Harry had gone, she was going, she had no doubts about that. She would like to believe in an afterlife, but if there wasn't one, who was she going to complain to? *No refunds.*

'I thought you might be moving into sheltered accommodation,' Joy said, fishing. 'Or one of these places with a warden.'

'A warden? What kind of place?' Hedi was offended. 'Some prison, you mean?'

Joy frowned, as if she suspected facetiousness. 'You know I try my best to keep an eye on you, but I worry about you, with you being on your own now and with the stairs and everything. Up and down, up and down! I have many interests to attend to as you know, but I can't relax for thinking you could have a fall at any moment. I'm not always going to be here for you to call on.'

'But why would I call on you? When have I ever done that?' Hedi demanded. 'Never!' The whole notion of asking Joy for help appalled her. 'For your information, I too have many interests to attend to. And just so that you know, I am going to be using those stairs a lot in the coming days. I will try not to be so negligent as to have a fall that might inconvenience you. Now, excuse me please.'

She stepped inside the hallway and slammed the front door behind her. The hallway was dark, with no natural light to illuminate it. Momentarily blind, Hedi assumed that Joy would stand aside to let her pass. But she didn't, and Hedi bumped straight into her. It was a surprisingly soft collision but Joy let out a shriek.

As Hedi groped for the banister, Joy found the light switch.

'There was no need for *that*,' she called after her accusingly as Hedi made her way up the stairs.

Hedi's heart was thumping in distress. As clear as day, she could hear Harry's warning voice in her head, rueful but loving: *You be careful, my girl.*

5

THEA

Thea was still sitting on the wooden jetty, the sun hot on her head, looking down at the water and smiling as a swift, shadowy shoal of fry swam past her feet, when the phone rang. She snatched it up. 'Thea Lewis.'

'Hello, Martin Evans, here,' a man said in a rich Welsh accent. 'I was just serving a customer, I was. To tell you the truth, I'd forgotten all about that sign for The Hideaway. The cottage has been empty for a couple of years now and to be honest with you, it's in a state of neglect.'

'I know,' Thea said. *And I don't care*, she almost added, glancing up across the meadow towards the house, white and square through the striped green screen of grass. She kicked her legs in the water. 'I'm here now, actually.'

'In that case, call round, and I'll give you the key so you can look round. I'm in the village, my greengrocer's is next to the church.'

'Okay. Where's the village?'

'Turn right out of the drive and it's four-hundred yards down the road. You can't miss it.'

Thea went back to the car. She drove past a sign: *WELCOME*

TO *BEAR CAVE*. She saw a woman in a trench coat walking a dog and she pulled up to ask her if she knew where Martin Evans's shop was.

The woman nodded and pointed up the road. 'See the chapel? And the grocer's next to it? That's Martin's shop. I've just come from there, as it happens. Bread and cheese,' she added, patting her bag. 'He does a lovely Caerphilly.'

The small row of shops included a charity shop, a bank and a newsagent. The greengrocer's had a colourful display of fruit and vegetables arranged outside it. Inside, it smelled of freshly ground coffee.

The grocer was cleaning cheese crumbs from a marble slab. He was a tall, even-featured man in his sixties with short grey hair in a neat side-parting and he smiled at her as she entered the shop. 'You must be the young woman I've just been speaking to.'

Thea was so nervous that she plunged straight in with the main thing on her mind. 'First of all, how much is the rent?'

'I was looking for a hundred a month – bills on top, mind.'

'A hundred a *month*?' Thea repeated, wondering if she'd got it wrong. 'I could take it for a month.'

'You'd better have a good look at the place, first though. Two problems – you can't get a phone signal in the house, and I'll tell you another thing that puts people off.' He hesitated as if he was confessing to a misdemeanour. 'There's no Wi-Fi.'

'Ah. Okay.'

'Well,' he said, shrugging, 'there you have it. It's not to everyone's taste, is it? People expect a phone signal and Wi-Fi when they're on holiday, don't they?'

Thea found herself nodding. 'Yes, that's true.' He was, she thought, the worst salesman ever.

'It's a shame because it's a beautiful place. Peaceful. A house doesn't like to be empty. It loses faith in itself. Take your time and have a good look around, get the feel of it. See what you think.' He reached under the counter. 'Here's the key,' he said, dangling it by a length of string. 'Take your time. There's no rush, I don't close till five thirty, but if you miss me, just drop it through the letter box.'

Thea took the key. 'Thank you, that would be great. Can I ask, is anyone else interested in it?'

Martin Evans chuckled. 'Don't worry, if they start queueing round the block, I'll tell them you were first in line.' He said it in a kindly, reassuring way that made her smile.

With the key in her hand and feeling dazed, Thea headed back to her car. She felt slightly unreal and reckless, as if she was doing drunk internet shopping. It was that same kind of thrill, of acting out of character with no inhibitions. Sitting behind the wheel, she opened her hand and looked at the key. Her plan had been to head towards the sea. But there was no harm in having a look inside, was there, just out of curiosity – *why not?* And then she could drop the key off again with a cheerful thank you and tell him that he was right, the place was not quite suitable for her needs or something equally polite.

But as Thea drove back along the road and bumped down the dirt track again, she had the same feeling as before: that she was coming home. She passed the small wood on the right, a mix of deciduous trees carpeted by last year's leaves, and she was back at The Hideaway. There was the cottage nestled in the grass. She felt emotional. Tears pricked her eyes, and she was overwhelmed with gratitude at the beauty of the place. She felt the same intense blend of happiness and sadness that she experienced watching the dawn break or witnessing kindness.

Once more, she waded through the long grass to the red door. The key turned easily in the lock and the door opened. The kitchen was dusty and warm with sunlight. Cooker, sink, a log burner in the corner, a sofa and chair with green bamboo-print covers, a fold-up wooden table with four dining chairs slotted beneath it.

She went through to the bedroom with the bath under the window. The other room, at the back, had a bed and a chest of drawers. It was cooler, shadier with the woods behind. The green leaves dappled shadows on the wall.

Hang on a minute. Sitting on the edge of the bed, something occurred to her. Martin Evans had said a hundred a month, not a hundred *for* the month. *The place has an outside loo,* Thea thought. And no Wi-Fi or phone signal.

What about Adam?

Why couldn't he leave things as they were? They wanted different things.

He'd asked her to think about it, so she'd driven away – driven here – without a plan.

She walked around each room again. *I love it*, she thought, tucking her hands in her jeans. She went back into the room with the bath, looked through the window and continued her conversation aloud. 'Tell you what. If I shouldn't take it, give me a sign. I don't mind what kind of a sign, as long as it's obvious. I'll leave it up to you.'

She gave Fate a good few moments to think about it.

There were apparently no objections.

Thea suddenly felt a feeling of release, as if a weight had lifted off her. 'That's settled, then,' she said. The roadworks, the hand-painted sign, the good feeling, the trusting landlord, she was being funnelled into a new life that she'd never expected.

She walked back to the greengrocer's, and as Martin Evans was busy, she put some apples and plums in a couple of paper bags and joined the queue to pay.

'Apples, plums and one Hideaway,' she said with a smile when she got to the counter.

He laughed and weighed the fruit. 'You know, I had a feeling you'd say that. You look as if you've fallen in love.'

And that, Thea thought, *was what it felt like*, as if she'd fallen in love with the place. 'Can I pay you the deposit tomorrow, with the first month's rent?'

'Oh, no, there's no need for a deposit. Pay me the rent at the end of the month when you've got your money's worth. It will be nice to have someone living there. It'll need a bit of an airing, but it will do it good to be lived in again. My wife will pop round in the next hour and bring you some clean bed linen and towels, and she'll give it a once-over for you. There should be enough wood by the stove to keep you going for a while in this weather. Is there anything else you want to know?'

'What's the name of the place across the estuary? It's a kind of long white building overlooking the water.'

He smiled. 'That's the George III Hotel. Part of it once belonged to the old railway station that used to run along the banks towards the coast. The railway's gone now but the signal is still there, as a reminder, a salute if you like, to its past. It's a beautiful place, and serves good food, too. You can drive there over the toll bridge but, mind you, it costs 8op and it closes at six thirty, so you might find you have to walk back.' He smiled cheerfully. 'Although in my opinion, that's no hardship.'

'No, I agree.'

'And now, may I ask you something?'

Thea twirled the key on the end of the string, thinking he was going to ask for references. 'Yes, of course.'

'Your name,' he said, 'Thea Lewis. I wondered if you had family connections here?'

Thea laughed. 'No, not that I know of. I wish I did! But I feel as if I've been drawn to the place because I had this dream that I was on a long sandy beach and...' she paused and gave a self-conscious, one-shouldered shrug. She didn't want him to think she was all woo-woo. '... I came to see if I could find it.'

'In that case, you're nearly there.' He put the two neat brown packages of fruit on the counter in front of her. 'Carry on going along this road, six miles or so, and you're going to come to

a beautiful stretch of coast, even if I do say so myself. Miles of
sand and sea. Your dream place.'

Thea looked at Martin suspiciously but he seemed perfectly
serious. She laughed. 'Okay. Thanks.' She put the key in her
pocket and picked up the fruit.

Martin's wife drove up shortly after Thea got back, bringing
with her a vacuum cleaner, dusters and polish, kitchen spray,
sponges, fresh bed linen and towels.

'I don't know what he's thinking,' she greeted Thea, 'letting
you move into the place when it hasn't been touched in months!
That's men for you! I'm Sian.'

'Thea. Thea Lewis.'

'I tried to call you to say I was coming, but there's no signal.'

Sian Evans looked a lot younger than her husband – early
fifties, Thea guessed. She had rich brown hair, cut short. She
was wearing a tan-leather waistcoat over a blue check shirt and
jeans. Her face was open, free of make-up, brown from the sun.
She radiated efficiency.

'Let's start with making the beds,' Sian said. 'I always think
the bed is the most important part of the house, don't you?'

Thea laughed. 'I've never thought about it.'

'A good night's sleep and you can tackle the world,' Sian
said. She picked up a pillow and buried her face in it. 'I was
worried it might be damp, but it feels fine. See what you think.'

Thea buried her face in it too. 'Fine,' she agreed.

Between them they unfolded the white bed linen and made
up the beds. Sian plumped up the pillows and Thea fluffed the
duvet.

While Sian wiped down the surfaces, Thea vacuumed,
getting all the cobwebs out of the corners. It was funny how
cleaning a house made it feel like home, she thought as they
worked.

Sian tackled the bath and hung the red towels over the side. She stood back admiringly. 'There! It looks better already!' She took the yellowing notice out of the window and folded it up. Then she checked through the cupboards. 'There's enough china and cutlery here for four. It was supposed to be a holiday let, but the whole Wi-Fi thing put people off staying. To be honest, it was the first thing they'd ask. "What's the password?" Right! We've just got the windows to do and clear the cobwebs out of the privy then we can have a coffee to reward ourselves.'

'I'm afraid I haven't got any coffee yet,' Thea said. 'I can offer you apples and tangerines, though.'

'Martin's made you up a welcome pack. Milk, tea, coffee. Biscuits too, knowing him. He likes his biscuits.'

'In that case...'

Sian was taller than Thea, so she cleaned the outside of the windows and Thea cleaned the inside.

'Look at that!' Sian said, folding up the cloths when they'd finished, while Thea picked cobwebs off the feather duster. 'It makes all the difference to let the sun into a place.'

They sat by the table to drink the coffee and Thea became aware of Sian's inquisitive gaze.

'Have you come far?'

'London.'

'This is a change for you, then!' Sian sat, her head cocked, waiting for Thea to continue the conversation, and when she didn't, she prompted her. 'Broken heart?'

Their eyes met, and for a moment Thea was on the brink of tears. Kindness always affected her that way. 'Yes,' she said. 'That's right.'

'I thought so. Time out, right? It helps if you can disconnect yourself for a while. Absence makes the heart grow fonder and all that. Just because it's a cliché doesn't mean it isn't true. Don't let him back into your life too soon, give him time to realise what he's missing.'

She made it sound delightfully simple. Thea stirred her coffee thoughtfully. 'It's not exactly what you think.' She wasn't ready to talk about it yet, and even if she did, what could she or anyone say to make it better? 'But you're right about taking time out. I feel as if I've just got to come to terms with things. It's easier to block them out in a way by keeping busy, but it's like a stampede going on in my head. I thought if I could find some space and light to be calm in and find some sort of way to sort it out...' She rested her cheek in the palm of her hand.

'Don't worry. You'll find it.'

Sian said it with such conviction that Thea laughed. 'Maybe I will. I hope so. My friend says I'm running away.'

'So what if you are? Sometimes in life, running away is the right answer.'

'Yeah. Never looked at it that way before.' Thea looked at Sian's tanned, confident face and got the feeling she was speaking from experience.

Sian finished her coffee and got to her feet. She unplugged the vacuum cleaner and retracted the lead. 'I'll take this back with me but I'll leave the cleaning things under the sink for you.' She smiled and looked around. 'This place used to be a pigsty.'

'It was trashed?'

Sian laughed. 'No, it was an actual pigsty. The farmer had to give up the pigs because he got too fond of them. He's more a cow man, now. You'll see them on the marshes keeping cool. Well! I'll be off.'

Thea followed Sian outside to her car. 'Thank you,' she said.

'No, no, don't mention it,' Sian said.

Thea watched her drive off. She thought, going back into the house, it was true, it did make a difference having the windows cleaned. Everything was shining, bouncing back the light. She walked around it. It was small, compact, like a play-house, and she couldn't believe her luck.

This is mine!

She lay on the bed, with her hands behind her head. The bed was soft, the linen was fresh. Right by the window, the breeze blew the purple foxgloves so they bobbed and tapped on the window. From here she could see the trees on the hill in the distance, and a strip of blue sky.

Thea had no timetable to keep, no phone to distract her and no one in the world to worry about. She stretched her arms out like a starfish and felt the tension slowly leave her muscles. In a word, she felt blissful.

But that was about to change.

6

HEDI

Hedi was sitting on the floor of the living room, making her way through two towering piles of photograph albums. The task was depressing. And puzzling. Some of the photographs they'd kept baffled her, especially the views. She stared at them blankly. *Views of where, exactly?* Of places she had no memory of ever having been. In any case, how could you reduce a mountain to a print? You admire a mountain for its majesty. To reduce it flattened it to nothing.

There were photographs of Maggie through the years: *happy, happy, happy – where had it gone, that happiness?* It had disappeared with her childhood.

And there were black-and-white pictures of Hedi and Harry outdoors, sitting on a tree trunk, taken on his Kodak which had a timer. It was like looking at two strangers, both of them formally dressed in suits. Hers was bottle-green, she recalled, and the skirt came below the knees; she remembered it well. She stared at these for a long time, feeling that if she stared hard enough, she could return into their heads, and into their thoughts. *Those smiles! Were we really that happy?*

'Yes, Harry my boy,' she murmured. 'We were, weren't we? Most of the time, we were.'

There were groups of people, too, with her and Harry amongst them, all of them smiling around a table, glasses raised. *Who were they?* She'd forgotten their names and now there was no one to ask. Snuffed out of her memory like a dead match.

It had been elastic, their relationship. Many times over the years they'd pulled apart, but at a certain point, thank heavens, they'd always snapped together again. The tension had never gone to breaking point. It had come close, though. On her fortieth birthday, after too much wine, after the guests had gone home, she'd said to him, 'If you're ever going to leave me, Harry, do it now, while I've still got time to find someone else.' Because she'd seen the way he looked at... no, it was no use, the name had gone. One of the guests, anyway; younger than Hedi was. *Cheryl?* Vivacious, extrovert, with curly brown hair to her shoulders. An actress with an amateur theatre company. Radiating energy and sex appeal, as Hedi remembered it, her face close to Harry's, her hand on his arm. She'd felt a furious, burning agony.

Go to her now, with my blessing.

Meaning: *get the pain over with. I saw the way you looked at her.*

And Harry's face. What could you really tell from a face, anyway? Considering it.

She had a flash of the feeling of *them and me*. Why didn't she think to fight for him? It was as if she had had no power.

You must remember, I was familiar with that feeling.

It was unlike the easy job of getting rid of the books, to which she had said goodbye without a qualm. With the photographs she felt a compulsion to scrutinise each one before she threw it away. It might contain clues to the meaning of life, like a giant jigsaw puzzle. You could only see the whole picture once the puzzle was complete. There! That flash of red, which could have been a sweater or a rose, turns out now to be a smile.

Better minds than hers had pondered the meaning of life.

Procreation. The survival of the species. Maybe that was all it was.

We made a very poor show of procreation.

Hedi's thoughts jumped to Maggie, and what she'd said, that they were already dead to her, and she felt that hurt again. It wasn't in her heart, but in her stomach. She tensed.

Can't stomach it.

They were both cut from the same cloth, mother and daughter, quick to lash out and quick to recoil.

For a moment, and this was a cruelly satisfying idea, Hedi imagined just giving up and leaving everything for Maggie to sort out. Let her clear up the mess, keep what she likes and get rid of the rest of it. Leave it for her to do.

'Why is there so much stuff?' Maggie had asked them repeatedly during her adolescence. 'Why do you have to keep everything?'

And one day, she'd come home from school with an answer. She was gleeful and puffed up with pride about it.

'It's because you're war babies. And you keep trying to stuff me with food because there was rationing, that's right, isn't it? You're old and you're still living in the past.'

Hedi remembered the way she'd stood there, flushed with adolescent insight, as if she'd finally found the key to understanding them.

Harry, overhearing, had startled them, jumping to his feet with such force that his chair tipped backwards and his tea slopped into his saucer. He'd said something that made Hedi think he was going to tell Maggie everything.

'You want to know about the past?'

'No!'

The idea was horrendous, as if they were pulling Maggie with them into the abyss.

No!

'Go on, hit me,' Maggie had said defiantly through her confused tears.

Why had she said that? Harry had never hit her, or even raised his voice to her.

That was my job, Hedi thought.

She remembered Maggie leaving the room, slamming the door, running upstairs, sobbing – you could hear those sobs even through the fitted carpet, and Harry's eyes had been fierce on hers, gripping her hands so tightly that it hurt.

'She needs to be told,' he'd said.

Hedi shook her head now, because all these years later she had never changed her mind about keeping the past a secret from her. Why would anyone let a beloved child get even the briefest glimpse of evil? Letting it into her life with all the confusion of feelings so tangled up together that it was impossible to unpick it.

It had been their duty to protect her.

Isn't this exactly what she was doing now, protecting her from the distasteful chore of reality, clearing up after the dead?

You've been dead to me for years. Maggie's words echoed through Hedi's mind.

Maggie hadn't wondered about it, hadn't made any attempts to contact them, hadn't come to the house – even though it was her inheritance, after all.

What had happened after the 'war babies' incident?

Who knew? She didn't imagine there would have been an apology. That was one thing Hedi had taught her daughter, wasn't it?

You never apologise. Because an apology required an explanation and secrets were meant to be kept.

Hedi hadn't thought that the process of clearing out the apartment would be so time-consuming. Her first instinct had been to let it all go, sweep it all out, but she hadn't reckoned on her own curiosity. Now she was surrounded by papers and photographs and knick-knacks. She wanted to look at everything before she flung it, and each thing she looked at was a memory. Some were faded and colourless, but others were startlingly vivid. This was her history, the mess she was sitting in the middle of.

'Or in my case, *herstory*,' she said aloud, smiling to herself. It was still a matter of pride to tell a joke in the language not her own.

Hedi's smile faded. History was meant for the people who followed to learn from, but she couldn't imagine that Maggie would want anything of theirs, not now she'd spoken to her.

You're dead to me.

'Ach,' she said, feeling the wound that the words had made. How could a daughter have said that and not known how deeply it would hurt?

Unless hurting was the point, in which case, Maggie had judged it well.

When she walked out of their lives, they had waited for her to come to her senses, because she had the baby and she was twenty years old and she would need their help, sooner or later. They would wait until she was ready to come back.

And apologise.

Yes, ready to apologise, that was what it had all been about. Because on the matter of food, or the lack of it, Hedi was an expert. *How could a nursing mother last on an apple and a couple of yoghurts a day? Impossible.* The very idea alarmed her.

If only she could see me now, Hedi thought with grim humour. *Nothing to eat but my words.*

7

THEA

A few days later, in the early evening, Thea was sitting on the jetty in the sunshine, her feet dangling in water so cold that it gripped her ankles like a vice. Holding her red hair out of her eyes, she looked across to the far side of the estuary where the brightly coloured bunting of the George III Hotel was flying in the warm breeze.

The river glittered and dazzled against the blue of the sky and she tilted her face to the sun. Despite sunblock, a pattern of freckles had appeared across the bridge of her nose, but one of the benefits of being a recluse was that there was no one around to judge.

She had just come to this satisfying realisation when her phone buzzed. It was almost intrusive and she stared at it warily for a moment where it lay on the warm wooden slats. The vibration was giving the mobile a kind of momentum – it was steadily creeping its way to the edge of the dock. Thea grabbed it before it fell into the river. 'Hello?'

'It's Maggie,' her mother said crossly. 'Where on earth have you been? I've been trying to get hold of you for days! I've been out of my mind with worry!'

This, to Thea's mind, sounded unlikely. 'Sorry,' she apologised, just in case she was being cynical. 'I'm having a break and there's no signal in the place I'm staying.'

'What do you mean, having a break? Have you lost your job?'

'No. It's summer so the school is closed. I mean, I'm on holiday.'

Maggie blew her nose noisily, and at length, as if she had a bad cold.

Thea waited patiently for the nose-clearing to finish. 'You sound awful,' she said sympathetically. 'Are you okay?'

'No. Thea, I've had some terrible news,' Maggie said. 'Are you sitting down?'

'I am,' Thea said, suddenly alarmed. 'Are you all right? What's going on?'

Maggie took a quivering intake of breath. 'Harry's passed away. My father.' She was silent for a moment, letting the news sink in. 'Hello? Thea?'

'Yes?'

'I didn't even know he was ill,' Maggie added irritably, as if it were Thea's fault. 'Hello? Did you hear me?'

'I did.' Thea realised Maggie didn't have a cold after all – she was crying. Which was confusing, to say the least. She watched a canoeist paddle towards the bridge in the distance. The red of the craft trailed a long crimson reflection in the bright water. 'I don't understand. You told me your parents died a long time ago,' she said. She knew that it was the wrong thing to say. Her mother liked her to keep on-script.

'Thea, you've got a memory like an elephant when you want to,' Maggie said sharply.

'Mmm.' It wasn't the kind of thing a person would forget: that they had no family, that it was just the two of them. 'I'm sorry about your father.' Thea had never met him, nor her grandmother, because Maggie had fallen out with them a long time ago. She used to say they were estranged. That was how she put it. 'My parents and I are estranged.' It sounded irredeemably formal. And then when Thea reached her twenties and wanted to meet her grandparents, Maggie told her they were dead. She'd only ever had a hazy idea of the kind of people they were, her impressions coloured by their failings as parents. 'How are you holding up?' she asked gently.

'I wish things had been different.'

'Yeah.' Thea guessed her mother probably felt guilty. It was too late to patch things up and she must be full of regrets. Thea knew all about regrets. She watched the water lapping against the riverbank in little glossy waves.

'I've got a favour to ask you,' Maggie said.

'What?'

'Go to the funeral for me, will you, Thea?'

Thea was silent for a moment, taken aback by the request. *Now* she got it. 'You're not coming back for it?'

'I can't, can I? You'll have to go on my behalf, as my representative. See it as an opportunity for you to meet your grandmother, at least briefly, before it's too late. I give it a month.'

Thea could hear a tinkling noise which sounded suspiciously like ice cubes being swirled in a glass. 'Give what a month?'

'Before Hedi joins Harry. They've always been inseparable. I've always said, "when one goes, the other will go." Haven't I always said that, James? Oh, never mind. It's the truth, anyway.'

'You think Hedi will die of a broken heart, you mean?' It was unlike her mother to sound so sentimental.

'You know what they were like. Joined at the hip.'

'How would I know that? I've never met them.'

'Don't start,' Maggie said sharply. Her voice rose in pitch. 'I'm grieving. You don't seem to realise what it's like for me. I thought they were dead, and now one of them really is.'

Thea tried to find the logic in this statement and gave up.

Way over on the other side of the estuary, a green convertible was driving away from the hotel. The driver's dark hair was blowing behind her like a banner. She looked utterly carefree.

'Where is the funeral?'

'In London. Golders Green Crematorium, tomorrow. Two o'clock.'

'London? That's where they live?' Thea ran her hands through her hair in frustration. She could have passed them in the street and never known it. 'Why didn't you...' She bit off the rest of the question because what was the point in pursuing it? 'It's a bit sudden.'

'Yes, well, Thea, if you'd bothered to answer your phone before now you'd have got the message earlier, wouldn't you? Speak later, the taxi's here.'

Maggie hung up, leaving Thea staring at her mobile, her emotions all churned up. She got to her feet, feeling light-headed, and she bent over to let the blood rush to her head. Her hair swept the wooden planks of the dock. Beneath the slats she could see the dark water with fish taking refuge in the shadows. The wood was warm under her feet, the sun hot on her shoulders. She walked up and down to shake off the feeling, making overlapping patterns out of her wet footprints.

Harry had died; her grandfather with the red hair, who she'd never known and now never would know. Her grand-mother, Hedi, was all alone and grieving.

What she knew of them was filtered through her mother's emotions. According to Maggie, they should never have had children, because they were crazy in love and only needed each other. Maybe she was right, because after Maggie, there were no more babies; their family was complete. To be fair, Hedi had been well into her forties when Maggie was born.

Despite being loved 'up to a point' as Maggie grudgingly put it, she had told Thea that she had felt permanently misunderstood. Her relationship with her parents was superficial, a perfect veneer. She always felt there was a barrier between them, the way they shut her out. And it showed in Maggie's defensive behaviour. On any shopping trip, for instance, she always found someone to argue with, either for getting in her way or not serving her quickly enough or for some other minor misdemeanour that Thea was unaware of. Maggie was acutely sensitive to her own feelings whilst being completely insensitive about others.

'And that,' one guy had said sadly on the day they waved goodbye to him and his swimming pool forever, 'is the very definition of a bully.'

Thea stepped off the jetty and waded back through the grass to The Hideaway with an ache in her heart. Obviously she would go to the funeral; there was no question about that. She would meet her grandmother, and hopefully forge some kind of a relationship with her. She didn't really believe Hedi would follow Harry soon after – this sounded like some romantic notion of her mother's, and maybe even a convenient one.

Thea would go back to the flat first and find something suitable to wear.

Going into the kitchen, she told herself firmly: *It doesn't matter what you wear*.

Yes, it does, her inner voice contradicted her. *You're meeting your grandmother for the first time. Of course it matters*.

Would she be expected to wear black? Something smart, at least. One thing she'd found out since becoming a recluse was that the less she did, the less she wanted to do. She felt very safe doing nothing. She liked being left alone. Even when she went to Martin Evans's shop to buy food, she tried not to meet people's eyes in case they started up a conversation.

She hadn't always been like this. She'd had a normal life once – friends, a boyfriend who loved her.

It was already hard to remember how those days felt. It seemed like another life, one that belonged to someone else.

Before Thea went back to the house, she got her phone out again and checked on the times of the trains back to London. She found she could catch one from a stop just up the road to Birmingham, and then get a connection from Birmingham to London. She was too late to do it today because the journey took five hours, which was cutting it fine. She would have to go early in the morning. Couldn't go to the flat first.

Thea remembered that Bear Cave had a Heart Foundation charity shop. She hurried to the village and looked through the shop window. 'Something black,' she said softly to herself. She went inside, feeling shifty, as if she'd gone there shoplifting. She checked that her tote bag wasn't open, because if it was, what if something were to fall into it? Her gaze swept across the racks of clothes.

'Can I help you?'

She jumped in alarm and averted her gaze. 'Me? Oh, no thank you. Just looking.' She risked a glance at the woman. She was in her seventies, stocky, with grey hair and a gentle smile. She looked like the kind of person who would attend funerals. 'Actually, yes,' she said. 'I need something to wear for my grand-father's funeral.'

The woman's eyes grew pink with tears. 'What an awful time for you. A great loss.'

Thea felt like a fraud. 'I didn't actually know him.'

The woman was warm with sympathy. 'No? But you're paying your respects. He'd appreciate that. I always think a coat and a dress go well together. You need to feel warm on such a sad occasion and some of those churches are shockingly cold even in the summer. Or would you prefer a suit, a little black suit?' She was already sliding the hangers along the rails, pulling out garments and draping them over her arm. 'Will you be wearing a hat?'

'No, I don't think so.' Thea bit the edge of her thumbnail. 'Do people wear hats at funerals?'

'It depends on your personal taste. Some people are hat people,' the woman said. She gave Thea that consoling smile again. 'Don't worry, you'd know if you were. No hat. Do you need to look at shoes?'

'Shoes.' Thea pinched her lower lip thoughtfully. *What are you going to do, wear trainers?* 'Yes, please. Size four.'

The woman took everything through to a dressing room in the corner, swished back the green curtain, hung the clothes up and put the shoes on a chair. 'Call if you need me,' she said. 'I'll be right here.'

Thea looked at herself in the full-length mirror and held her hair away from her face. Her eyes looked very green without mascara, but the overall effect was nondescript and forgettable.

She stripped to her underwear, tried the black dress on and put the black coat over it. Both garments fitted, more or less. She looked like a stranger to herself, someone you'd see in the street heading for a bus stop, hurrying home with their supper and some cat food in a nylon shopping bag.

'Knock-knock!' the woman said from behind the curtain. She moved it back a little and peeked through. 'Ooh! You do look smart! I've found you some shoes! Slip these on.'

'*These*' were black patent court shoes.

'There! Haven't they made a difference? Now you've got the look!'

The look being that of a woman going to a funeral. Yes, she couldn't argue, she had the look, all right. 'Thank you for your help.'

'Now try on the suit. I'll find you a blouse to go under the jacket, ivory, perhaps? Give it a bit of a lift?'

'No, there's no need,' Thea said quickly. 'You've been very helpful, and these are perfectly fine. I'll take them.'

'You're easy to please,' the woman said, but she seemed disappointed. 'Still, you'll have bigger things to worry about at this sad time. I know what it's like to lose all interest in your appearance, grief does that to a person. I'll let you get dressed again.'

Thea hung up the clothes, put her jeans and T-shirt back on, checked the prices on the labels, quickly worked out what her ensemble was going to cost and took everything to the counter to pay.

Her heart was pounding as if she'd been running but her ordeal was almost over. She put the clothes into her bag and was turning to leave when the woman said suddenly, 'I know who you are! You've moved into The Hideaway, haven't you? Martin's place?'

'Yes.'

'Not too lonely for you, is it?'

'No. It's perfect.'

The woman looked at her hopefully but Thea couldn't think of anything else to say.

'I'm Daphne,' the woman said. 'I hope the funeral goes well, or at least as well as it can do. Don't worry, your loss will get easier in time. Things tend to, I've found.'

'I hope so,' Thea said.

The following day, Thea returned to London by train and made her way to the crematorium chapel. As there was no one around, she went inside.

Sombre music played softly on a sound system.

An elderly, white-haired woman dressed in black was standing at the front of the room with one hand on the casket. She was looking down at the spray of flowers threaded with white birch twigs. *Hedi.*

Thea slid into a seat at the back, not wanting to disturb her. But she looked so alone, so lonely, that she changed her mind and got up again. It was ridiculous, rather than polite, to sit this

far away from her own grandmother. She could at least intro-
duce herself, she thought, before anyone else turned up.

She checked her phone for the time and her heart sank. Five
minutes to go, and unless everyone else was going to turn up
right on the dot, it was going to be a very small gathering.

Her black patent court shoes clicked loudly on the wooden
floor, and the old woman turned eagerly. Her face was half
hidden by a black net covering her hat. She too was wearing a
black coat and black patent court shoes. Beneath the net veil,
the only feature that Thea could see clearly was her mouth, red
lipstick carefully applied. Hedi gave an 'Oh!' of surprise.

'Hedi? I'm Thea, Maggie's daughter.'

'My girl!' her grandmother said in a strong accent which
Thea couldn't place. She turned to look past Thea and her
shoulders drooped. 'You're alone?'

'Yes. Maggie's in New York at the moment. She would have
come otherwise, I know.'

Hedi shrugged. 'Maybe,' she said, her voice distant. 'I truly
hoped, despite...' She pressed her quivering lips together and
turned back to Thea. 'But *you* came. Well then.' She held her
arms out. She was small woman, small enough that Thea's chin
was level with the top of her head. As they hugged, her black
satin pillbox hat was knocked to one side. Hedi stood back,
replaced it at a jaunty angle and raised the black net. Her eyes
were fierce and dark, gleaming with emotion.

'Your hair! Look at the shine, like polished copper,' she
marvelled. 'I never thought to see this hair again, it's Harry's
hair as it used to be. And your eyes, too, are like Harry's, green
as gooseberries. You know gooseberries?'

'Yes, I know them,' Thea said.

The funeral celebrant appeared from a side door. He
smoothed his thinning hair back, straightened his tie, glanced at
his watch and asked Hedi courteously, 'Are you expecting any
other mourners?'

Hedi raised her chin proudly. 'No, it's just us.'

The music started playing and the funeral celebrant stood at the lectern and said a few words of comfort. His amplified voice echoed loudly around the empty room. He read a poem that Harry liked, which ended:

> *The woods are lovely, dark and deep,*
> *But I have promises to keep,*
> *And miles to go before I sleep,*
> *And miles to go before I sleep.*

Thea felt Hedi trembling against her as his words rang out, and she tucked her arm in hers.

Hedi frantically turned back to Thea. Her shoulders drooped and in a gesture of resignation she covered her face with her hands. The celebrant guided them both out of the room and they stepped into the red-brick, sunlit courtyard which was lined with flowers.

Hedi pulled herself together. 'That is that,' she sighed. *Thet is thet.*

As they left the courtyard, a line of glittering funeral cars disgorged a new set of mourners.

Hedi stopped to watch them for a moment. 'So much misery,' she murmured.

Thea was about to tell Hedi that she would head back to the tube station, when the old lady grabbed her wrist.

'Let's go to eat now, shall we? It is, in the circumstances, the only civilised thing to do, don't you agree? And all arranged.' Her expression was hopeful.

'Sure.' Thea nodded.

'Good,' Hedi said. 'See? I have a taxi waiting.'

The taxi took them into the heart of London and stopped outside Claridge's.

They entered a world of instant luxury: soft beige carpet

underfoot, art deco mirrors, an extravagant sculpture hanging from the ceiling like some exotic sea creature. Music drifted from the grand piano: plaintive and beautiful.

Hedi was very businesslike. She had booked a table. As the waiter courteously took them over to it, Thea could see it was set for four.

'You can get rid of these,' Hedi said to him, waving her hand. 'It's just us two, after all.'

In a moment, the extra place settings were cleared away. The sommelier presented a bottle of champagne; Hedi looked at the label and nodded with a little smile of amusement. As the waiter poured it, she raised her black net veil and folded it over her hat, her dark eyes meeting Thea's.

'I have been sorting out old photographs,' she said. 'I bought this for Maggie, but you might like it.' She opened the gilt clasp on her handbag and took a photograph out of the red leather address book which was keeping it flat. 'Here.'

Thea looked at it carefully. It was of Maggie looking ridiculously young and very slim, her dark hair tied up in a blue scarf, holding a baby in her arms. *Me.* The baby's wispy hair shone rose gold in the sunlight. They were laughing on a yellow beach, against the background of a deep blue sea and a pale blue sky.

That beach – it seemed familiar. Thea shivered, as though someone had walked over her grave.

'You would of course be too young to remember it,' Hedi said. 'But it was the most perfect holiday, the four of us together, a family.'

Thea felt her heart being squeezed with emotion. 'I know it sounds strange, Hedi, but I sort of do remember it,' she said, choosing her words carefully. 'I dreamt about it recently, a beach like this one. I was happy in the dream.' She looked at her baby self closely; one chubby hand on her mother's bikini top, laughing at the camera, showing pink gums.

'You were always happy,' Hedi agreed fondly.

'Where is this beach in the photograph?'

'This was in Wales. Harry was Welsh. We had Maggie late, as you know, but Harry's parents were still alive to indulge her, and they doted on her. We all did. We had got to the age when all the turmoil of living was in the past and then she came and she was our delight, our passport into the future.'

'Did your own parents ever meet her?' For a moment, it seemed the wrong thing to ask. Hedi's eyes reddened with tears. She shook her head sharply.

'No. They did not.'

A few moments passed and Hedi picked up her glass and delicately sipped her champagne. 'I have made many mistakes in my life,' she began, but she didn't finish the sentence. Her eyes met Thea's. 'Your mother has told you all about Harry, I expect. And you didn't know him, but you came to pay your respects. I am so grateful.'

'I wanted to come.' Thea sat back in her chair as the waiter spread the linen napkin on her knees. 'It was nice to hear the things you said about him. I liked the poem.'

Hedi put her champagne flute down carefully. '"And miles to go before I sleep."' She smiled. 'I don't have many miles to go now, thank God.' Her dark eyes met Thea's. 'Don't look so startled!'

'I hope you're wrong. I was just thinking, we've got a lot of time to catch up on. It's not too late, is it?'

Hedi turned and looked around at the other diners.

For a moment, it seemed that she wasn't going to reply and then she turned back to face Thea, her napkin crumpled in her hand.

'But you see, Thea, I'm ready to go,' she said regretfully. 'I have pushed death away many times in my life, but he is standing by the door, waiting for me to say my goodbyes. He has been very patient for all these years, lurking in the shadows, but now he is in full view, and not hiding any more.'

Just then, the waiters brought their afternoon tea; it was arranged beautifully on a cake stand.

'Eat!' Hedi said magnanimously. 'Enjoy!'

Hedi took eating very seriously, closing her eyes in appreciation and humming with pleasure.

Thea found herself smiling with delight because the sandwiches were delicious and she hadn't realised how hungry she was.

'What is your occupation?' Hedi asked during a pause.

'I work in a school,' Thea said.

Hedi brightened. 'Just like my father! He too was a teacher!'

'Was he? Actually, I'm not a teacher, I'm a school secretary.'

'But you're an intellectual, it's obvious a school would employ an intellectual,' Hedi said firmly.

Periodically the champagne in their glasses was topped up and when there was only one pink macaron left, Hedi glanced at her watch. She dabbed her mouth with the napkin and sat back. 'This has been most pleasant,' she said. 'I hope you will remember this day with fond memories.'

'I will.' Thea nodded and met Hedi's gaze, seeing love in her dark eyes.

She was suddenly tearful. It was as if they'd always known each other; there was an intimate bond in the way that they recognised each other. It was a good, warm feeling.

'I can come and visit you again if you'd like,' Thea said. 'Let me give you my phone number.'

'How wonderful of you to suggest it, but I regret there won't be time. This is our goodbye.' Hedi leant across the table and took Thea's face in her warm hands. Her breath smelled sweet, of jam tarts, and she kissed Thea's forehead. 'My sweet girl. I've upset you. Don't be upset.' Changing her mind, she picked her handbag up, took out the small red address book and gave it to Thea. 'Put your number in here if you wish.'

After Thea had written it down, she handed the book back and said, 'Will you give me yours?'

Hedi ignored the question and said, 'I have two taxis waiting for us right now. Tell your driver where you want to go. Don't pay, I have an account. When you think of Claridge's, think of Harry and me.'

Thea nodded, unable to speak.

Outside the hotel, the cabs were waiting for them, engines running. Before she got into hers, Thea and Hedi stood face to face, with too much to say and not enough time.

Impulsively, Thea hugged her grandmother. It wasn't the polite hug that she was expert at but a warm, fierce one from the heart.

Hedi's face was impassive despite almost being lifted off her feet.

Thea felt indescribably sad and wished she could be as practical and as matter of fact as her grandmother about their parting. 'Goodbye, then.' But as the cab pulled away, she saw Hedi pull down the veil of her pillbox hat to hide her tears.

8

HEDI

As Hedi got out of the taxi after leaving Claridge's, she saw Joy standing in the front yard taking photographs of the rubbish bags, which, surprisingly for this time in the afternoon, hadn't yet been collected.

Despite being curious, Hedi was in no mood to speak to her neighbour. It had been a tiring day, full of emotion, and so she blanked her and headed up the stone steps, taking keys out of her handbag.

But as she opened the front door, Joy called to her in her high, sharp voice, 'Excuse me, Hedi, they haven't taken these rubbish bins. You know why? There are too many of them. You need to ring the council.'

Hedi stared down at her through the blurry dark veil of her hat. 'So? Who cares? Let them take them next time.'

'That's in two weeks!' Joy exclaimed. 'You can't leave them like that for two weeks, they'll attract rats.'

Hedi felt anger surge through her in a hot, unstoppable wave. 'Too late for that,' she said furiously. 'I can see one rat sniffing around already.'

Joy shied back. She narrowed her eyes to look at Hedi, and she seemed to register the deep black of mourning.

Hedi braced herself on the threshold, taking deep breaths to keep herself calm. She waited to see what would happen. It could go either way now. Joy could back down out of respect or she could pretend to be suddenly colour-blind and carry on saying her piece.

Encouraged by Hedi's silence, Joy obviously decided to opt for not backing down.

'You know what this mess is called?' she asked, waving at it. 'It's fly-tipping. It's against the law.'

'Pff! Nonsense! You are making me angry with your accusations,' Hedi replied crossly.

She heard Harry's calm voice in her head.

Is that so?

'Yes, it is so!' she snapped.

'What is what so?' Joy asked, confused.

Hedi felt dizzy. She steadied herself against the door frame and wondered if maybe she had drunk too much champagne. Even sharing it with Thea, it was half a bottle each, and on an empty stomach too because some time had passed before their afternoon tea had been brought to them on that little bone-china stand. It had been a good funeral, yes, she was qualified to say that, and Thea standing with her, together. What a surprise that had been, and no awkwardness, just a beautiful feeling. How proud Harry had been to have a granddaughter with red hair.

'I'm making an official complaint,' Joy stated, jerking Hedi back out of her thoughts.

'Shut up!' The adrenaline flooded through Hedi in an unstoppable rush. 'You are an ugly person. I would like to crush you under my foot and kill you,' she said, gritting her teeth.

'Is that a threat? Did you just threaten me?'

'Stupid nonsense,' Hedi muttered going up the stairs to her

flat. 'The woman is crazy and what have I ever done to her that she starts her bullying now my husband is dead?'

Inside the flat she felt disorientated. *No books.* The place seemed bigger, huge, as if she'd dwindled.

Hedi's phone buzzed in her handbag, a reminder to take her afternoon blood thinners.

She went to the kitchen and took out the warfarin. She looked at the yellow packets closely as if she was seeing them for the first time. She took the packets to the lounge and popped the blue pills out and the brown pills out, one by one, and laid them in tidy rows on the little wine table, a pleasant and mindless way of passing the time. *Fly-tipping, was she? Attracting rats, was she?* Well, if Joy asked, she would inform her kindly that she was now obligingly killing them off.

She went downstairs, expecting Joy to appear at any moment, but for the moment she had retreated. Hedi emptied the pills into one of the bin bags for the rats to find or ignore, as they chose.

Tomorrow, a man was coming for the sofa, the armchairs, and the wine tables. They would take everything except for the beds. No one wanted the beds because of health and safety, although they hadn't been able to explain to her what made a bed such a dangerous item.

The men would take all the furniture and she would ask them to move her own bed into this room and she would use it to sit on, and to die on. Hedi would put it right here against the wall and turn her face away from the window. She would retreat into herself until she left the bed, the room, the house, the city and the Earth behind her, to enter that new realm where her beloved Harry was waiting.

She smiled. She wasn't afraid.

9

THEA

The following week, Thea was walking along a public footpath overgrown with cow parsley when her phone vibrated. It was call from a London number she didn't recognise. 'Hello?'

'Social Services. You have been named by Hedi Lewis as her next of kin. I'm one of the social workers on her case.'

'Is she all right?' Thea was apprehensive as she looked towards the estuary.

'That's what I'm calling you about. A neighbour has reported concerns about Hedi's welfare. She's been acting in an aggressive manner towards her, and she's been seen outside in her nightwear. She's neglecting herself.'

Thea felt defensive. 'She's just been widowed. She's grieving. She and her husband, Harry, were very close.'

The social worker took in a deep breath and Thea realised she was smoking.

'It's not as simple as that. Life's not that neat, I'm afraid,' she said, exhaling. 'We think it's in her best interests to go into residential care where her needs will be met.' A siren drowned her out for a moment. Once it had passed, she added, 'She's in her nineties, so it probably doesn't come as much of a surprise to you that she can't look after herself.'

'I don't know if that's true. She seems to know what she's doing.'

'When did you last see her?'

'Last week, at Harry's funeral.'

'Hm. That's what you call your grandparents, is it? Hedi and Harry? Not Granny or anything?'

'No.'

'Oh. Anyway, we're going to have a meeting,' the social worker said. 'We think you should attend. Of course you don't have to be here, but as Hedi's next of kin it's often quite helpful if you come, so we can talk about it together and make sure we're all on the same page.'

'Will Hedi be at the meeting?'

'Doubtful. She won't get out of bed. That's what I mean by neglect. And she won't eat. Luckily she's got a neighbour keeping an eye on her because she hasn't left the house in days.'

'But you said she saw her out in her nightwear?' Thea picked a daisy nestled in the grass. She twirled the stem, watching the white petals blur around the yellow calyx.

'Broadly speaking,' the social worker said patiently, 'she hasn't been much of anywhere. The neighbour thinks she's not eating.'

'And is that not allowed, to stay in bed and not eat when you've lost the husband you've been with most of your life?' Thea wasn't being challenging, she was just curious.

'No! If Hedi can't self-care, then we'll do it for her.'

'It wouldn't be self-care then, would it? Out of interest, how do you feed someone if they don't want to be fed?'

'Through a tube. It would be in her best interests. It's not very pleasant. And after that, there's no going back.'

'How is feeding her through a tube in her best interests if it's not very pleasant and there's no going back?'

'It will keep her alive.'

It sounded a bit of a catch-22. Thea decided not to ask the next question that immediately came to mind. *What if she doesn't want to stay alive?* It seemed strange that, like it or not, you were forced to carry on living when you didn't really want to. *But was wanting to die a rational response?* And Hedi did want to die. She had told her so at the funeral.

Unexpectedly, tears filled Thea's eyes and she felt a rush of grief for the grandmother she barely knew.

'Hello?' The social worker said sharply. 'You still there?'

Thea cleared her throat. 'Yes. I'm still here.'

'You can't look after her,' the social worker said, 'if that's what you're thinking. It's not a one-person job.'

'No, I suppose it isn't. Look, if it's a meeting about Hedi's future, then Hedi should attend, don't you think?' Maybe the meeting would make Hedi see things differently and pull herself together. 'She deserves to have a say in it. I wouldn't want to do it behind her back, and I definitely wouldn't want to make any decisions on her behalf. Can't we do it at her house?'

The social worker hesitated. 'One moment. I'm just going to put you on hold.'

Until the social worker mentioned it, it hadn't occurred to Thea to offer to look after Hedi. They might be part of the same family but they barely knew each other. However, now it was a kind of them-and-us situation, she felt a kind of obligation. Maybe she could do something for Hedi, give her something to live for. But even as Thea considered it, her courage left her. It was a big responsibility and 'not a one-person job'.

Maggie should be doing this, she thought.

The truth was, even if Maggie hadn't gone to New York, she would never have taken on the problem of Hedi.

'You still there?' the social worker asked.

'Yes, I'm still here.'

'We'll meet you at Hedi's. Give me your email address and I'll send you the details.'

A couple of days later, Thea went back to London. She rested her head against the train window, feeling nervous about seeing Hedi. She didn't want her grandmother to feel ganged up on, but that was the feeling she'd got from the social worker; a kind of righteous disapproval, as if she and Hedi were breaking rules that they didn't know anything about.

No matter what, she would make it clear to Hedi that she was on her side. But there was always the chance that social services were right, and that residential care was the answer. Hedi must be lonely, living by herself after all these years with Harry. They might find her a good home where the inmates played chess and discussed literature.

Inmates?

She shivered. 'Residents,' she said aloud, correcting herself, catching the eye of the woman sitting opposite her.

The woman sitting opposite looked up from her phone. She seemed kind.

'Social services want to put my grandmother in a home,' Thea said.

'Has she got dementia?' the woman asked sympathetically.

'No. She's... lost the will to live. Her husband died not long ago.'

'That's tough.' The woman added brightly, 'But some of those places are very nice. They have hairdressers on-site, and activities, like making Easter bonnets, and regular bingo sessions. It can be a fresh start.'

'Are you a social worker?' Thea asked suspiciously.

'No, no.'

There was an awkward silence, as if they both regretted the

intimacy of the conversation. The woman picked up her phone
again and Thea looked through the window, noticing her own
reflection against the background of fields and buildings. She
wondered what she was getting herself into.

Hedi lived in East Heath Street. Thea walked there from
Hampstead tube station. She knew the road quite well because
it bordered the Vale of Health, but she'd never really taken
much notice of the houses.

It was only about a mile and a half from where Thea had
lived with her boyfriend and she felt a new surge of resentment
towards Maggie. All this time Hedi and Harry had been living
quite close to her without Thea knowing it. Her life would have
been different if they'd been part of it.

She walked up the stone steps, pressed the buzzer and
waited.

A face appeared in the ground floor window, and the
window opened. A woman with grey hair held back by black
hair grips popped her head out. 'She won't answer, you know.'

'Excuse me?' Thea said. Just then, the intercom clunked
into life.

Hedi said, 'Who's there?'

'Thea.'

Hedi buzzed her in.

Thea walked up the flight of pale blue carpeted stairs to
find Hedi waiting for her by the open door, wearing a man's
tartan dressing gown that was much too big for her. Other than
that, she looked fine. Her white hair was neat, and her scarlet
lipstick perfectly applied.

'*Thenk Gott* you've come,' Hedi said with relief. 'I've had
officials calling me non-stop.'

'I know. I've been trying to call you myself.'

'I turned the phone off. Ring ring! Ring ring! That's all it does!'

'That is the nature of a telephone,' Thea said drily.

'Smart Alec. These officials, they expect me to answer their questions, and do they answer mine? No! Why can't a person die in peace if they want to? Anyway, you're here now. You can tell them.'

Their footsteps echoed on the bare floorboards and Hedi led Thea through to a room that was empty except for two blue-and-white striped deckchairs in the middle of it and the bed pushed up against the wall.

That was it.

Thea looked around in astonishment – *how could Hedi be living like this?* There were empty bookshelves and no furniture, no pictures on the walls, although Thea could see the ghosts of where they'd been from the nails and paler squares on the light-blue walls. 'Where are all your things?' Her words bounced back at her hollowly.

'Sit, and I'll tell you.'

Thea sat in one of the deckchairs and held her bag on her knees. 'Is all your stuff in storage?' she asked.

Hedi tucked her hands in her dressing gown pockets and looked surprised. 'Storage? No, what would be the use of that? I paid people to take it away. Why not, I can't take it with me. Why should anyone have the burden of clearing up after me once I've gone? It makes sense to do it myself, doesn't it, it's only polite.' She lifted her chin and ran her hand down her throat. 'It's a Swedish custom. I'll tell you something about the Swedes, they are intensely practical people. I know this from experience. *Ektually*, I lived in Sweden for a little while.'

'Did you?' Thea looked around doubtfully. This was starting to look like a hideous mistake to have the meeting here. 'What will the social worker say when she sees the place is empty?'

'Probably what she said last time. "You might be depressed, have you seen a doctor? He could give you something to take, prescribe some antidepressants,"' Hedi said, mimicking her. 'I am flattened and crushed by my loss. They want to give me something to take the pain away? Why would I do that? I owe Harry my heartbreak.' Hedi stood over Thea and took her hands in hers. 'You understand, don't you, I am ready to go,' she said, squeezing her fingers tightly, their eyes locking. 'You know how it is. I've had enough now. I'm tired. I want to be with my husband. The truth is, I thought I'd be dead by now.'

'Yes, I get that,' Thea said desperately. 'But if you go, Hedi, I will never get the chance to know you. I'd like us to have a relationship. Does that count for anything?'

'Now you are humouring me,' Hedi said, letting go of her hands. 'But you're sweet.'

Sunk into the deckchair, Thea wondered how to retrieve the situation. 'How do you feel about the meeting with the social worker?'

'I don't want to meet her. I refused to attend, so now she's coming here. Pah!' She folded her arms, letting out a puff of exasperation. 'I just want to be left to die in peace, is that so hard to understand?'

'No.' Thea chose her words carefully. 'I don't think you should tell them that, though, because they will argue that you're not doing what's best for you.'

'I *am* doing what's best for me.'

'I know you are. But it's against their job description to let you die happily. It's against the law. You've got to live miserably instead.' She tried to make a joke of it.

Hedi didn't smile. '*Exektly*,' she said, tightening the belt of what was probably Harry's old robe. She sighed, and it seemed to come from deep inside her soul. Her gaze rested wistfully on Thea and she gave a faint smile. 'That hair, so much like his when he was young,' she said softly. The intercom buzzed and

Hedi went to answer it. 'Oh, it's you,' she said to the visitor ungraciously.

Thea got up out of the deckchair and attempted to look as if this whole situation was perfectly normal.

The social worker's name was Charlotte Green. She had short blonde hair and she was wearing a brown trouser suit, very businesslike. Her eyes widened as she took in the empty room.

'This is how you're living?' she asked, shooting Thea a meaningful look.

Hedi rolled her eyes. 'It's a free country.'

'Where do you sleep?'

'In my bed, where else?' Hedi replied. She sounded bored.

'You don't mind if I look around?'

'Why should I mind?' Hedi once more retied the belt of her plaid dressing gown and showed the social worker around. Their footsteps echoed loudly on the floorboards.

Thea stood awkwardly with her weight on one hip. She felt like an intruder, and the social worker's attitude was brisk and domineering, almost bullying, as if she was determined to make Hedi confess that she couldn't look after herself.

She hated herself for wondering if maybe the woman was right.

It was an awful thought, and one that she hadn't considered until now. Thea had taken Hedi at face value as intelligent, lively and self-possessed. But these empty rooms – well, it didn't look good.

Moments later, Hedi and Charlotte Green were back from a tour of the apartment.

Hedi folded her arms and pressed her lips together stubbornly, as if she'd suddenly taken a vow of silence.

The social worker sat down in the deckchair and took some papers out of her briefcase. She started to write a few notes which were almost certainly not arguments in Hedi's favour.

'Is there any food in the fridge?' she asked, looking up at Thea.

'I don't know, I—'

'Why do you want to know?' Hedi asked her belligerently. 'Are you hungry?'

The social worker struggled out of the deckchair – it was impossible to get out of it in a businesslike manner – and went into the kitchen.

Thea heard the suck of the seal as she opened the fridge, and the cushioned puff as she closed it again.

Charlotte Green came back into the room and leaned on the back of the deckchair. 'Obviously my recommendation to you both is to consider that the time has come for Hedi to admit that she's not coping. We have a duty of care. The neighbours are worried. When they saw her furniture being carried out, they thought she was being burgled. And I've had a report to say she goes out in her nightwear.'

'Which neighbour?' Hedi asked crossly.

'I'm not at liberty to say.'

'I know who. That nosy Joy.'

'That's not the point.'

'Sure, I put the bins out in this dressing gown. I like it, it's comfortable.' Hedi wriggled her shoulders and turned up the shawl collar. 'Smells of Harry,' she said.

It was impossible to read the social worker's expression, but she didn't exactly look impressed. She turned to Thea. 'How long are you staying?'

'I've just come up for the day.'

'Well,' Charlotte Green said briskly, 'I'll get the ball rolling and we can see where they've got vacancies. You'd be surprised how often rooms come up. Hedi, once you've got company and a regular meal plan, and your medical and emotional needs are met, things are going to look a lot brighter, I can assure you.'

Thea saw the panic of betrayal in Hedi's eyes and she

turned away quickly, rubbing her temples – she was getting a headache and although she knew that the day wasn't going to go well, she hadn't expected it to plunge into a nightmare quite this quickly.

Obviously, rationally, Hedi would be better off being looked after – she could see that – but she still felt sick with guilt. Hedi couldn't live in a practically empty flat, even if it did still have a bed in it. While she understood Hedi's reasoning for getting rid of her furniture and possessions, it only made sense in the light of her conviction that she was going to die imminently.

But as she seemed in perfect health, the chances that she was going to die anytime soon were slim to zero.

Thea was looking at a dead fly on the windowsill, half waiting for Hedi to argue in her own defence, but her grandmother was uncharacteristically silent. *It could be,* Thea thought hopefully, *that Hedi is also coming to the conclusion that this is for the best.*

She turned to say something. A cloud passed, and the sun shone in through the window, throwing their dark shadows across the room. Hedi's shadow looked very small. She was staring helplessly at the floorboards, her shoulders rounded in resignation, her thin, pale neck jutted out from Harry's robe, her white hair curling at the nape. She looked frightened, like a child who had done something wrong and didn't know what. Thea's heart went out to her.

She glanced at Charlotte Green the grown-up: stony faced and implacable as she wrote her notes.

Thea's stomach was tense with anxiety. *What was the right thing to do for Hedi? What was the answer?*

No use pretending. She knew perfectly well what it was, and had known, reluctantly, from the start, ever since the shock of seeing the bare flat.

She had to leave The Hideaway and come back home to London. Carry on with her normal life and her normal job.

Promise to visit Hedi every day after work, make sure she had
company and a meal in the evenings... see if she could get some
of the furniture back. Thea felt her spirits sink. But yeah, she
could do that. She was only giving up a holiday, after all; the
seductive attraction of being somewhere else, living a different
life for a little while.

A new life.

Wasn't that what Hedi wanted, what her death wish
amounted to, a new life, an escape from this one?

Suddenly it was the same feeling as jumping off a rock into
the sea – after the visceral reluctance, the plunge itself was easy
enough. It was time to stop wondering what the best decision
was and look at it from another angle. She was living with guilt
as it was, wishing that she had altered the course of a relationship. Not any more. She cleared her throat, and her voice came
out slightly hoarse. 'I think you need a holiday, Hedi. You can
come and stay with me if you like,' she said. 'We'll have a
change of scenery, company, fresh air—'

Hedi lifted her head and looked at Thea in surprise, her
dark eyes wide. 'Where would we go?'

'Near the sea.'

Hedi was quick. She gave a sharp intake of breath. Then
she shook her head. '*You hef plens.* I don't want to put you out.
At your age, you're free, having fun. No, no. Impossible. I
couldn't impose.'

For a moment, Thea felt sweet relief flooding through her,
and confusion. *You hef plens?* But at the same time she'd seen a
spark of hope in Hedi's dark eyes, behind the bleak desperation.
It was enough.

'I haven't got any plans, really. Where I'm staying, it's
peaceful. You'd like it, I think.' She could come for a break, and
Thea would see Hedi through the worst of her grief until they
were both strong enough to come home. She would drive them

back and they could stop by IKEA to buy the basics. It would be like setting up a flat again. It might be fun.

'One moment,' Hedi said, holding up her finger. She walked out of the room and the floorboards bumped and creaked. The neighbour in the apartment below banged on the ceiling. It echoed like a gunshot. 'That Joy! See what I have to put up with?' Hedi said over her shoulder.

'Look here,' the social worker said briskly to Thea once Hedi had left the room, 'she's not your responsibility. No offence, but this is not a one-person job, do you hear me?'

Thea nodded. 'So I've been told.'

'And,' Charlotte Green added pointedly, 'for your information, may I remind you that assisted dying is against the law, if this is the route you're thinking of taking.'

Thea flushed. 'What are you talking about? That's an awful thing to say! I don't want Hedi to die! I want to give her a reason to go on living.'

The social worker looked at her steadily for a few moments.

Probably they were trained to be sceptical, Thea thought, trying not to blink. She had the impression she was waiting for her to crumple and back down.

'Okay,' Charlotte said finally. 'I'll be liaising with social services in your area so that they can keep an eye on things. They'll pay you a visit when Hedi is settled. Any problems, you get in touch with them.'

Hedi came back into the room carrying two small, well-worn tan-leather suitcases. 'I have everything I need,' she said. 'This small case I will leave to my daughter, Maggie.'

'Maggie is my mother,' Thea explained. 'She's in New York with her boyfriend.'

The social worker raised her eyebrows. *Of all the problem families*, her expression implied, *this was up there with the best of them.*

· · ·

They bought Hedi's train ticket from one of the machines at Euston station; it took an inordinately long time to because of the bustling crowds, and because Thea was carrying the two striped deckchairs that Hedi had insisted they bring with them. Then they had to join a queue, and Hedi wanted a one-way ticket.

Hedi was wearing Harry's tartan dressing gown over her black coat because the suitcase was full. She was also wearing the black pillbox hat with the net veil. Her wallet was tucked under her arm. She was tapping the screen with her credit card. 'Tell me,' she said briskly, waving the card at Thea, 'where does this go?'

'In that slot there, but just a minute,' Thea cautioned. 'Before you do that, it's a lot cheaper to buy a return. Don't ask me why, it's just the way the rail system works – it doesn't cost much more than a single.'

'But what's the point? I'm only going one-way,' Hedi said firmly.

'Yeah—' This was awkward.

'Makes no sense to buy a return,' Hedi said stubbornly, tilting her chin. 'I shall be gone soon to join Harry.'

'Okay, yes, but...' Thea checked the time. They had ten minutes to catch the train, so she gave up arguing. 'A single it is,' she said. 'Now you can insert your credit card. We'll have to hurry, or we'll miss it.' Hedi collected her ticket. Thea picked up the leather suitcase. It was surprisingly light and they hurried through the crowds towards platform thirteen and got on the train just as the whistle blew.

Thea put the suitcases on the luggage rack by the door and leant the deckchairs against it.

'Don't leave the suitcases there! Someone will steal them,' Hedi said crossly. 'That small one contains items of great value.'

'Does it?'

'Of course. Pah! Why else would I bring them?'

'Sorry.' Thea retrieved the cases and put them on the empty seat next to her. She sat down, relieved they'd caught the train and relieved to have got a seat. For a moment, she and Hedi looked at each other in that tired, expressionless way that strangers do, eyes skimming briefly across each other's faces.

Hedi closed her eyes, her chest still heaving from the exertion. Her black veil was caught up in the waves of her white hair. She looked pale, defeated and slightly deranged.

Thea felt a pang of pity for her grandmother. For all that she was putting up a good fight, her control over her life had been taken out of her hands, firstly by the social worker and now by Thea herself. She couldn't believe that Hedi had agreed to it. They'd kind of rushed into this without any discussion and she knew what that felt like, to have things happen to you when you hadn't instigated them.

She felt a sudden panic. She was responsible for Hedi. What if her grandmother got ill? Or what if they didn't get on? The Hideaway was fine for one person, but for two – how would they get away from each other if they needed to?

And the other worry that Thea had to face was what would happen if Hedi was right and she did die at The Hideaway? What would she do? How would she cope?

She got to her feet quickly, as if she could shake the idea off. She disguised it as a stretch. Now that she was standing, she could see the buffet car in the next carriage, bathed in a red glow. She edged out of the seat, glancing at the small suitcase with its valuable contents. She was intrigued, the cases themselves looked battered enough to belong in a skip.

At the buffet car she ordered two coffees and asked for a couple of miniature bottles of Scotch which she had spotted on a shelf behind the till. As she was helping herself to milk and sugar, she remembered Charlotte Green the social worker's expression when she came back from snooping in Hedi's fridge – *how humiliating for Hedi!* – so she also bought two egg salad sandwiches and two slices of fruit cake. The buffet car manager put everything neatly into paper bags and Thea carried them back to her seat. As she put them down on the table, Hedi jerked awake with a cry, her eyes wide with fright. Then she saw the bags and looked at them with interest.

'I was hungry,' Thea said. 'Voila!' She took out the coffees, and divided the milk and sugar sachets, the sandwiches, and the cake, and then the two little bottles between them.

'*Thenk you*,' Hedi said with a happy smile.

Thea poured the whisky in her coffee cautiously and then – *just go for it* – emptied the whole lot in. Hedi did likewise, and then she picked up a sandwich. 'Egg salad, my favourite,' she said.

'Mine too.'

That was something they had in common. It was amazing, Thea thought as she ate, the power that food has to make the world look a little brighter and problems a little smaller. That, and the restorative effect of the spiked coffee.

They shared the fruit cake and put all the wrappings in one of the paper bags. They didn't talk much after that, but it was a happy silence, not an awkward one. They looked through the windows and commented from time to time when something particularly caught their eyes – Friesian cows in a field, a string of brightly coloured narrowboats, a castle on a hill.

The train rocked them gently. As they got nearer to The Hideaway, Thea dared to feel that everything might be all right.

It was dark when they reached their destination. The trees cut black shapes in the turquoise sky. No one else got off the train.

Hedi looked round at the name of the station, Bear Cave, illuminated by a single light. She let out a cry. 'I know this place!' she said. 'I know it well.' She hugged herself. 'This is the exact village where Harry was born.'

'Seriously?' Thea felt the hairs prickle on her arms, even though it was a warm evening. 'How weird is that!'

'Maybe it's not so surprising,' Hedi said philosophically. 'We have come full circle. And you are living here now?'

'I'm just on holiday.'

Hedi shrugged and nodded. 'A fine place to come.'

They went down the road and crossed the bridge over the stream and walked along the high street. Passing the shops with their windows dark, their reflections were as faint and insubstantial as two ghosts. 'There's the bank,' Thea pointed out. She was thinking about the leather suitcases and she wondered again about the contents and whether they would be safe in the cottage, even for a short space of time. 'I wonder if we could rent a safety deposit box,' she said. 'Is that still a thing?'

'What for?'

'For your valuables.'

'Listen, don't worry about my valuables. They are only of value to me.'

'Oh, okay. You keep them for sentimental reasons?'

'Is that why I hang on to them?' Hedi wondered aloud. 'Nothing more than that? Sentimentality? Who knows. Maybe.'

'It's a good enough reason,' Thea said.

'If you're on holiday, where is your home?'

'In Highgate in London, not far from you, as it turns out.'

'Ah.' Hedi was thoughtful. 'Just across the Heath. Maggie didn't tell you where we lived?'

'No.' *She said you were dead.*

They were walking down the track in the cold shadow of the black woods, the gravel crunching under their shoes. Hedi shivered.

'Are you all right?' Thea asked her, putting the deckchairs down for a moment. 'Am I walking too quickly?'

'A little. Give me a moment.'

They had come to the end of the track. The small white

cottage seemed luminous in the dark. 'Look! There's The Hideaway,' Thea said proudly.

It was so pretty; it lifted her mood like nothing else. She
loved the way it seemed to be growing out of the ground. She
took her keys out of her pocket and opened the door.

Hedi followed her into the kitchen and looked around
tiredly, with a faint smile. She rested against the pile of wood by
the stove.

She looked exhausted, Thea thought with alarm, like a
woman who had made a huge effort and was now at the very
limit of her strength. She put Hedi's cases on the table. 'Come
and sit down. I'll make some tea. I've been sleeping in the front
bedroom, but you can have it if you like. It's brighter in the
mornings. The other bedroom faces the woods. I can swap the
sheets.'

'No need.' Hedi smiled faintly. '"The woods are lovely, dark
and deep". Yes, maybe... maybe I'm ready to sleep now. I will lie
down. No need for tea. Show me to the bathroom, if you please.'

'The toilet is outside, I'm afraid.' They went back outside. It
was pitch-black. Night noises echoed over the water beyond the
jetty. Thea switched on the flashlight and led them by the
dancing circle of torchlight.

Hedi went in first. After a few minutes the toilet flushed,
the water ran in the butler's sink, and she came out, blinking at
the dark, and held the flashlight while Thea went inside.

Back in the house, Thea locked the door and Hedi went
straight to the bedroom. She took her shoes off, and her hat, and
she lay on the bed with her arms crossed over her chest. She
looked too tired to speak, and she just nodded and gave Thea a
faint smile. 'Thank you.'

Thea hesitated in the doorway. 'Do you want me to switch
the light off?'

'No. Maybe close the door.'

'Sure. Sleep well.'

10

THEA

While Hedi slept in the back bedroom, Thea got a fire going in the wood-burning stove. She wasn't ready for bed – she felt too wired to sleep. Sitting forward on the green bamboo sofa Thea watched the flames take hold, her hands pressed together like in prayer, trying to collect her thoughts. It was strange having someone else here. She had felt safe on her own, but now she felt the heavy weight of responsibility. It had been a surreal kind of day and there were all sorts of things going through her head. It was so strange that Harry came from Bear Cave, such a coincidence, and she'd found it by chance. If it hadn't been for the traffic lights she would have driven straight through the village without giving it a second thought.

Hedi had told her on the day of the funeral that they had visited Harry's parents when she was a baby, and that they'd doted on Maggie. She wondered if their love had somehow stayed with her, somewhere deep inside, imprinted on her subconscious, and that's why it felt like home. *I could blog about it*, Thea thought, *see if anyone else has had a similar experience.*

She thought of Hedi lying down on the bed in Harry's tartan dressing gown, her arms crossed over her chest, pale as stone. Thea had never been responsible for another person before. And now she was in charge of an adult who she barely knew.

Funny how I never think of myself as an adult.

And Hedi – she didn't know her well enough to make a judgement. She seemed slightly eccentric – it was impossible not to notice the strange looks that they'd got, Hedi in her black hat and dressing gown – and definitely misguided, clearing out her house so thoroughly. Didn't know anything else about her except that she had a death wish and she'd loved Harry passionately and intensely. She thought of the way her face lit up when she spoke about him, as if she'd moved from this dimension to a better one.

She would look forward to getting to know her over the course of the holiday.

Thea looked at the small leather suitcase on the kitchen table, the one that contained the valuables. What exactly was in it? She wondered what Hedi regarded as valuable enough to keep, bearing in mind the ruthless way she had cleared the house of everything bar a bed and the deckchairs.

She could risk a quick look, but the suitcase was probably locked, anyway. Shame, really.

She stood up and went over to the table. The tan leather was scuffed, but it retained the soft gleam of age. Thea ran her hands over the smooth, cool lid.

Or maybe it wasn't locked. There was one way to find out. She clicked the lock open. Thuk! It seemed a very loud click and Thea quickly glanced at the bedroom door, but the silence was so deep it seemed to hum.

Opening the suitcase, she saw it contained a disappointing jumble of odd things: coins, medals, a man's watch, a metal bowl with dents in it, and some sort of artisanal spoon that looked as if it had been made from a tin can. 'They are only of value to me,' Hedi had said. There was also a yellowing document sticking out of the little cloth pocket in the lid, possibly Hedi and Harry's marriage certificate, something like that. None of her business, anyhow. If she wanted to know about Hedi, she could ask her.

She slid the document out of the pocket anyway and held it for a moment without looking at it. It trembled in her hand. The wood crackled and burned in the stove, making her jump. Time passed, a lot of time, it seemed. An old saying came to her: *Idle hands are the devil's workshop.*

Hey! she argued with herself. She wasn't *that* idle. She'd been to London and back twice in a couple of weeks when she was supposed to be on holiday, which wasn't part of the plan at all.

Go on, read it, you know you want to.

Yeah, why not.

She unfolded the document.

Straight away, she saw it wasn't a document, it was a type-written letter, folded for so long that the words along the creases were hard to read. But she read it anyway.

SPECIAL ORDER OF THE DAY

by Lieutenant Colonel MW Gonin RAMC

I wish to thank all ranks of the 11 (Br) Light Field Ambulance and every member of 567 Coy American Field Service Unit who have worked with us so closely, for what you have done since coming to BELSEN concentration camp on 17 April 1945.

You undertook what, for this unit, was the thankless and unspectacular task of clearing BELSEN concentration camp. Our American friends and yourselves, with the British Red Cross service, have moved well over 11,000 sick from BELSEN. To do this, sixty-three of you have worked for a month amid the most unhygienic conditions inside huts where the majority of internees were suffering from the most virulent diseases known to man. You have had to deal with mass hysteria and political complications requiring the tact of diplomats and firmness of senior officers. During the first ten days in the Concentration Camp and before any organised attempt had been made to feed the sick in those huts, you distributed 4,000 meals twice daily from what RSM MARNO could scrounge by initiative and subtlety.

You have, without hesitation, acted as undertakers, collecting over 2,000 corpses from the wards of the hospital area and removing them to the Mortuary – a task which the Royal Army Medical Corps can never before have been asked to fulfil.

The cost has not been light: twenty of you contracted Typhus – a disease causing great personal suffering. Thank God all the patients are doing well.

One of us will never leave BELSEN – the dawn attack by the German air force on our lines was the price he paid to come here.

Life can never be quite the same again for those who have worked in the Concentration Camp but you will go with the knowledge that the 11(Br) Light Field Ambulance has once again done a good job.

Wm Gonin

Lieut. Colonel RAMC

'Wow,' she whispered softly, her heart full, her eyes blurring with tears. Suddenly she was startled by Hedi coming out of the bedroom.

'Thea, where is my case?' Hedi looked from Thea to the letter in her hand. 'Hey! What are you doing with that?'

'I just—'

'Give me that letter,' Hedi said coldly. 'It's not yours to read.' She took it carefully out of Thea's hands, mindful of its fragility. Then she slapped Thea hard and viciously across the face.

It was so unexpected that Thea cried out in shock, her face burning from the impact, and from the shame.

'Hedi, I'm sorry,' she pleaded.

'How *could* you?' Hedi's eyes were dark with furious anger. 'You were right. I should have bought a return ticket as you said. Tomorrow I'm going back to London.' She folded the letter up and put it back into the pocket of the case, closed it and took the case to her room.

Thea braced herself, expecting Hedi to slam the door, but her grandmother closed it carefully, which was worse. Thea heard her dragging a chair over, making sure she didn't sneak in and root through her possessions while she was asleep.

Can you blame her? Thea rubbed her sore cheekbone. *What have I done?*

11

HEDI

Hedi sat on the chair and leant back against the door, her heart racing painfully. She looked out at the dark looming woods, hugging her case to her chest, the taste of woodsmoke in her throat.

Bitter tears rolled down her cheeks, hot and caustic. The skin of her palm stung like a nettle rash. All these years she and Harry had kept Belsen a secret, and now her granddaughter had torn off the covers, leaving her naked in the light of the revelation.

Harry! What do I do?

He had told her many times that there was no shame in it, not on her part. Survival had been the thing, the *only* thing, and praise God, they had both survived to live their lives happily together without looking back. On the rare times that they brought up the subject, that was what they agreed on: *no looking back.*

She banged her fist on the case, her face screwed up with rage. *How dare Thea?* She was furious with her, burning up with anger.

Is that so?

Harry's voice came to her perfectly clearly, the calm in the eye of the storm.

'It is so,' she protested in a small, tight voice clogged with tears. 'It *is* so.' But her anger was losing its power and she rubbed the tears from her eyes with the edge of the tartan dressing gown and took a deep, shuddering breath.

So now she knows.

What had she seen in her granddaughter's startled expression? *Guilt – quite right, too.*

And alongside the guilt, tears.

Hedi knew she shouldn't have kept the letter. It was bound to be read. What was she going to do, eat it on her deathbed? She should've burnt it.

But it was a fine, moving letter of thanks and appreciation, covering in just one page the heroic magnitude of the long month that went by after liberation, with the heartbreak, the death, the pain, the hope, the love, the transformation that took place during that extraordinary time.

Without Harry, she would not be here today. Maggie would not have been born. And therefore, ergo, Thea would not have been born either.

Just as she came to this conclusion, Hedi heard a choked sob in the other room.

She was flooded with remorse. *What am I thinking! The girl has been so kind!* Travelling all that way to the funeral of a man who was a stranger, except by blood. Offering Hedi a holiday and her freedom when the social worker wanted to lock her up. Buying sandwiches and whisky. She was a good, decent person. *So Thea read the letter – so what? Curiosity killed the cat, satisfaction brought him back.*

At least go in and talk to her.

It was Harry's voice again. No, it was her own voice for once, one she barely listened to, the voice of reason. Hedi got up, put the case down on the bed, removed the chair from against the door. Opened it.

Thea was sitting on the bamboo sofa, her arms resting on her knees, head bent, shrouded by her auburn hair.

'I apologise,' Hedi said softly, standing in the doorway. 'It was unforgivable of me to slap you, and you have been so kind to me.'

Thea raised her head. Her face was puffy, strands of hair sticking to her cheeks. That red mark.

'I'm sorry too,' she said. 'I don't know why I did it – I don't usually... I'm usually very respectful.'

'I know that,' Hedi said briskly. 'Of course, it's plain, anyone can see it in you. Don't cry! I'll put the kettle on.' Well now, here was something she could do. The kettle was half full already and she switched on the gas. Cups, saucers, sugar. Milk from the fridge. She busied herself, wondering what to say and where to start.

When she turned back, Thea was sitting at one end of the sofa, generously making space for her. Not like her mother at all.

'Here.' Hedi give her the cup and sat next to her. 'You know the saying "curiosity killed the cat"?'

Thea bit her lip. 'Yeah. Of course.'

'"Satisfaction brought him back." You know that bit?'

Thea shook her head.

'If I explain the past,' Hedi said, 'it might bring you back, you see?'

'You don't have to explain.'

Hedi shrugged. 'Too late. The cat is out of the bag.' *The ket is out of the beg.* 'It is better that I tell you the truth of it now, but the choice is yours. To hear, or not to hear. You see, I am taking the coward's way out, to leave it to you to choose.'

Thea broke eye contact. She hooked her hair around her ear and sipped her tea. Then she asked, 'Does Maggie know?'

'No. Never. She was so perfect... We didn't want to sully her with that knowledge. We wanted her to see that life is beautiful and full of love, which it has been, you understand me? Look at all this,' she said, spreading her arms wide to include Thea and the kitchen around her. 'We wanted her to trust in the goodness of life. She shouldn't have had to worry about what had happened to us or what we'd seen.' Hedi sighed. 'I don't know, it seemed for the best at the time. Things always do, don't you find? People who'd been in the camps seemed to divide into two schools of thought: those that talk about it to the world, witnesses to what happened, and those who put the past behind them. Harry and I put it behind us. The older we got, the less of our life it took up. You know... percentage-wise, as Harry would put it.'

'Oh.' Thea's eyes searched for hers again. 'The letter, that was to Harry, wasn't it?'

'That is correct. April 1945. The war was still raging in its death throes.' Hedi closed her eyes for a moment, visualising it. 'And an extraordinary thing happened. The Germans approached the British lines waving a white flag of truce. They needed assistance. Their request was simple. The hospital in Bergen had been overtaken by a virulent typhus epidemic, and when the war was over, which would surely not be long, the sick patients would leave in their thousands and head back to their homes; not only to Germany but to Holland and France and Belgium, taking the typhus with them.' She opened her eyes and looked at Thea. 'You understand? Europe, already devastated by war and hardship, would face a pandemic. They wanted the British to help them restore order and guard the patients.' Hedi paused and gave a wry smile. *Patients.*

'So Harry and his group of men were ordered to change out of their battledress and into their dress uniforms. A ceasefire zone was established around the camp. And the British drove through enemy lines in enemy territory, waving white flags of truce. Hoping for the best.'

Hedi's cup trembled and clattered in its saucer. She put it on the floor. 'That day was the day I got my first sight of him in his uniform, with his blazing red hair and his gentle green eyes and his clean soap smell.' Clasping her hands on her lap to steady them, she looked into the flames, at the wood burning red in the stove, remembering.

12

HEDI
BELSEN, APRIL 1945

Hedi left the deep, dark comfort of sleep, her young bones pushing against her thin flesh, and woke into the half-forgotten and pleasurable sensation of heat and humidity.

Pressed up against Magda on the middle tier of the wooden plank bed, the heat was Magda's fever, and the dampness was Magda's sweat. Although the warmth was welcome, it was also fierce, like standing too close to a fire. For a moment, Hedi didn't move, she just lay there listening to the groans, whimpers and death snores of the other prisoners, her filthy shirt clinging to her back. It wasn't a bad feeling. Let's face it, she'd had worse.

Reluctantly, Hedi opened her eyes and saw with fresh eyes the terrible state they were in. Each time, it took her by surprise. Brief periods of sleep cruelly wiped her mind clean, and on waking, reality returned with incredible violence. For a moment, her gaze connected with the gaunt, blank stare of the woman lying on the other side of her. That woman had been here so long she had forgotten her own name. Her only identity was her number.

Black, vacant eyes met hers and locked. And then suddenly,

in their lifeless depths Hedi saw a dangerous flicker of amusement. The woman threw her head back and laughed.

Hedi lay still and stared into the woman's wide-open, cavernous mouth. Maybe it wasn't a laugh. It sounded like a squeak of rusty hinges. A laugh or a scream, they looked the same these days.

She realised it was getting dark. That was strange. 'Where are the Kapos, do you think?' she asked the woman. 'They're late. Shouldn't they be here, beating us already, getting us out for the evening roll call?' Everyone hated the Kapos. They were prisoners, the same as them, but working on SS orders. They were brutal and cold-bloodedly cruel. Still, Hedi felt oddly indignant. The camp was run on routine. She felt as if she were the strict teacher and the Kapos were pupils unexpectedly late for school.

The woman's dark eyes were watchful. She didn't reply.

Hedi turned carefully on her wooden plank to tell Magda that the Kapos hadn't come.

Magda was twenty-four, but in that glance, Hedi saw her as she would look when she was an old lady, eyes sunken, moving behind the lids, her thin, tight skin glistening like a pearl. She was wrapped in a blanket. She had typhus, spread by the lice in the seams of their clothes. Now that Magda had got rid of her clothes, the lice lived in the blanket instead.

Hedi had a fear, a horror, of Magda dying. Who would she have left if she went?

Magda had been an attractive woman when they'd first met in the freight carriage, with thick brown, shoulder-length hair and full lips. They'd been told they were lucky to be going to Belsen. Belsen was not a concentration camp. Internees were exchanged for prisoners of war. They were currency.

'You can be my little sister,' Magda said furtively to Hedi as they were crushed together. 'You remind me of her, a little.'

Hedi was wary. 'Where is she?'

Magda averted her eyes. 'We got separated.'

Hedi didn't trust Magda. Nothing personal; she didn't trust anyone. 'You might find her again. And then you won't want me.'

Magda gripped her arm. 'Tell me, how old are you?'

'Seventeen.'

'Okay, so she's just fourteen. You'll be her big sister. We'll be the three sisters.' Magda's face altered, her chin puckered, her mouth turned down. She was crying silently.

Hedi stared at the pure brightness of the track of Magda's clean tears. She shrugged. 'I suppose I could be your sister if you want it that much,' she had said. 'At least,' she added, 'I could give it a try.'

What did it matter, really? They were heading for the end of the line, the terminus. They all knew that.

Now, six months on, it was evening roll call and the Kapos were late.

Hedi was on the point of waking Magda when she thought, *leave her to sleep*.

She got down from the bunk, twisting at the last moment to avoid a pool of excrement dripping between the slats. Typhus did terrible things to the human gut. The disease was raging through the camp, turning the huts into cesspits.

She could hear a Kapo's voice outside and there was something strange about it. Instead of barking commands, it sounded almost normal, like voices you might hear in a village, from people walking past, passing the time of day. She rubbed a hole in the grimy window and watched inmates hobbling by, their heads supported by a scaffold of bones.

'Hey, come and look!' Hedi announced to whoever in the hut had a mind to hear. 'Everyone's heading to the *Appellplatz* for the roll call. We should go!' That was how it was, day after day, the sick, the dying, the starving, the weak and the insane, they all gathered in the yard in rags, standing in that desolate place with a cold easterly wind blowing, shivering for four hours in all weathers at the mercy and whim of the brutal Kapos, who in turn were at the mercy of the SS who were ruled by Camp Commandant Kramer. She turned back to face the room. 'Hurry! Let's go! We'll be in trouble!' They were creatures of habit. Why would today be any different?

The gaunt woman climbed down, also avoiding the puddle of filth. She elbowed Hedi out of the way and put her eye to the clear spot in the grimy window and looked out.

'Something is going on,' she declared after a moment. 'Come! Let's go see!' She bared her teeth in her skull. 'After all, what can they do but kill us?'

Suddenly from outside the hut there was a burst of gunfire.

Neither of them flinched. They were fatalistic, that way.

It hadn't put off the other prisoners, either.

Through the clean patch in the glass they watched the skeletal women shuffling silently in the direction of the *Appellplatz*. Their faces were vacant. Prisoners in the camps didn't have expressions. They didn't have the energy for them, and besides, they no longer had the muscles necessary to form a frown or a smile.

And the other thing was, they didn't have feelings. Well, you couldn't. What was the point of them? It was easier to choose what you saw and what you didn't see, and to try to keep sane. Their whole view of life depended on them looking through the small clean hole that remained in their souls.

Hedi and the nameless woman glanced at each other. They were curious. Beneath the apathy, that most basic of human instincts survived: the desire to find out what was going on.

Outside the wooden huts, the path to the *Appellplatz* was piled high with bodies waiting to be buried, a tangle of limbs. Hedi saw them and didn't see them. A woman paused to lean on them as if they were sandbags, regaining the last of her strength before moving on.

Hedi and the nameless woman were too weak to lift their feet as they walked. Their bones weighed them down. Their shuffling sounded like a whisper, kicking up dust.

Suddenly a voice blared through a loudspeaker and they stopped dead.

'*IHR SEID FREI!*'

Hedi was confused. The announcement was German, but the accent wasn't.

'YOU ARE FREE! WE ARE THE BRITISH ARMY! STAY CALM! FOOD AND MEDICAL HELP IS ON ITS WAY!'

Hedi and the woman looked at each other, mouths agape, understanding the words. They danced around in Hedi's head, but the notion was too enormous to absorb.

'What's he saying? We are free? That's what he's saying?' the woman asked.

'Sounds like it,' Hedi replied doubtfully. 'Look out!'

An army jeep was driving slowly towards them followed by a silent crowd of the starving. The women stumbling after it were waving their arms and wailing without sound, without tears, too weak to cheer.

The car was manned by British soldiers, one holding the megaphone and repeating the message. '*IHR SEID FREI!*' And bizarrely, Camp Commandant Kramer was sitting in the vehicle with them, his scarred face tight with contempt, his hand on his gun.

Hedi moved back cautiously to avoid being knocked over in the scuffle. She backed into a birch sapling. In a rush of gratitude she snapped off a young branch and threw it with all her remaining strength at the car as it passed.

A British soldier caught it and as he did so, he looked straight at her, his jaw muscles tense. Compassion softened his green eyes, and he held the leafy branch up high and saluted her.

Under his cap, his copper hair shone bright in the sunset. When Hedi blinked, it left a green afterglow on her retina.

Next to her, her nameless companion collapsed to her knees in the road in a prayer of thanks, kissing the tyre tracks left in the dry earth. It was a mistake, really, because for a few moments, she couldn't get up again.

When the woman finally got to her feet, she said purposefully, 'Right, let's get some potatoes.'

Hedi shivered. It was spring, and still cold. She was ready to return to the relative warmth of the hut. 'Why? Why should we? Did you hear them? Food is on its way!'

The woman snorted. 'There are 40,000 of us in this camp. How long is it going to take that handful of soldiers to get around to us, of all people?'

Hedi agreed with her reasoning. They shuffled to the potato patch, and found they weren't the only ones to have thought of stocking up. They joined their fellow internees in digging in the dirt, furtively, but not furtively enough because suddenly the Kapos were on them, guns aimed. They started firing.

A starving girl next to Hedi dropped to the ground dead, spilling her haul around her. Hedi, ears ringing, flattened herself against the earth, eyes squeezed tight as she prayed. *Please! Not now. Not yet.*

More shots were fired, but this time they were warning shots, fired in the air.

'Stop!'

The British soldiers were back. They were angry, challenging the guards. 'What the hell are you doing?'

Hedi's heart was pounding with relief. She got to her knees cautiously, spitting the dirt from her mouth.

The Kapos turned on them indignantly and tried to make the Tommies understand. They were only killing the troublemakers. They had to keep order, didn't they? It was their job!

Otherwise there would be rioting! The prisoners were stealing the potatoes!

The soldiers had seemed impassive the first time they drove past, but now, as they confronted the Kapos, their emotions showed.

'Look at them! They're living skeletons,' the commanding officer reprimanded him, his face flushed with anger. 'This is not a hospital, this is a horror camp.'

'So?' asked the Kapo, confused.

The nameless woman was on her hands and knees, gathering the dead woman's potatoes. Hedi joined her, clutching them to her bony chest, hunching her shoulders against inevitable blows as they hurried way, but the Kapos were too busy arguing with the British to bother with them.

'Did you see the look of disgust on that officer's face?' Hedi asked, troubled, as they shuffled back to the hut.

'How could I miss it,' her companion said.

Back in the hut, they announced the good news.

'The British have freed the camp!'

'They are bringing us food and medicine! And look!'

They were holding the potatoes to show them, dusting the sandy soil off them.

Hands reached out weakly. Even Magda, burning with fever, dangled her arm over the plank. The ones who lay still were dead.

Hedi held her bounty close and considered her options. She could use these potatoes to barter with, as well as to eat. She had enough to last her for weeks if she guarded them well, she could keep them until they shrivelled and started sprouting.

But already her crazy companion was distributing hers, one in each trembling, outstretched hand.

Hedi hesitated, but she understood the gesture. It was an

act of faith; they were free! Free to be generous! It was a dizzying feeling. She felt as if her shrivelled heart was cracking open to reveal something good.

She put two in the bubbling pot to cook and climbed back onto the plank next to Magda.

'Here,' she said.

Magda gave a faint smile. Their dark eyes met. 'Thank you.'

In the same way that water takes on a wonderful sweetness when you are thirsty, the raw potato tasted magnificent. There was the satisfying crunch, the juice, the way the starch lined the roof of a sore mouth and coated the teeth. 'Eat, Magda,' she prompted.

The woman who had forgotten her name lay on the plank next to her, chewing.

Ah, Hedi thought, *she is not so crazy after all.*

The woman sensed Hedi's gaze. 'You know something?' Her eyes looked huge and bottomless. 'A heart or liver would go well with these potatoes,' she said speculatively.

Hedi was appalled to feel the saliva rush into her mouth.

It had been just a rumour to start with, that people were cutting open the dead for their organs. But there was evidence of this on the piles of bodies, and one of the Kapos had been shot for selling kidneys from door to door to the local villagers.

'Maybe,' she said. 'But now we are free. We can be civilised.'

'Freeeeee,' the woman said, stretching out the word with great satisfaction. 'What are we going to do with our freedom?'

'As soon as I've had enough to eat, I'm going home,' Hedi said.

'Home,' the woman repeated, as if she was feeling her way around the word. 'Who will you find waiting?'

'I'll know when I get there.' Hedi felt a moment's unease.

'Maybe no one,' the woman said, as if she could read her thoughts.

The sun set behind the trees. The stove flickered shadows around the hut. The woman's eyes looked like holes in her skull.

'What will you do?' Hedi asked her.

'I will go and look for my husband.' She flinched, as if the memory physically hurt.

'What's his name?'

'Karl.'

Hedi was surprised. 'You can remember his name, but you forgot your own?' She propped herself up on her elbow where the sores weren't too fresh.

'It's strange,' the woman agreed, wrapping her potato up in her blanket, saving some for later.

'Don't worry. When you find your Karl, he will tell you what your name is.'

'Perhaps.'

With food in her belly, Hedi was ready to take on a fresh problem, the subject of her companion's identity. It was an important thing to know – not right now, perhaps, but in the future. 'God has called you by your name,' she said. 'If He calls you and you don't know it, how will you know to answer Him?'

The woman didn't seem too troubled by the question.

What a terrible thing to forget your own name, Hedi thought. Everything had been taken away from them: their freedom, their families, their possessions, their looks, their pride, their self-respect, their free will, their health. All they had left of themselves was their identity, and without that... Her thoughts tailed off and she looked up at the plank above her. It was very narrow to hold a row of people, even thin ones. She hadn't noticed it before. How could that be?

But then, it was very unusual to have the freedom to lie here doing nothing, without fear of reprisals.

The Kapos hated them, but even more, they hated them doing nothing. It frustrated them. Nothingness was a final state of mind that some women retreated into through apathy when they could find no will to go on.

Once they went into it, there was no enticing them out, not with food nor threats nor pain. The Kapos could punish them horribly, kick them, torture them, flay them, but it made no difference. They had turned their face to the wall and gone somewhere deep and unreachable to die, which was frightening and impressive to watch.

Hedi had never got to that place yet, but she knew it was there, accessible, if she needed it.

So far, she had lived from day-to-day, not with hope, exactly, because this place destroyed it very quickly, but with stubbornness. 'I wonder when they'll bring the food and medicine?' she asked.

'Trust me,' the woman with no name said knowingly. 'We're in for a long wait.'

No sooner had she said it than they heard British voices outside.

'Ha! You're wrong!' Hedi said triumphantly. 'They've come! I can hear them outside right now!'

The door of the wooden hut opened, letting in the cold light. Five young soldiers in khaki uniforms came in a few paces, led by the man with the copper hair and green eyes, the man who had saluted her. They were carrying stretchers.

But moments later it seemed as if they had walked into an electric fence because they suddenly jerked to a halt and walked straight back out again, letting the door slam behind them. There was the unmistakable sound of retching from outside.

'That was a flying visit,' the nameless woman said drily.

Hedi's blood rose to her cheeks in shame.

A new voice whispered weakly, 'If I'd known they were coming, I would have made them tea.'

The nameless woman threw back her head and gave a screeching, rusty laugh.

'What will we do now?' Hedi asked in a panic. 'Have they abandoned us?'

Just then, the door opened again, and the soldiers came back inside the hut, smoking cigarettes. The cigarettes burned red and the blue smoke rolled across the ceiling. Hedi inhaled deeply. It reminded her of her father. It also, she guessed wryly, disinfected the air a little.

The soldier with copper hair pursed his lips and dragged on his cigarette, making a little warm glow. He blew out a pale stream of smoke.

Hedi hoped he might recognise her as the girl he saluted with the branch, and say something, but he didn't. Of course he didn't. *Living corpses all look the same. It must be hard to tell that she was even a woman.*

'Right!' he said cheerfully, 'this is the plan. We're going to clear out the dead from here to give you more room. We'll bring you some food, and we're going to clean the huts and commence a delousing operation. Once you've had a bath and a few hot meals...' His voice faltered and he fell silent. He breathed in deeply through his nostrils and cleared his throat before continuing, '... a few hot meals inside you,' he continued steadily, 'you won't know yourself.'

'Huh. She doesn't know herself now,' Hedi said gloomily of her companion.

'It's true,' the woman nodded. 'I've forgotten my name. Have you got a cure for that?'

The soldier gave a faint smile. His gentle green eyes swept Hedi's and rested on her. Then he too left and went outside. He lowered his voice, but the inmates could hear the men's voices through the cracks in the wooden door.

'Let's get the dead out,' he was saying. 'Then we'll transfer the sick. And the rest, the ones who are fit, we'll feed.'

'Fit? Mate, they're zombies. How can humans be that thin and still alive?'

'They can have my rations. They're welcome to them. I've lost my appetite,' the third solder said.

The news that they were fit came as something of a surprise to the living corpses left behind. But they'd been promised food, so they didn't complain much.

Once the dead had been stretchered off, there was more room in the hut. It was still a disgusting place to be, and Hedi tried not to get too optimistic about the future. You couldn't trust anyone, there was no point in trying. She left that to the naive. She herself knew better. 'You hear what he said, Magda? They're going to bring us food. You'll soon be well.'

They were waiting for their food, and they didn't have to wait long; when it came it was biscuits, potatoes and milk, and stew from a tin. There was so much food that Hedi thought at first her portion was for all of them. She ate it quickly, too quickly, and licked her metal bowl, satisfied for now. Then she helped Magda to eat hers, holding the spoon to her lips. 'Good?'

'Good,' Magda agreed, opening her mouth like a baby bird. After a couple of mouthfuls she let her head drop. 'No more, Hedi,' she whispered. 'You have the rest.'

Hedi stroked Magda's hair gently out of her eyes and looked down at the food left in the bowl. She put her face over it to inhale the savoury aroma. *She said I could have it.*

Undecided, she lay back, rested the bowl on her hollow belly, comforted by its residual warmth, and reviewed the day. They were free, and they were being looked after.

'Soon we'll be home,' she said to Magda.

How would she get there? She had come here by train. How civilised that sounded, compared with the reality! So, she thought logically, she would go back by train, too. She could imagine her parents' faces when they saw her!

Hedi's thoughts clouded over – she didn't know where her parents were. But as she herself was still alive, it was likely they were, too. If not likely, then it was certainly possible. It was their stubbornness that she had inherited, after all. She looked across at the woman with no name. 'What about your parents? Will they be waiting for you?'

'No.' The woman laid her bony forearm across her forehead, covering her eyes. 'They were shot.'

'Oh. Sorry.'

The woman snorted with anger. 'Why do you say "sorry" like that? It was a quick, clean death and they died with a full belly. What more could you want?'

'I was just being polite,' Hedi said, hurt by the woman's harsh tone.

'Ah well, you're young.'

It was true. 'Too young.' It filled Hedi with dismay to think of all the things she hadn't experienced, and maybe never would. She thought of the British soldier, how clean and kind he looked. 'I've never even kissed a boy yet.'

'No? Hey, don't worry, you will one day. Underneath that dirt and with a bit of flesh on your bones I expect you'll be quite pretty, really.'

'Do you think so?' Hedi would like to believe it. She said doubtfully, 'The soldier vomited after he saw us.'

'That was because of the smell, not us.'

'The smell. Yes, you're right.' Hedi didn't notice it any more, and so she tended to forget about it. 'When you were seventeen, had you kissed a boy?'

'Yes, I kissed Karl. In an orchard. Then I had a nosebleed.'

Hedi was puzzled. 'Why?'

'Who knows? Maybe it was the excitement.'

'Just think, even now, Karl might be on his way home.'

The woman considered the statement. 'No. The war's not over yet,' she said finally. 'We would have been told.'

'You think you know everything,' Hedi said irritably, scratching her infested head. 'Why would Commandant Kramer allow the British to free the camp if we're still at war?'

The woman thought about it. 'Ask yourself this. Did he look like a defeated man to you, being driven around in that car like a dictator with his fat stomach and his scar and the fire of Nazi devotion burning in his eyes?'

She's right. *It's not over yet*, Hedi thought.

13

HARRY

Late that evening, Harry Lewis and his men returned to their new quarters in the Panzer Training School in Belsen. They mustered in the German Officers' Mess, as well stocked as a gentlemen's club.

Despite the comfort, Harry had never felt so tired or so dispirited. He ran his fingers through his hair. What were they doing in this hell? He was well acquainted with the horrors of war, but nothing had prepared him for the sights they'd seen that day.

The description of Belsen as a 'hospital' was just a ruse. It was a concentration camp. He'd heard rumours about the camps, but as both sides employed propaganda, he had believed it was just another extreme example aiming to convince them of German brutality.

Then he thought of the girl in the silent, shuffling crowd, her cheeks hollow, her huge grey eyes with pure light in them, throwing the branch to him with the last of her strength. And later, in the filthy hut, he'd seen her again, vivid with life, despite being crammed into those human pigeonholes with an upturned tin bowl as a pillow. The memory moved him and gave him strength. *That's what this is for.*

He looked up at Derek. 'It's going to be a big task,' he said simply, thinking of the sight, the smell, of the unburied dead.

Derek swallowed his water the wrong way and once he'd recovered from choking, he started to laugh. 'That's what we're here for, chum.' All of a sudden, he stopped laughing and he was sober again.

'This girl, when we came in...' The thought of the girl cleared Harry's mind. It was no different from a lot of choices he'd made in life. Which puppy to keep. Which motorbike to buy. Which branch of the Armed Forces to join. Which woman to save.

He couldn't make a difference to everyone, but if he could make a difference to one person, he would have done something worthwhile with his time here.

'No fraternising,' Derek reminded him, wagging his finger.

'Yeah, I know the rules.'

Bill Corley came to sit next to Harry. His weary face was pale and the stubble showed dark on his cheeks. 'We've got a dickens of a job ahead of us,' he said. 'This place is beyond belief.'

He was about to say more but the colonel called them to attention and addressed them, thanking them for volunteering to join the armed convoy through enemy lines, at the request of Commandant Kramer. It had been risky, he acknowledged.

Too true. Harry's heart had been in his mouth. He'd watched the defeated, disillusioned faces of the German soldiers as the British convoy rumbled through the battle-scarred countryside. *We're all scared*, he'd thought. *We've all had enough.*

The colonel informed them that the hundreds of Wehrmacht guarding the camp had now been recalled to battle.

The good news was that it would leave more space in Camp Two for the sick when they transferred them from Camp One.

'We're going to have the place cleaned up, and get the people fit for discharge. Our priority is to feed the living and dispose of the dead,' the colonel concluded. 'One final point.' His face was grim, and as his men waited for him to continue, he gave one of his rare smiles. 'Gentlemen! The bar is open.'

It was the best news Harry had heard all day.

14

THEA
PRESENT DAY

In The Hideaway, Thea saw Hedi's eyes moving under her veined eyelids as she remembered the past.

Hedi fell silent and rested her cheek against the green sofa cushion. Her tea was undrunk, cold in the cup.

Thea crouched towards the last bit of warmth ebbing from the stove. The shifting logs had burned down to grey ash. She wondered how Hedi had managed to keep this story a secret from Maggie all these years, leaving such a massive chunk of her life out of the picture. She knew why. *She was perfect.*

But she could understand now why Maggie's determination to diet after Thea's birth had been incomprehensible to Hedi, even forty-five years on. That's exactly how she might have felt if she'd seen a starving woman shot dead right next to her for scrabbling for a few potatoes.

Hedi opened her grey eyes, emerging from her memories. In her lined face her eyes were as bright as those of a young girl. She smiled at Thea. 'Harry was such a handsome boy.'

'Was it love at first sight?'

Hedi considered the question carefully. 'I wasn't thinking so much of love right then – what use was that to me? Easy to see you've never been hungry, God be praised! Food was all I could think about, licking the bowl clean and anticipating the next meal. We had bottomless appetites for food. Desperation turns people into animals. We had been living like animals for a while. I thought of him a lot though... he was a bright spot in my day.'

Thea wanted to ask Hedi what had happened to Magda, but at the same time she was not sure she wanted to know, especially this late at night. Instead, she said, 'That day that the British came and the camp was liberated, it must have been a relief to know you'd been rescued, and the bad times were over.'

'Over? Not quite over,' Hedi said. 'The war hadn't ended at that point.' She glanced at her watch. 'It is very late and that is a story for another day.' She looked around and got to her feet unsteadily. 'Tell me, where is the flashlight? I will go to the privy before bed.'

'I'll come with you,' Thea said.

Outside the cottage, the night was still and the air was fresh and cool on her skin. Light flooded out of the windows, making picnic-blanket squares on the grass. Above them in the black sky glittered a scattered profusion of stars.

In the cathedral resonance of the dark, an owl hooted, and the sound echoed across the water.

'You know, I love night-time,' Hedi said, listening.

'Me too.' Thea took the old woman's arm. 'If you look over there beyond the jetty you can see the hotel on the other side of the river.' She shone a long cone of light at it. 'We should go there for drinks one evening, right?'

In the distance, the George III Hotel was lit up, bejewelled with coloured bulbs. Their reflections danced and glittered on the black water. The faint sound of music reached them on the breeze. It looked exciting, enticing, and Hedi laughed with delight.

Thea was relieved. It seemed as if things were all right

between them again, better than all right, and she felt immensely grateful. She hated conflict.

Curiosity killed the cat, satisfaction brought him back.

As she stood waiting for Hedi outside the peeling door of the privy, she knew she would never see her the same way as she had before, not as the selfish Hedi that her mother resented, nor as the wife so wrapped up in her husband that the couple excluded their own daughter.

That image had been overlaid by a sadder, more poignant one. Hedi and Harry were survivors. As the letter to Harry had stated: *Life can never be quite the same again for those who have worked in the Concentration Camp.* But she understood Hedi's reasoning. Truth could be a burden. Was it better to be seen through the prism of pity, or misunderstood for hiding the truth?

Inside the privy, the chain of the toilet cistern clanked and the tap in the butler's sink turned on before Hedi opened the door and came out shaking the drips from her hands. 'Your turn,' she said cheerfully. 'I will keep guard for you.'

Thea sat on the loo and looked up at the ceiling where the shadows were shifting. A moth was batting itself against the light bulb. The spiders were busy adorning the corners with cobwebs once more.

When she came out, Hedi was pointing the wavering flashlight towards the hotel. She sighed deeply. 'It's beautiful,' she said, and they stood there a moment longer in the rustling night air before going inside.

15

THEA

Next morning, Thea woke up from a dream about the sea that was so real she could taste the salt on her lips. She felt a surge of excitement and opened her eyes. It was daylight, and all was quiet. She closed her eyes and tried to sink into the dream again, forcing herself deeper into the freedom of a blue sky, the mint-cold waves lapping at her feet, the breeze ruffling her red hair.

Something important had been about to happen just before she woke up. It was at the same time urgent and solvable. It was to do with her boyfriend, Adam. He was wearing paint-splattered navy overalls, his long brown hair held out of his eyes by a band.

'Hey!' she'd yelled to him.

He glanced across, surprised, and grinned. 'Hello,' he said. He came over and looked at her with steady, hazel eyes.

They were an unusual colour, and in the dream she'd wondered how it was that she'd forgotten about them. 'I'm glad you've come,' she'd said with a little laugh and the weightless happiness and sense of purpose thrilled her.

But already the memory was fading irretrievably. Well, why wouldn't it? It was just a dream, after all. Her subconscious had bypassed the logic, her suppressed emotions, her regrets. She missed him and she wanted to cry, mourning what they had. Why did he want to change things?

I wish...

She groped for her phone and checked the time. Eight forty. Early, but not too early to get up and face the day. And not just the day, but Hedi; a virtual stranger with a dark story to tell.

My grandmother.

It must be equally strange for Hedi, Thea thought. She'd been uprooted, forced to change her plan to die peacefully, if that was really something one could plan. She had seemed pretty sure about it, and Hedi, as Thea had discovered last night, was more familiar with death than most people.

Thea lay awake listening intently for signs of life in the next room. All was quiet. She wondered if she should check on her.

This must be what babysitting feels like, she thought. A sense of responsibility mixed with nervous uncertainty. Not that she'd ever babysat before, but she was guessing the emotions were probably similar.

She got out of bed and went quietly into the kitchen. The two blue striped deckchairs were leaning against the wall, where they'd left them the evening before. The kettle was cold. Thea stared at it, wondering whether the sound of it boiling would wake Hedi up. She quite liked the privacy.

She took a chance. Sitting at the small wooden table staring at her coffee, Thea had the idea, on and off – yes, she knew it was ridiculous – that she should check on Hedi in case something had happened to her while she herself was going about her normal business.

Time passed.

She checked her phone. Hedi had been asleep for fourteen hours now.

Thea got up and listened by the door in the hope she would hear her grandmother breathing, but unfortunately Hedi seem to be a remarkably silent sleeper. Thea hadn't even heard the bed creak. It had to be a good thing, didn't it, that Hedi was catching up on her rest. It showed she felt comfortable and safe. The previous day had been strange for them both.

Despite this, Thea couldn't settle, and she wondered if she dared to go out to take her mind off it. Hedi might sleep for ages yet. On the other hand, she might wake up completely disorientated and need reassurance. She decided to leave her a note on the back of an envelope.

Gone down to the jetty.

There. Done. She added:

It's straight ahead as you leave the house.

Thea dressed, made another coffee, and carried it along with the striped deckchairs down to the jetty. She set them up facing the sun. For such heavy and cumbersome bits of kit, they were surprisingly comfortable. It was like sitting in a hammock. She closed her eyes, her thoughts bathed in the red light of her eyelids.

She was disturbed from her thoughts a short time later by Hedi, wearing black, carrying two mugs of coffee like a waitress. Thea watched her through the fringe of her eyelashes as Hedi put the mugs down silently, took her shoes off and placed them neatly together. Then she straightened up, shielding her eyes from the sun, and after a moment's indecision walked briskly to the end of the jetty. As she stretched her arms out, Thea sat up, suddenly alarmed. 'Hedi!'

Her grandmother didn't hear her. She stood motionless, arms raised, looking across the shimmering water.

Thea got out of the deckchair. She hurried along the boards. 'Hedi!'

Hedi turned quickly. 'Thea!' she said, surprised. 'I thought you were sleeping.' Her expression altered. 'What's wrong? You look upset.'

'I thought you were... going to fall in,' Thea said lamely, patting her racing heart.

'Did you? And you were coming to rescue me? Sweet of you,' she said defiantly, 'but I don't need rescuing.'

'Okay! Good to hear,' Thea said.

They stood looking at each other awkwardly. Thea scooped her hair back and tied it with the band she was wearing around her wrist while she tried to think of something to say. *Nope. She had nothing.*

Hedi, too, was looking thoughtful, running a finger along her lower lip. 'The weather is mild,' she said at last.

Thea squinted up at the sky, as if she hadn't noticed. 'Yes. Very mild.' She wondered if Hedi regretted oversharing. She wondered if she should bring up the conversation and say something reassuring. She wasn't sure what.

Hedi turned back to look at the water.

'Um, I'm going to the shop in a minute,' Thea said, desperate to break the deadlock. 'Do you want to come with me?'

Still with her back to her, Hedi shook her head. She seemed mesmerised by the water. 'No, thank you.'

'Okay.'

They were as distant as strangers but now with new, added worry. *I've made her my responsibility, I'm committed,* Thea thought in amazement. She'd acted without thinking, for once. Maybe that wasn't a bad thing. That's where she went wrong, usually, overthinking everything. 'I'll get enough food for a couple of days,' she said. 'Is there anything you particularly fancy?'

Hedi looked at her over her shoulder and her eyes gleamed. 'Wine?' she replied cautiously.

Thea laughed at the conspiratorial way she said it. She realised they were feeling similar emotions – two strangers sharing a house with a whole lifetime of conversational pitfalls to catch up on. 'Yeah, wine, definitely,' she said. 'Red or white?'

'Up to you.'

'Okay. Red, then.'

Hedi clapped her hands, and just like that, the distance between them closed up. '*Ektually*, I was going to say red!'

And I thought we had nothing in common, Thea thought cheerfully as she headed back to the house.

That evening, after supper, without really discussing it, Hedi grabbed the half-empty wine bottle and her glass. 'I'm going to sit on the jetty,' she announced. 'I would like to watch the sun go down.' She held Thea's gaze as she said it.

Thea saw the invitation in her eyes. She picked up her glass, still half full. 'I'll come with you.'

Hedi smiled. 'Wonderful!' she said. Her smile faded. 'I have a confession I want you to hear. I have never spoken about it to anyone, not even to Harry.'

She went outside, and Thea grabbed another bottle. She had a feeling she was going to need it.

16

HEDI

BELSEN, APRIL 1945

Hedi raised her head from the upturned metal bowl that doubled as a pillow and turned her head towards Magda. The truth burst in on her thoughts like sunlight. *We are free!*

She stared at the knobbly vertebrae protruding from the skin of Magda's neck and saw the slow rise and fall of her blanket. Hedi felt Magda's bowl on her stomach, as if she had remained completely motionless in her sleep. She took hold of it as it wobbled, but it was surprisingly light and she realised it was now empty.

Strange. How had that happened? She looked around and saw that the woman without a name was staring at her, her eyes glinting from the cocoon of her blanket.

'What's wrong?' the woman asked.

Hedi picked up the empty bowl to show her. 'Look! Someone ate Magda's food.'

'Don't look at me,' the woman said. Her eyes slid pointedly towards the bunk nearest the door and stayed there. 'Who is the fattest of us?'

Hedi raised her head and looked at the bunk by the door, the bunk where the fresh air leaked in, where blonde-haired

Lena Martens lay snoring softly. She was making the most of the unaccustomed lie-in, one pink arm dangling off the edge of the plank.

Hedi envied her. Lena had been a nightclub singer in Berlin. She had once had a seductive body and her voice was low and thrilling. She had been doing better than most, using her curly hair and her pretty smile to persuade the guards to do favours for her. How she returned the favours, Hedi wasn't exactly sure, but she would disappear for an hour at a time and come back hard-eyed and silent.

Hedi let her head fall back on the bunk. Her heart raced with the effort of holding it up. If she was Lena... she lifted the neck of her shirt to look at her breasts. They'd gone. She was all ribs now. If she had been supplied with the same equipment as Lena, she too would use it to her advantage. Why not? They all had their own ways of staying alive.

Her mind went back to the subject of the missing food. 'You think Lena took it?' She felt a rush of indignation. Strange how they still had morals in this amoral place, at least when they chose to. 'I'm going to ask her if she ate Magda's meal.'

'Huh! Good luck with that.'

Hedi got out of bed and edged past the filth that had pooled in the centre of the hut. She stood next to Lena's plank and saw, enviously, she was lying on a sawdust mattress. 'Hey,' she said, poking her. 'You! Lena!'

Lena raised her head. She opened her eyes reluctantly and squinted up at Hedi. 'You woke me up,' she said accusingly.

'Did you eat Magda's food?'

'Yes.'

'But that was Magda's!' Hedi said indignantly.

Lena gave her a strange, shameless smile. It wasn't humour or even cruelty. It was worse – there was no emotion behind it at all. 'If she wanted it, she would have eaten it like the rest of us. The smell of it was tormenting me and keeping me awake. Anyway, we'll get more today so what's the problem?'

Hedi wanted to argue with her. It had taken a lot of effort not to eat it herself, and she'd used all her willpower for what? But at the same time, there was something about Lena, some star quality that desperately made Hedi want Lena to like her. 'I suppose that's true,' she conceded. She gave up, went back to her bunk and reported to the woman with no name. 'You're right, it was her.'

The woman grunted. 'Told you. She's got no morals. You know why she's here? The SS caught her sleeping with the enemy.'

For a moment, Hedi was confused about who the enemy was. 'She was sleeping with Tommies?'

'No, no. Communists, Jews. Not exclusively – don't get me wrong. She's worked through the whole of the Wehrmacht in her time, if you ask me – she's generous, that way. How about you? How did you get in here? Are you secretly also a nightclub singer, under the dirt?' The woman gave a screeching laugh at her own joke. It was harsh and piercing, like a gull.

Hedi stretched her lips over her teeth in a smile. 'I'm not interested in that sort of thing. My father was reported for listening to BBC broadcasts.' *Trying to get a balanced view*, was how he had put it, *away from the propaganda*. He was a reasonable, thoughtful man, an intellectual, slow to anger. She wondered if he was angry now.

A few days previously, Hedi, when they were still unaware of the events to follow, had asked the nameless woman what she wished for most in the world.

'To be a Kapo,' the woman had replied.

Her answer had surprised Hedi. But what could she say, it was the woman's wish. Hedi had been waiting for her to return the question, because she herself had a long list of wishes to keep her going, the first among them to be home with her mother and father again, just as things used to be. And then after that, to eat her mother's home cooking, and wear a pretty dress. She would wear it to a dance and turn heads and meet a good-looking boy who was, like her, a little shy.

But the nameless woman still didn't ask and so she'd said nothing and kept her list to herself. She had a feeling the woman found her annoying.

They both turned over on their stomachs and looked up, distracted by voices outside. The door of the hut opened. Hedi blinked as the light flooded in, and then looked at the visitors eagerly. Four big Hungarian men came in with stretchers, their wide faces impassive. One of them stopped to stare at Lena, caressing her cheek with his thick fingers.

'What's going on?' Hedi asked them, propping herself up, eager for information.

'We have come for the dead,' one of them replied in English. It looked as if he was winking at her grotesquely but in fact one of his eyes was swollen shut. 'The more, the better.'

'Don't say that!'

'Listen! You're going to enjoy this.' He gave Hedi a bitter, satisfied grin. 'The British have made the SS chief undertakers. They got them working last night, burying the corpses. When the guards fled, they locked the rest of them up overnight. They're back out working this morning.'

'You're crazy. I don't believe you,' Hedi said firmly. 'They would never agree to that.'

'Who said they agreed to it? But it's true. Men and women alike.' The soldier turned to his friends, eyebrows raised, and they smirked. 'Don't ask me why, but they don't seem to think much of their new roles. Right. Let's get started.' He jerked his head at the men. Two of them grabbed the nameless woman by the arms.

'Idiots!' she protested feebly, smacking them away. 'I'm not

ready for burial yet! Come back tomorrow!' She pulled her
blanket over her head.

It was depressing, Hedi thought, watching them take the
bodies out, to see how many more of the women had died in the
night.

When the Hungarians were satisfied that the remaining
occupants of the hut were all alive, at least for the moment, they
wheeled the cart away.

Lena slipped out after them, swift as a shadow.

'Did you hear, the SS are burying the dead,' Hedi said to the
woman with no name who was still under the blanket.

'I know.' She uncovered her face again. 'I heard. I'm not
dead, and I'm not deaf either. It's about time, that's what I say.'

The crematorium had seized up a few weeks ago through
lack of fuel. After that, the SS had tried injecting the dying with
petrol to make them burn better, but they had given up on it as a
bad job and let the dead pile up where they lay.

Now, the SS were being put to work. Hedi felt the slow,
satisfying creep of vengeance warming her shrunken heart. A
word seemed to flash in her head. The word was: *retribution*.
'Let's go and see, shall we?'

'Give me a moment,' the woman said. 'I have to check my
busy diary. I may have plans.'

'Of course,' Hedi said politely. 'I understand. Take your
time.'

'As it turns out, you're lucky. I'm free this morning.' The
woman eased her scabbed legs out of the bed, wobbling as she
steadied herself. She wrapped her blanket around her shoulders
and they hobbled out into the early morning air, heading for the
burial pits.

The camp was well hidden from view. Around the huts was
the barbed wire and beyond the barbed wire were the dark and
lovely woods, rustling like the sea.

As Hedi paused to catch her breath, she looked at the trees

swaying their branches against the blue sky and for a moment she was filled with hope.

The burial pits were behind the crematorium in the north-west of the camp, in full sunlight. As Hedi and the woman made their way unsteadily past the building, they heard the screams of a crowd coming to them on the breeze, screams of delight against the rumble of machinery. The nameless woman's grey blanket fluttered behind her like a cape as she shuffled a little faster, kicking up dust.

They crossed their arms over their chests for warmth as they shuffled along.

'I'm going out of respect,' Hedi said piously, almost believing it, but it wasn't only that – as they walked towards the pits, they could hear shouting and goading, and the sheer thrill of what was happening energised her. The tables had turned!

What the Hungarian said was true. Members of the SS, men and women, were pushing carts piled with corpses, and Hedi looked at them as they passed, their expressions a blend of anger, shame, disgust.

'You've taken our jobs!' the woman cackled, and she nudged Hedi with a bony elbow.

The rumours were true, and it was sweet; the tables had turned.

Hedi's heart was racing discordantly with jerky little beats of effort as she hurried alongside her. And what an unbelievable spectacle they came across.

A bulldozer was digging out the dirt and in the morning sunshine, the SS were carrying the corpses from the carts to the huge pit, sweating miserably in their dark uniforms, jeered by the crowd.

Hedi covered her nose with her hands because the smell was indescribably bad. Over the tops of her steepled fingers she stared hard at the scene; at the British, at the SS, at the dead, and at the vengeful crowd around her that she had now become a vengeful part of. This burial pit was an offence, a sacrilege against life that each and all of them were witnessing, and yet, oh yes, it was powerfully satisfying, too. She raised her feeble voice in a cheer, because what a tremendous event this was!

The nameless woman nudged her. 'I don't know about you, but personally I feel the British are being extremely helpful, the way they are using the points of their bayonets to offer encouragement,' she said, her eyes gleeful.

The Tommies were expending all their frustration, anger and despair on those who had inflicted the horror.

'They are certainly persuasive.' Hedi scanned the faces of the soldiers hopefully and with a sudden jerk of her stomach she saw the man with the red hair shouting and jabbing viciously at the bearers, his green eyes burning with hatred, pouched from tiredness. He looked crazy. It was as if that calm, emotionless face that he had worn the day before had been peeled away to reveal the loathing beneath. At every jab, the crowd cheered him on.

The jeers were from a motley crowd of inmates, mostly women, a hundred or so crowded together. The SS officers were tossing bodies from the carts into the pit, looking sick to their stomachs, their expressions twisted in a grimace of disgust. The smell of putrefaction was as thick as a cloud. The sturdy SS women were crying pitifully as they worked, wiping their snot on the sleeves of their black uniforms as if the scales had dropped from their eyes and they had only just noticed the horrors that they had colluded in.

'Look at them,' Hedi said as they tumbled the bodies into the pit. 'Look at the tears streaming down their cheeks.' Despite herself, she felt a pang of pity. 'See how sorry they are, the women, now they realise what they've done,' she said.

The woman snorted. 'Don't be fooled! Sorry for themselves, that's all that is. It's too late to be sorry now.'

The scene was ugly and shocking, and Hedi felt the feeling

rising up in her like a mighty rushing wind, thrilling and sickening. They had been starved, beaten, kicked. *Now let them have a taste of it! See how they like it!*

'Face what you done!' a voice cried out.

Hedi and the woman joined the cheering, howling crowd, and the noise was deafening, uplifting. too. Hedi started shouting along with them because it was all so very satisfactory to behold the enemy being treated with the same brutality it had meted out. She watched a reluctant SS guard get prodded into the pit and as he tried to climb out the crowd jeered and laughed. Hedi jeered too and then suddenly, something came over her, and it was as if she had stepped out of unreality into reality.

She stopped shouting as suddenly as if she'd been gagged. She stopped seeing the soldiers and instead she saw –

The dead. The older corpses looked shapeless, colourless, unformed, as if they'd been carved out of soap. But the more recently dead still looked like themselves. Her heart broke for them. They had been so close to freedom, so close. The pain and the horror was so violent that it was physical and she started shivering in shock. She tugged the woman's arm. 'I'm going back to the hut,' she said.

'Why?' The nameless woman looked at her in surprise and then she shrugged. 'Please yourself. I have something that I must do.' She pushed her way feebly to the front of the crowd.

Hedi could see her approach the lip of the pit. She heard her let out a wild screech and she aimed a kick which connected with the back of an SS officer's knee and caught him off balance. He stumbled once, twice, and then disappeared into the pit. They saw his hands appear as he scrabbled to climb out again as though the hounds of hell were after him. The little crowd laughed and cheered at the spectacle, and two women grabbed the nameless woman to stop her from falling in on top of him.

Hedi felt full of shame. She had never been able to understand hatred, not until now. Yet here she was, as cruel and
heartless as they were, raising her fist, jeering, vilifying.

Is it this easy to hate? she asked herself as she looked at the
SS women that had made them live in fear for so long.

The body of a small girl was tossed in. Hedi heard a mother
in the crowd scream in agony. It wasn't just vengeance that was
fuelling the crowd, but grief too. Seconds later the mother
jumped in the pit to hold her child and she was dragged out by
inmates. At once it was too much for Hedi, too much, and the
feeling of excitement evaporated. She felt as if she had woken
up from a dream and found herself in a nightmare. She shuffled
back to the hut, miserable, trembling, and full of disgust. Her
mind soon went to the next big event of the day: food.

Food! Suddenly that was all she could think of, she was
obsessed by it. It would at least fill the hole that the dismal
scene had caused in her. Back inside the gloomy hut, she passed
Lena who was lying on her plank again, her eyes shut. She
groaned and her pretty face was contorted with pain.

'Are you all right?' Hedi asked. 'Where did you go?'

'None of your business,' Lena said hoarsely.

Hedi shrugged. 'I know that.' She climbed up on the plank
next to Magda for comfort and stroked her tangled dark hair
away from her eyes. 'Wake up, Magda,' she said to her softly.
'The SS are burying the dead. The clean-up has started. We'll
be getting more food in a minute, and you will soon be well
enough to join your little sister.'

Magda's eyes flickered open. 'Have you seen her?' she
whispered.

'Yes, I think so,' Hedi lied. 'Almost certainly I've seen her.
She looks like you, I think.'

Magda gave a weak smile, and Hedi rested her forehead
against her friend's neck, asking God for forgiveness for the lie,

and waiting for her to say something more, but Magda had sunk back into the fever-hot restlessness of sleep.

Hedi sighed then turned over the other way, her back against Magda's spine.

She looked at the empty space next to her. The nameless woman hadn't returned. How satisfied she must have felt as she watched the SS officer topple, and how unafraid.

Her train of thought was interrupted by the sound of Lena retching, followed by the splattering of vomit. The smell and the duration of it was astounding, and Hedi grimaced, wondering how it was possible to throw that much up from an empty belly.

Unless, of course, her belly wasn't empty.

Just as she thought it, the door of the hut opened and the nameless woman was back, steadying herself against the frame before entering. Just as well, because she stopped herself just in time to avoid walking through the vomit on the floor. Despite her malnourished frailty, her brain was quick. Without hesitation she looked accusingly at Lena who was hanging limply over the side of her mattress, drool dripping from her mouth.

'Eaten too much, have we?' the woman asked sympathetically. And then her tone changed. 'You! Hedi! Have the soldiers brought the food yet?'

'No, not yet.'

'I see. So then. Lena, did you eat our food?' she asked sternly.

Lena wiped her mouth with the back of her hand. She shook her head and said thickly, 'So what? You weren't here.'

'I'm here now, aren't I?'

'There wasn't much,' Lena said miserably. 'The inmates in the cookhouse helped themselves to it first.'

The woman with no name curled her lip in disgust. 'It looks plenty to me, you piece of dirt.' She grabbed Lena's hair and pulled her off the plank so that she fell into her own regurgitation.

Hedi covered her eyes, she couldn't bear it. She had seen enough violence. Her heart was beating wildly in her chest as if it was trying to escape her body. Suddenly it seemed as if their liberation was nothing more than a new way to torment them. They had been filled with hope that all this was over but still it went on interminably, and now they had emerged as the monsters they had loathed for so long. 'Don't,' she pleaded. 'Please stop.'

Eating all the food had robbed Lena of her strength, and Hedi listened to her cry out and whimper with each blow as the woman beat her. The woman stopped suddenly. She made a screeching noise, but Hedi realised she wasn't laughing, she was crying.

It's too much, she thought wildly. *Our hearts are breaking.*

The nameless woman came back to her bunk. She leaned over her board for a while with barely the strength left to climb on it and then, grunting, dragged herself up by force of will and turned her face towards the wall.

Lena was lying on the floor, groaning in agony.

Hedi was frantic to leave, to get out as soon as she could, once she'd had some food. Why shouldn't she? *Ihr Seid Frei!* The best words in the German language!

Well then. If she was free, she would get out of here and find her own food. Fastidiously, she lowered herself onto the filthy floor, clinging onto the bed frames for balance until she reached Lena who was blocking the doorway. Anger flared inside her.

'Move!' she ordered her.

'Help me,' Lena whispered.

'Move, or I'll beat you myself.'

Lena whimpered like a whipped dog and didn't or couldn't move.

Hedi stepped over her, treading on her soft, yielding thigh, using her as a bridge to keep her feet clean.

She left the hut with a feeling of relief and looked around cautiously.

The screams of the crowd were drifting on the air from behind the now-defunct crematorium, and she heard a gunshot. Her empty stomach clenched painfully with tension. *Now what?*

Others were trudging along, coming and going purposefully but with no urgency. She shuffled along the path beside them, past the empty potato patch with its earth churned up, past the cookhouses. She hesitated. Could it be true that the cooks were inmates who were eating all the food? But suddenly she was only hungry for freedom. She had now reached the barbed-wire fences that separated the camp from the SS compound. She stared at the view through the spikes. How neat it looked through there, and how clean! There was a lot of activity, soldiers coming and going, Germans and British and Hungarians together. She waited for someone to challenge her and the inevitable repercussions, but nobody took any notice of her. *Strange! I've become invisible*, she thought with interest.

Invisibly, she continued through the military bloc towards the camp gates without being questioned, until she reached the gates. They were huge, like the gates of a fort. Although they were open, when Hedi looked around she could see guards in the watchtowers. She stood still, frozen, waiting to be shot at any moment. The breeze wrapped her striped shirt tight against her legs. She was a fearful child.

Her heart was pounding with exertion and anxiety. *Go on*, she told herself. *I dare you.* As she stood shivering, she felt her strength draining away from her wasted muscles. *What are you waiting for?* She put one foot forward, testing. The next got her through the gates. One step, then two, and without fanfare she was standing on the main road between Bergen and Winsen.

The breeze was cold and fresh, clearing the smells of the hut from her nostrils.

Hedi stood on the road savouring the sudden solitude. All this space to herself! And no one even close to her! She stretched out her arms to their limits. She was free to think her own thoughts without them being interrupted by moans and whimpers.

The trees were coming into leaf, and in the meadow, yellow wildflowers nestled in the green grass. The birds were singing around her, their songs following their own joyful tunes. She narrowed her dazzled eyes. In the distance, a little cluster of buildings gave off grey smoke from their chimneys. The village was a totally unexpected, like some vision from the past. She hadn't expected such a sight to still exist. For these past months, her reality had been the only reality. Looking at the houses, she imagined the people living inside them, ordinary German citizens just like her, going on with their normal lives as best they could. *How could that be?* she marvelled. But it gave her hope for her own family's survival.

Her legs began to tremble. She didn't have the strength or muscle to walk any further, so she remained on the road where she was, a little way outside the gates, with all this space around her, reluctant to return.

In the distance, a strange, hunched figure of a young woman wearing a coat and a ragged headscarf caught her eye. She was hurrying along the road towards the camp, holding something protectively in her arms. As she got close, Hedi knew she couldn't have been in the camp for very long because she didn't look too bad, really; she still had a layer of fat on her cheeks.

The woman was gleeful and when she got a few feet away from Hedi she said mysteriously, 'Do you want to see what I've got?'

'Yes.'

The woman opened her coat with her free hand and

revealed a bundle of speckled feathers. 'It's a chicken!' She was holding the chicken's head under its wing. It had gone into survival mode and was playing dead.

'Where did you find it?' Hedi asked, stroking the warm, soft feathers with her finger. It was plump, too.

'Down there.' The woman pointed back the way she'd come. 'At the farm.'

'Truly? Did the farmer give it to you?'

'No, he didn't exactly give it to me, but he didn't try to stop me, either. They're scared of catching typhus. There are signs all along the highway, warning people to keep away.' She pushed Hedi's hand away. 'That's enough stroking,' she said possessively. 'Go and get one for yourself.'

Hedi looked across the fields and considered it. First, there was the long walk and then there was the effort of chasing a chicken and catching it, and, also, maybe this time the farmer would fetch his shotgun and wouldn't be so scared. 'I won't bother,' she said airily. 'The British are giving out food. In our hut, we've already had a meal.'

The woman laughed cynically. 'I hope you enjoyed it. It might be your last. Haven't you heard? The stores are empty. The inmates rioted last night and took all the food except for that rock-hard black bread. They fell on the place like locusts! Hundreds of them!' She shrugged. 'I don't care. I've got my chicken.' She nursed it for a moment in her arms. 'Trust me. You should go and get one for yourself. Seriously.'

Hedi bit her knuckles, dismayed that the stores were empty. She would have been perfectly content to eat the hard black bread. She wasn't fussy.

The woman hurried past her back into the camp and Hedi turned to follow her. She noticed the barbed-wire fencing and the gates, seeing them clearly from this side for the first time.

She decided to make a detour to the cookhouse to see if what the woman had said was true. A soldier opened the door, releasing a savoury-smelling cloud of steam. 'What can I do for you?'

'Is it true that you've run out of food?'

'No.' He gave her a faint smile and cocked his head. 'You want something to eat?'

It was the strangest question she'd ever been asked in her life. 'Yes please.' And then, as if life had played a cruel trick on her, she said with a plummeting heart, 'Only I haven't brought my bowl.'

'Don't worry, I'll get you one. Eat it slowly, mind. Your stomach's not used to it yet. Wait here.'

Sure enough, moments later he was back at the door with a mess of thin stew. It was hot and very tasty, and she drank it straight from the dixie and ate the meat on the bottom with her fingers, humming with pleasure, savouring the warmth and the taste.

Eating the food cheered Hedi. When she'd finished, her stomach felt full and tight, painfully so, really, but for some reason she was still hungry.

'Better?' he asked.

'Yes, thank you. From now on, can I just come here and ask for food?'

He chewed his cheek and studied her thoughtfully. 'Didn't you get any today?'

'Lena ate it. She ate everyone's.'

His eyes hardened and he whistled. 'All right. Tell all those in your hut who haven't eaten and can make it here to come and see me. My name's Jeff. Can you remember that?'

Hedi nodded. 'Jeff.'

'That's right.'

'But – what if they can't make it here? My sister is very sick.'

'You can take some back for her. Tell her to hang on in there. We're going to be evacuating the sick to hospitals on the twentieth.'

'What date is it now?'

'The eighteenth.'

'In two days, then.'

'Correct.' He went to refill the dixie.

Hedi could feel the stew settling in her stomach, spreading warmth and satisfaction around her whole body. She could still taste it on her tongue. It was bringing her senses back to life, like a light switching on.

When she got back to the hut with Magda's food, the smell of human waste hit her. She shuddered in disgust. She covered her nose with her arm and went inside. Lena's mattress was empty.

The woman with no name was lying on her back with her eyes shut.

Hedi climbed on her plank and nestled close to Magda, knowing that after the twentieth, she wouldn't see her again for a little while. She smoothed Magda's matted hair from her hot forehead. 'In two days, you are going to the hospital where you will soon be well. Eat, keep your strength up.'

Magda's face was expressionless, but there was mingled love and pain in her huge eyes. She raised her head and took a few spoonfuls of the watery stew.

'Good. Listen, I will come and visit you. Have you had enough? You can have some more later.' Hedi put the bowl next to Magda and got down from the plank again.

She nudged the woman with no name. 'Hey! Guess what,' she told her excitedly. 'They're giving out food at the cookhouse. You just have to ask Jeff for it. See? I've brought some for Magda. And the sick are being transferred to the hospital in two days' time, on the twentieth.' She was proud of being the bearer of this good news, and she expected it to be well received.

The woman opened her dark eyes. They rested in their sockets like pebbles in a hole. 'Lena's dead.'

It felt like a slap, harsh enough to make Hedi cry out. She

glanced back at the empty plank. *No more Lena?* She was the healthiest, the plumpest of them all, with her pink skin and her blonde hair. It seemed impossible that she was dead after that short time.

She asked fearfully, 'Did we kill her?'

'Not you. You didn't do anything.'

'That's true.' *But I walked on her.*

'Don't forget, she tried to starve us,' the woman added reasonably.

'True—'

The woman said, 'She was sick. She was still on the floor when that Hungarian came back because she hadn't turned up for their, er, rendezvous, if you know what I mean. Despite the state she was in, he picked her up in his arms, held her close and cried his eyes out like a baby.'

Hedi didn't know what to make of the statement. 'So?'

'What do you mean, so? She had someone to cry over her, that's what I'm saying. That's nice, isn't it?'

Hedi agreed that it was very nice. She thought of the way Lena's soft, vulnerable body had felt under her weight.

'And now,' the nameless woman said, rubbing her hands, 'I'm ready to eat.'

17

THEA

PRESENT DAY

When Hedi stopped talking, Thea looked up at the balmy night sky. It was giving way to a deep velvety blue and the stars were fading. Dawn was not far off. A breeze was stippling the water, shattering the reflections of the hotel lights into pieces. Thea glanced across at Hedi. She was sitting very still and it was impossible in this light to make out her expression.

Listening to her story, Thea had veered from guilt to justification to guilt again. Would she herself do the same? She wondered if Hedi was expecting absolution. She wasn't sure it was hers to give.

Hedi turned to look at her and Thea saw the pale curve of her cheek and the dark glint of her eye.

'Say something to me,' she demanded, her voice shrill.

Thea had thought at one point during the story that Hedi's experience was unimaginable. It wasn't true though because she could imagine it only too well. 'It's getting light,' she said. 'We've been here all night.' She felt around on the jetty for the second wine bottle and upended it into her glass. A couple of drips and that was it. 'We've finished it,' she said in surprise.

She had never wanted another drink so much in her life. She put the bottle down and finished the dregs from her glass.

'Never mind that. Say something about Lena.'

'I can't.' It felt like a make-or-break moment and Thea shook her head. 'I don't know what to think.'

'Think? Don't think! You have to know! Tell me what you feel! You have feelings, don't you?'

'I suppose I feel sorry for her. We all like to think the best of ourselves and I want to imagine I'd have helped her to her feet and cleaned her up. But I'm glad... or not glad, but satisfied because she paid for her selfishness. Karma, right?'

'It's true that if she'd shared the food, she wouldn't have died. The death rate doubled, tripled, in the days after the Tommies came. There was an obsessive compulsion to eat. Those that were fit ate the food of the unfit. The unfit died of starvation, and the fit, with access to unlimited food, died because their shrunken stomachs and hearts couldn't cope. Karma,' Hedi repeated the word thoughtfully. She looked up. 'So you don't blame me?'

'No, I don't blame you. How could I?' The words came out spontaneously in a rush.

Hedi got out of the deckchair and held out her hand to Thea. She drew her close and they walked arm in arm along the jetty towards the house, through the shimmering grass, bleached colourless by the dew.

When they got inside, the fire was out, but the kitchen was still warm.

'Are you cold? Shall I make us a hot drink?'

'Not for me, I'm ready for bed now,' Hedi replied. She was avoiding Thea's eye. She headed to her room.

Thea felt she'd let her down. 'Listen, I'm glad you told me that story,' she called after her.

'Why?' Hedi asked.

'Because I know you better now.'

Hedi's eyes softened and she gave a brief laugh. 'For better or worse. Good night, Thea.'

'Sleep tight.'

Lying in bed, troubled by her thoughts and unable to sleep, Thea watched the room gradually regain its definition as the dawn broke and daylight seeped in through the window. She desperately wanted to talk to her mother about all this. She imagined telling her Hedi's story. Knowing Maggie, her first reaction would probably be: *I'm her daughter! Why didn't she tell me first?*

To which Thea could reply, truthfully, *I sneaked a look in her bag and found a letter…*

On the other hand, maybe it was something she should keep quiet about until Hedi died. Of course, by then it would be too late for Maggie to do anything about it in the way of a reconciliation. It could be that she wouldn't want to, anyway. *They have been dead to me for years.*

The knowledge felt like a burden, but it was a burden that she and Hedi now shared the weight of. That had to be a good thing. Every family had its dark side, she thought. She turned over with a groan and buried her face in the pillow. Finally, blotting the world out, she fell asleep.

When Thea woke up, Hedi's bedroom door was open but the cottage was empty. Thea went to the window and saw a flattened trail through the grass of the meadow leading down to the jetty where the deckchairs faced the river. She could see steam rising from a mug on the decking.

Hedi had left a mug with a spoonful of instant coffee in it waiting for her to add water. The kettle was still hot.

As Thea sipped her coffee, she wondered what the day would bring. The sky was a clear blue and it might be a nice idea to drive to the sea, walk along the shore and maybe have a swim in the ocean. She checked her phone – it had just turned eleven. She wondered how Hedi was feeling this morning. Her long-hidden memories had been stored away all this time like linen in a trunk, their colours vivid and untouched by age. Or were they spoiled and moth-eaten, smelling of neglect? Hard to know.

She had a quick shower, dressed in white shorts and a red sleeveless T-shirt, and took her coffee out to the jetty to join Hedi. The dew had burnt off and the sun was warm on her shoulders. 'Morning!'

'It's so peaceful here,' Hedi greeted her with a happy sigh.

'Gorgeous, isn't it,' Thea said, sitting next to her. 'I thought we could go to the coast today. We could find a quiet beach and maybe take a picnic with us. What do you think?'

Hedi frowned and pursed her lips. 'A quiet beach?' she asked doubtfully.

'It was just an idea. Is there something else you would like to do?'

Hedi brushed her snowy hair away from her forehead and gave Thea's question some thought. 'Maybe, yes,' she said at last. She looked suddenly shy. 'It sounds crazy, I know. No, forget it, I couldn't possibly say...' she said, flapping her hands.

Amused, Thea said, 'Okay, I've forgotten it.'

'Huh. Since you insist,' Hedi said with some dignity, 'I would like to go to the fairground.' She gave Thea a sidelong look.

Thea burst out laughing. 'I was not expecting that. But, great! I love fairgrounds!'

'Good! Me too! Harry and I used to visit Hampstead Heath fair in London. All the music and the flashing lights! It was so exciting. You know it?'

'Yes, I know the one.' Thea was relieved at the return of Hedi's good spirits, and she said cheerfully, 'Hedi, you're full of surprises.'

. . .

They set off after lunch, heading for the village of Fairbourne. Thea parked on a headland, just a short walk away from the ferry across to Barmouth.

For some reason, Hedi didn't take the news of the ferry crossing that well. 'We're going by boat?' she asked, alarmed when they headed in the direction of the sign. 'No. Definitely not. I can't do it.' She tightened the belt of Harry's dressing gown. 'You didn't tell me about the ferry, Thea. They sink, you know,' she said sternly. 'They have a reputation for it.'

'I think you'll be fine on this one.' They held on to each other as they clattered across the shifting pebbles down to the waterside. 'There it is, across there. Where those people are.'

A short distance across the water was the grey stone harbour, lively with people drinking coffee by the tables, dog walkers, children crabbing – dangling their lines into the water. A motorboat was moored up by the steps and a little group of people were getting onto it cautiously.

'That little boat?' Hedi squared her shoulders. Then she laughed. 'I suppose it's not so far to the other side. If it sinks, I think I could paddle there.'

'That's the spirit.'

The boat chugged towards them on an indirect route, negotiating buoys and moored dinghies; within moments, the captain was putting down his wooden gangplank and the passengers got off. The captain welcomed Hedi and Thea aboard, and gallantly helped Hedi to a seat.

Five minutes later, after chugging across the water, Thea and Hedi disembarked on the other side and climbed the harbour steps.

. . .

They walked along the promenade beside the sandy beach where deckchairs billowed in the breeze and donkeys plodded amiably with children on their backs.

Hedi laughed suddenly and clapped her hands. 'I can hear the music,' she said.

And there just ahead of them on the other side of the road was the fairground, gaudy in all its glory, strung with flashing lights, a bright whirl of colour and movement declaring itself in a cacophony of contrasting sounds, punctuated by squeals of delight from adults and prowled by surly, self-consciously nonchalant teenagers.

The aroma of sugary pink candyfloss mingled with burgers and frying onions. Proud fathers carrying unwieldy stuffed pandas under their arms were trailed by their children, triumph on their faces and ice cream around their mouths.

Hedi and Thea wandered around the stalls. Hedi stopped to offer encouragement to a boy who was hooking yellow ducks into a basket and to a mother who was flinging hoopla rings around like Frisbees.

She came to a stop by the waltzer, the gilded cars still swaying from the momentum of the previous ride. 'Shall we?' Hedi asked, going up the ramp and getting into the car. She sat down and patted the red vinyl seat. 'Come on, slowcoach! Sit!'

'Coming!'

Tucked behind the safety bar, they held on to it as the ride started at a sedate pace.

A good-looking, dark-haired man jumped on with them and took their tokens. 'Scream if you want to go faster!'

He span the car so hard that they did scream, and they clung on, excited and breathless. As the waltzer whirled with increasing speed, they couldn't hold on any longer, and they slid along the red vinyl seat until they were both squashed together at one end, crying with laughter, until the ride slowed down and they sat in the swaying car limp with exhaustion until it came to a stop. Weakly they got off the ride still chuckling and wiping their eyes.

'And now, I will buy my dearest granddaughter an ice cream,' Hedi said. She looked up at Thea, one eyebrow raised in query, as if she wasn't sure how the term would be received.

It was the first time she had used it, and Thea smiled, touched.

Hedi looked away and pinched her lower lip. She shook her head, as if she were having a silent discussion with herself. After a moment she said, 'I myself had an *Oma* whom I loved dearly.' She added softly to herself, 'It's only right that you should have one, too.'

'I'd like that very much.'

'Yes, I know,' Hedi said, pleased. 'And now for those ice creams.'

They ate them on a bench overlooking the sea, watching the waves curl and lace on the yellow sand. *I myself had an Oma.* It felt like a term of endearment, warm with belonging.

When Thea was first at school, the other mothers assumed Maggie was the au pair. For a while, Thea had been upset that she apparently had an 'old pear' and no mummy.

At Parents' Day, the nursery teacher, Miss Josie, brought it up with Maggie.

'She said what?' Maggie had rolled her eyes at the teacher. 'Don't listen to her. Thea, don't be ridiculous, of course you've got a mummy. I'm your mummy, you know that.'

'You're not Mummy,' Thea had replied, folding her arms indignantly, 'you're Maggie.' She'd been told so often enough.

'I'm still your mummy, but I'm not called "Mummy" because I've got my own identity,' Maggie had said patiently in her talking-to-idiots voice. 'My mummy and daddy are called Hedi and Harry because those are their names.' She glanced at the teacher. 'A lot of children call their parents by their names.'

'Actually, they don't,' the teacher said.

After eating their ice creams, they went for a walk around the town and stopped in a supermarket to get a chicken, some vegetables for the evening, and a couple of bottles of wine.

Hedi seemed subdued as they walked slowly back to the harbour.

'Are you all right?' Thea asked her.

'Actually I'm a little tired.' *Ektually*.

'Me too. We had a late night. How does this sound, I can go across on the boat and drive back round to pick you up. It will take me about half an hour, maybe, but you could stay here by Davy Jones's Locker and have a coffee while you're waiting.'

Hedi leaned on the railings and watched the motorboat pick up the little cargo of passengers. Then she looked across the road. 'You know, I will do that,' she decided.

'Great! I'll see you back here in half an hour.'

Hedi nodded, looking relieved.

'See you in a bit.' Thea wondered what it was that had caused Hedi to feel like that. But she had enjoyed herself and the main thing was that for the last couple of days she hadn't once mentioned following in Harry's footsteps. Today Thea had proved to Hedi that she still had plenty to live for, and she felt good about that.

18

HEDI
PRESENT DAY

Hedi waited until Thea was on the boat, and after giving her a cheerful wave she walked back into the busy town, enjoying being among people again. She was returning for a purpose – she wanted to buy something for Thea, a memento.

It was important that she give her something to keep after she'd gone, a souvenir of a happy day. Memories were all very well in themselves, but they were elusive, fugitive. Once she'd gone, Thea would be left with the suitcase containing a letter and the old watches and the metal bowl and spoon, meaningless items unless you knew their history. Memories were a lot easier to remember, good and bad, she'd found, when there was something material to pin them onto.

She passed an art gallery and stopped to look at the pictures in the window, pictures of the sea with frills of waves, *nicely done* she admitted grudgingly, but really, it could be any grey sea anywhere and it didn't seem to sum up her wholehearted enjoyment of the day.

A souvenir shop looked promising. Walking inside it, she dismissed the shell-covered trinket boxes and pretty mother-of-pearl jewellery dangling from a stand. She picked up a heavy granite ashtray that caught her eye. It had a ceramic gull perched on it, wings outstretched. The white of the gull contrasted nicely with the shiny black of the granite, and she was tempted, because it was a nice enough object, but then Thea wasn't a smoker, and what use was an ashtray otherwise?

Hedi left the shop empty-handed. *I will know it when I see it*, she thought. She glanced down an alley and saw a jewellers tucked out of the way, JONES AND SON written in curly gold lettering above the window. One half of the window displayed watches and engagement rings, while the other half was less ostentatious and little sign declared the trinkets to be pre-owned. A gold charm bracelet caught her eye. It was not the bracelet itself that grabbed her attention but one of the charms on it, which looked very much like a merry-go-round. The rest of the charms seemed rather commonplace: a telephone kiosk, a dollar sign, a horseshoe, a thimble. Yes, that was a merry-go-round, she was sure of it. The door had a notice: *Please ring bell and wait to be buzzed in.* Very well.

She pressed the buzzer and the door clicked open. Inside, the shop was rather dim. A silver tea set shone in a glass cabinet. Under the glass counter lay a line of pocket watches and chains. Gilded snuff boxes shone like bullion. Novelty bookmarks were arranged in a circle. As she was admiring this treasure trove, a thin, balding man emerged from a back room with his glasses at the end of his nose, polishing a silver candlestick. He put it down on the rubber mat on the counter and tilted his head to admire it. 'Looks better for a bit of loving care, doesn't it?'

'Wonderful!' Hedi said.

He smiled. 'How can I help you?'

'Now then,' she said, resting her clasped hands on the counter, 'I have seen something in the window that may appeal to me. A charm bracelet, but this is the thing. If the charm is what I think it is, I would like to buy it, but that one charm only.

You see, I have no need to be reminded of a telephone kiosk or a thimble.'

'You know what a thimble is? A kiss. *Peter Pan.*'

'Maybe so, but—' Hedi gave a one-shouldered shrug.

'Fair enough.' The jeweller went into the window and retrieved the bracelet, weighing it in his cupped hand. He undid the clasp and laid it flat next to the candlestick on the rubber mat.

'This is the one,' she said, pointing to it, 'this merry-go-round. I want it for my granddaughter. We have just spent the most marvellous day together.'

'Good to hear!' He smiled and span the horses on the charm round. 'I wasn't going to break this bracelet up. If I take that charm off, it will leave a gap.'

'I understand your dilemma. Ah, well.' Hedi's eyes gleamed. She wasn't a person to give up that easily. She added casually, 'I would need a gold chain to hang it from, of course.'

The jeweller tapped his fingers on the glass counter.

Hedi glanced at her little square watch with a blue leather strap, keeping her eye on the time. She needed to be back at the harbour when Thea turned up in her car, or else she would worry and have to find somewhere to park, and the whole reason she'd parked in Fairbourne in the first place was because parking was more difficult to find this side.

The gesture wasn't lost on the jeweller. 'I know what I'll do,' he decided. 'I'll substitute this charm with another one. Problem solved. What length chain?' He reached under the counter and produced the tray with the gold chains on, and while Hedi chose, he used his pliers to remove the charm.

'Belcher. A fine choice,' he said. 'Nice and strong.' He threaded the charm on the chain she had chosen, dangled it from his finger and offered it to Hedi for approval.

She took it in her hand and span the little carousel. 'Perfect,' she said, delighted. 'I am so pleased.'

The jeweller gave it a quick polish and put it in a blue velvet-covered box, and Hedi put it in the pocket of Harry's dressing gown and hurried back to the harbour to sit at a table and wait for Thea, bubbling with excitement.

She was drinking her coffee when Thea pulled up.

Hedi got into the car, her heart lifting as she looked at her lovely, generous granddaughter, large as life, with her beautiful copper hair. 'You are such a joy to me,' she said, feeling the sweet pain of love. She felt in her pocket. 'Here. I have a gift for you. Please accept it. Open it when you get back.'

For a moment, Thea looked surprised. She opened her mouth to say something, but her cheeks coloured and she tucked the box in her shorts. 'Thanks, Hedi,' she said softly, and smiled.

After they got back to The Hideaway, Hedi excused herself and went down to the jetty. She stretched her arms towards the white hotel across the water, her heart yearning. She sank back in the deckchair and sighed. She had wanted to tell Thea about Harry, about the man he was, the grandfather whose genes she had inherited. Those genes were a little diluted by now, of course, but she could see that Thea was the essence of him, the best part.

She closed her eyes and wondered if she had been wrong to start from the beginning of the story. *But where else does a story start?* If she was to tell it, she had to tell the good and the bad, no matter how bad the bad had been.

Funny that Thea had made no comment about Lena until asked. No comment about any of it, neither platitudes nor judgement; her calm, angelic features had not been unsettled or spoiled by it. She had seen no change in her attitude or demeanour.

At the time of telling it, Hedi hadn't felt guilt, but the

deepest shame. She wished she was as pragmatic as the nameless woman. *She tried to starve us.*

Deep down, Hedi had known at the time that it wasn't personal: that Lena wasn't trying to starve them but merely fill herself, but she agreed with the narrative anyway – Lena deserved their contempt.

She had expected Thea to condemn her. 'I feel bad about it even now,' she said softly to herself, feeling the breeze on her face.

Is that so?

This time, the phrase didn't bring her relief, but a kind of resignation.

What was done was done.

A blackbird pink-pink-pinked across the water and sang a glorious, intricate song of joy. Hedi smiled and opened her eyelids a little, just enough so she could look at the white, comforting blur of the hotel with longing and regret.

That evening, after a supper of chicken salad followed by apple pie, Hedi dabbed her mouth with the napkin.

Thea was playing with the gold merry-go-round charm hanging around her neck.

It was perfect.

'Time for our nightcap?' Thea asked.

Hedi smiled. 'Of course. It is our routine.' They took what was left of the wine to the jetty and watched the sun go down behind the hills, staining the water red.

She wondered with a pang of alarm if Thea needed the wine to numb herself against her revelations. 'You want me to carry on with my tale tonight?' she asked. 'Maybe by now you've heard enough. Just say.'

Thea smiled. 'I want to hear about Magda going into hospital on the twentieth.' She rubbed her thumb over the base of the glass and glanced up at Hedi again, her smile fading. 'It's important to talk, isn't it? Not just because I want to get to know you, but because you went through something terrible, and survived. Everyone likes to hear stories of survival.'

'Truly?' Hedi pursed her lips thoughtfully. 'Perhaps we find hope in them, I suppose. Talking brings it back as if it were yesterday. But is it not better to get over the past, leave it dead and buried, and move forward gratefully?'

Thea's green gaze was full of compassion. 'It's not dead and buried though, is it? It has stayed with you.'

Hedi felt tears prickle her eyes. 'You're quite right, of course.'

She felt very tired and very old. If she could lay the past to rest, perhaps she would find peace.

19

HEDI

BELSEN, APRIL 1945

Hedi opened her eyes to a new day full of the promise of ambulances. The sunlight cut through the dim squalor of the hut. Magda's hair was wet with sweat against her face. She was burning up. Hedi wiped her own damp cheek with the back of the hand and pressed her lips against Magda's bare, slick shoulder – she was hot enough to sweat steam. 'Magda? Can you hear me? You're going to hospital today. Just think! A bed for yourself and clean sheets and medicine for the typhus and hot, sweet milk with bread in.' *You know*, she thought wistfully, *that's almost worth getting typhus for.*

The woman with no name snorted from the plank opposite. 'Who said there would be hot sweet milk with bread in it?'

'It stands to reason. That's what my mother used to give me when I was ill. Why, what did you get?'

'Listen, when I was ill, I lost my appetite altogether. If I hadn't lost it, then I wasn't ill. It's simple.'

Hedi turned over to look at her. 'What's the matter with you this morning?'

The woman sighed. 'When we were liberated, we thought it

was a new beginning, didn't we? And yet, five days later, here we are, still living like animals in filth. I've had enough.'

'Don't say that!' Hedi felt a wave of alarm come over her. 'We've got food, haven't we? You'll feel better after you've eaten.'

'Yes, you're probably right.'

Hedi smiled. 'You've never said I'm right about anything before.'

'You never usually are.'

Hedi felt smug. Personally, she was feeling hopeful. She had dreamt she was home again, and her parents were waiting for her. 'Where have you been?' her mother asked in the dream. She had replied, 'I've been to hell but now I'm back,' and her parents had applauded her, their faces shining with pride, as if she had entered a gruelling race and seen it through to the end.

She enjoyed the feeling that the dream gave her, but at the same time she was afraid of it, because she knew it might not be real.

She wondered whether to share the dream with the woman with no name, but she decided against it because she would most likely ruin it in some way. 'Anyway,' she said, 'we should prepare ourselves for the ambulances.'

'What, pack a little suitcase, you mean? Toothbrush and scented soap?'

'You are too sarcastic sometimes. I mean, we must say goodbye to the sick. Unless – do you think they would let me go with her?'

'Doubt it. You're a lost cause. There's no cure for unwarranted cheerfulness.'

Hedi ignored her. 'You know, we should get our food now, before they come. I want to be here when they take her.'

'I agree.'

Hedi lowered her legs to the floor and looked for a clean

spot to stand in. But there was no avoiding the mess because the floor was covered in it.

The woman got down, too. For a moment, they stood face to face with their bowls and spoons and Hedi said, 'You know, you look a bit different today. Less...' she sucked her cheeks in.

'Funny,' the woman said, wrapping her blanket around her bony shoulders, 'I was thinking the same about you. You look less like a living corpse than usual.'

As compliments go, it wasn't much, and Hedi didn't like the idea she'd looked like a living corpse without realising it. Everyone else did, sure, but in her mind she looked like her old self. She scratched her head, feeling the lice bite.

As they passed Lena's bunk, Hedi noticed with regret that the mattress had gone. She should have taken it herself when she'd had the chance. She hated herself for thinking it. When they got to the cookhouse, there was a little huddle of people outside, and a different cook was ladling out the stew with good humour. It seemed somehow bulkier than she remembered. More meat and more turnips, Hedi judged. The inmates who had finished eating were talking about the ambulances coming – it seemed like a mantra on everyone's lips. With the sick being attended to, there was hope for them, because they would also have less chance of catching typhus themselves.

The cook told them that they could take food back to the hut for the incapable, if they could trust themselves to be fair about it.

Hedi and the nameless woman looked at each other.

'Feeding the sick will at least while away the time until the ambulances come,' Hedi said.

The woman agreed. 'They'll be glad of it, especially now that you've told them they will only receive bread in warm milk. They've suffered enough already.'

Hedi didn't care. She was used to the woman's sarcasm.

'And,' the woman continued sensibly, 'if they don't want it, we can finish it off.'

The cook came back with the container of stew. 'Don't let them overeat,' he warned. 'Until their bodies adapt, too much will kill them – and you,' he added pointedly, looking at each of them in turn.

They carried the container back to the hut together, with the woman grumbling all the way. 'We're dead any way we look at it, too little food or too much. When I leave here, I'm going to eat sausages and *sauerkraut* for the rest of my life and take the risk.'

As they went into the hut, the smell of food roused many women from their troubled dozing. Hedi and the woman distributed food in the bowls of those who could eat and tried to force it on those who couldn't. It was frustrating to see the food dribble back out of their mouths, but a couple of the women responded with gratitude and blessings. The French women said they could feed their own sick, thanks all the same.

Finally, Hedi returned to her own plank; she supported Magda's head and encouraged her to take a couple of spoonfuls. She slurped it off the spoon. Hedi was encouraged. 'Now you can try a piece of meat,' she said. 'It will give you strength for the day ahead. The ambulances are coming today, remember?'

Magda obligingly opened her mouth for the meat. Seconds later, her eyes widened in panic and she began to choke helplessly. Quickly, Hedi thrust her fingers in Magda's mouth and fished the meat out from the back of her throat. She put it in her own mouth, her heart thudding. She chewed it thoroughly and swallowed. 'I can see you're not ready for that yet,' she said, her voice high and fearful. She wondered suddenly if Magda had diphtheria, too. *Please, no.* 'Just hang on a little longer,' she pleaded. 'It's nearly over. The ambulances are on their way.'

20

HARRY

BELSEN, APRIL 1945

That same morning, Harry and Bill were in the barracks of the Panzer Training School watching eight hundred despondent Wehrmacht soldiers muster in the parade square in their camouflage jackets and peaked caps.

On the orders of their superiors, instead of being taken to a prisoner-of-war camp as they'd been promised, they were being returned to the German lines. Consequently they had been reissued with their MG54s and Schmeissers.

'Look at them, poor sods,' Bill said. 'They thought they were home and dry. They've lost the heart for battle.'

Harry scanned his eyes over their weapons and his heart lurched. Arthur, his younger brother, was still out there in the thick of war. But Arthur had always been the lucky one and there was no reason to think his luck wouldn't last. 'That's not a bad thing, if you ask me,' he said, lighting a cigarette and puffing on it. He narrowed his green eyes against the smoke.

'Fair point,' Bill said.

Harry could hear the distant rumble of the trucks approaching for the German soldiers. 'At least now we'll have room for the sick. We have to get things moving, the inmates are restless. I don't blame them. Apart from feeding them, we've made precious little difference. We've killed off as many as we've saved.'

It had, as it turned out, been a mistake to donate their rations to the cookhouse. The bodies of the starving had adapted well to the shortage of nourishment in their own infinitely mysterious ways. The sudden availability of plentiful food had caused the number of dead in the huts to rise astronomically. Even though the burials were almost constant, it was impossible to keep up and after five days their efforts had made precious little difference.

'Another three SS committed suicide last night.'

Harry stubbed out his cigarette. 'I heard.' He hoped they'd killed themselves out of remorse while there was still some humanity left in them, but he suspected that the reality was different. Losing their faith in Adolf must have been like being told there was no God. It made the future pointless.

The one exception in the camp was Commandant Kramer, whose eyes still burned with zeal for the Third Reich. He had been placed under arrest for killing inmates as they celebrated the arrival of the British.

Psychopath.

The Wehrmacht troops filed reluctantly into the trucks.

Finally, with them gone, Harry and Bill made their way back to the square. It was time to mobilise the ambulances.

The fleet was ready and waiting in the yard, and so was Lieutenant Colonel Gonin, his hands clasped behind his back.

'He looks grim,' Harry warned. *What now?* he wondered, his heart sinking.

The colonel called them to attention. He announced the news gravely. 'Men, the German army has left us a parting gift. They have sabotaged our water supply.'

There was a rumble of animosity. 'That's a rotten trick,' Bill said, 'even for them.'

Colonel Gonin raised his voice to be heard.

'Quiet! We are postponing the hospitalisation of the sick until we have a supply of clean water. Any questions?'

'Sir. How soon will that be? We promised them it would be today. The inmates are losing hope.'

'We'll get on to it ASAP, rest assured.'

'*ASAP*' *wasn't good enough*, Harry thought. The women had been hanging on to life by a thread, waiting for the twentieth. 'What are we supposed to tell them?'

'We will send the ambulances into the camp as planned, to keep up morale. However, for the time being they will return empty.'

Harry and Bill exchanged an incredulous glance.

'This is a joke,' Harry said bitterly under his breath. 'Poor devils. They're counting on us to keep our word.'

'Dismissed!'

21

HEDI

BELSEN, APRIL 1945

Hedi stood at the window of the hut and watched with excitement as the convoy of ambulances drove in. 'Magda, they're here at last!' she cried, clapping her hands. She squeezed her eyes shut and murmured a heartfelt prayer of thanks.

The woman with no name stared at the plank above her head and made no comment. After a few moments, she said, 'You know, I think I'm coming down with something.'

Hedi turned sharply to look at her. 'What do you mean?'

'My bowels feel loose.'

'Are you being serious?' Hedi asked, her heart sinking.

'I'm telling you,' the woman insisted, 'my bowels feel loose.'

'Stop saying that, you're making me ill.'

'I'm being polite! What am I supposed to say? I'm going to soil myself?'

Hedi shuddered. 'Well, anyway, don't say it again. I get the picture. Maybe you ate too much.'

'You saw what I ate,' the woman replied furiously. 'Who do you think I am? You think I'm Lena?'

Hedi cringed at the anger in her voice. 'Don't,' she pleaded.

'At least I haven't tried to choke people to death, not like you. I saw you, shoving that food into Magda!'

'I know.' Hedi climbed back up on her plank. She huddled close to Magda for comfort and pulled her blanket over her eyes, hiding miserably in the dark. She'd had enough. More specifically, she'd had enough of waiting. She felt as if she'd been waiting for months for one thing or another, waiting for her parents, waiting for food, waiting to be beaten, waiting to die, and now, waiting to start living again. She closed her eyes and resigned herself as she carried on waiting.

When it got dark, they heard a polite knock on the door of the hut.

'Come in, it's open!' the woman with no name called out.

Hedi uncovered her eyes hopefully and raised her head. The door opened. It was not the medical team, but two men in civilian clothes. A beam of light from a torch danced over her, and she blinked in the brightness.

'Hi, folks,' one of them said from the doorway. He had an American accent.

'Who are you?' the woman with no name said with contempt. 'Sightseers?'

'We're American Friends. Quakers.' His voice tailed off for a moment as he trained his torch on the woman. 'We're fixing the water supply.'

'What's wrong with the water supply?' she asked.

'It's been fouled.'

Hedi closed her eyes again and let her head drop back with a thud. That came as no surprise. She had seen bodies floating in the water tanks, women who had tried to get water to drink but had fallen in and drowned because they didn't have the strength to drag themselves out again. *I'm going to lie here forever,* she thought wearily, *with nothing happening, just people coming to look at us and going away again with a story to tell.*

'Don't worry,' the American Friend said. 'We're here to help.'

He closed the door again and the two men went away silently.

'Yeah, closing the door on us, that's certainly helped,' a weak voice came from the top bunk. 'He was letting the cold air in.'

'Hedi, you know something?' the woman with no name asked suddenly, poking her with her elbow. 'I don't believe there's a hospital. The British are going to let us die here, in these huts. They're going to finish what the Nazis started. Take it from me, they're being ordered to, by the SS. It's clear to me, now.'

Hedi turned her head and stared at her.

The woman's roving eyes were huge and glittering in the gloomy dark, and her manic gaze steadied and settled on Hedi.

Hedi was suddenly afraid. For some time, she had believed the woman had lost her soul because those screeches she used to give came from an inhuman place. But lately, she had seemed perfectly normal again and Hedi had come to the conclusion she'd been mistaken. True, the woman could be ironic and volatile but that was a long way from crazy. Now though, the woman's dark eyes were full of intelligent cunning. 'You know how they'll do it? They'll board up the huts so we can't get out and then...'

Hedi put her fingers in her ears. She couldn't bear to hear any more. But with her fingers jammed in her ears she could hear her heart galloping wildly, as if she was listening to it through a loudspeaker. It sounded as if it would explode with fear. She took her fingers out again and scratched her arms, shuddering. She could feel the lice crawling in the creases of her skin.

The woman in the top bunk hung her head over to look at them and said, 'Let me ask you, why would they do that?'

The woman propped her head up on her skinny wrist. 'Think about it. We're in Germany. We're still at war. And yet, the British come in and take over? It makes no sense.'

'That's true enough,' the woman in the top bunk conceded.

'But why would the SS let the Tommies treat them badly?' Hedi asked. 'If they were still in charge, that SS guy you pushed into the pit would have tortured you and then shot you, you know that.' For a moment, she found herself reliving the moment at the pit when the woman flew at him; the exuberant, shameful revulsion she felt as his knees gave way.

'I'm just telling you what I know,' the woman with no name said firmly. 'Take it or leave it.'

'I'll leave it, thank you very much,' Hedi said crossly.

But she slept restlessly that night, troubled by nightmares. In the early hours of the morning she fell into a deep sleep at last, and when she woke up she felt she'd time-travelled. The medical team was in the hut – one British medical officer and four stretcher-bearers.

She recognised the officer at once as the soldier with the copper hair. He was standing in a stream of brightness. He seemed all shine – his face, his belt, his boots. Suddenly she was wide awake.

'This is what we're going to do,' he announced. 'All those suffering from typhus will be moved to the medical unit immediately.'

'I've got typhus,' the woman who had forgotten her name said eagerly. 'I've had it for a few days now. My bowels are loose...'

Hedi frowned. *So she says.* The woman was covered in sores, it was true, but she seemed well enough.

Suddenly, everyone in the hut had typhus. *Herr Doktor! Herr Doktor!*

'My sister's got typhus, too,' Hedi shouted to the soldier, raising her voice to join in the clamour. She turned to Magda, lying close to her for the last time. She pulled the damp strands of tangled hair away from Magda's hollow cheeks. 'You're going to be safe now, and you'll soon be well again. Don't forget me, will you?'

Magda opened her eyes, and Hedi felt herself falling deep into the dark emptiness of her gaze.

There appeared a glint of recognition. 'Sister,' Magda whispered.

'That's right, Magda.' They lay cheek to cheek amidst the tumult.

The soldier called for silence. 'Listen,' he yelled, 'don't panic, we'll come to you each in turn.' He wiped his hand over his face.

Hedi was surprised when he came over to them first. He was clean and healthy. She inhaled deeply – he smelled of soap.

'This is your sister?' he asked gently, calming her with his green gaze. 'Let's take a look, shall we?'

Hedi levered herself from the bunk to give him room to examine Magda. She watched him as he gently moved the blanket covering her.

His expression altered, dimmed, like a cloud crossing the sun. Avoiding Hedi's eyes, he looked back at the stretcher-bearers and shook his head.

Hedi's breath caught in her throat because she knew what the gesture meant. She tugged the sleeve of his tunic. 'She's going to die, isn't she?'

He tucked the blanket carefully around Magda again. 'That's a typhus rash. She's very sick. Right now, we have a policy of only taking the women we can help.'

He said it in a gentle but matter-of-fact way that made her want to cry. His face was full of sorrow.

Please, her lips pleaded to him, but no sound came out. What was the point? He had a policy.

The soldier turned away, but then he hesitated and turned back again, settling his steady gaze on Hedi once more. His eyes were translucent, the colour of green glass, like sunshine through a bottle.

'How about you?' he asked her. 'You're okay, are you? No fever, diarrhoea?'

Hedi shook her head. 'I'm okay, thank you.'

He smiled. 'Good.' He seemed to come to a decision. He took out a skin pen from his pocket and drew a cross on Magda's forehead. 'We'll take this one,' he said to the other two men. 'Fetch her a fresh blanket.' And then he asked Hedi, 'What's her name?'

'Magda.'

'Magda, we're going to wrap you up and get you clean.' He unwrapped her from her old flea-ridden covering. For a moment, naked, all bones, Magda whimpered pitifully. The stretcher-bearers covered her up quickly with the fresh blanket and carried her out as if she weighed nothing. She had gone before Hedi had a chance to say goodbye.

The soldier came back to the woman who'd forgotten her name. 'Let's have a look at you.'

The woman opened her eyes a fraction and groaned weakly, letting her jaw hang open like a corpse.

The stretcher-bearers waited by the door for his signal.

'Scared you'll catch it?' the woman with no name said mockingly, in a miraculous burst of energy.

'We've been vaccinated,' the red-haired soldier replied mildly, as if she'd been talking to him. He opened the neck of her striped tunic and examined her skin carefully. 'Right,' he said at last. 'You haven't got a fever and the good news is, it doesn't look like typhus – in fact, you're remarkably fit in the circumstances. You've got scabies and pressure sores, but I think that's all – it's hard to tell under the dirt.'

The woman with no name didn't receive the news well. 'What do *you* know, Tommy? Are you even qualified?' she asked him crossly. '"Remarkably fit" indeed! Are you blind?'

'Don't worry, she's lost her mind,' Hedi explained to him. 'She thinks you're working with the Germans to kill us all. You're not, are you?'

'No, we're not,' he said sharply. He glanced at her and his green eyes softened for a moment. The corner of his lip dimpled momentarily in a smile.

'Great,' the nameless woman spat when he moved on to check on the other inmates, his skin pen at the ready. She watched him drawing a cross on those lucky ones who were to be taken to the infirmary. 'What did you tell him that for?'

'In case you were right.'

'Idiot! He's not going to admit to it, is he?'

Further into the hut there was some sort of lively argument going on.

'Those that we can help are our priority,' she heard the soldier say sternly above the noise.

The woman in the top bunk said knowingly, 'The French women don't want to be separated.'

Hedi watched the stretcher-bearers take out the patients cocooned in new blankets. The group of French women hobbled outside after them with the final patient evacuation of the day. She listened to them banging on the ambulance, wanting to be let in, too.

'Soon,' she said wisely, 'the sick will emerge from those blanket cocoons as butterflies.'

The woman with no name snorted. 'Never mind them, what about us?' she asked, but her voice was resigned.

Moments later the French women shuffled back into the hut, grumbling as the vehicles pulled away.

Hedi lay back and spread her arms. She had a little more space to herself now, as well as extra straw for her mattress. She felt a chill go through her as she remembered the soldier's shake of the head. Then she imagined Magda wearing clean clothes and sleeping in a clean bed, being fed milk and... Hedi suddenly remembered the food that was left in Magda's bowl from the night before. She hoisted herself on her elbows to check, but both the food and the bowl had gone. *Oh well.*

Still, she felt hollow and lonely now that Magda, her purpose in life, had been taken from her. She sighed and closed her eyes.

The woman with no name went to fetch the food from the cookhouse.

When she came back she shared it scrupulously, starting with Hedi, and finally came back to her own plank to eat her own portion.

They ate quickly, and in silence. When she had finished, Hedi licked her bowl and wiped a warm smear of stew from the tip of her nose with the back of her hand. She looked warily at the woman. 'Don't you just sometimes wish for a different flavour? Something green, maybe?'

'Hm. It's filling, but that's about all you can say for it. It's too bland for my taste.'

'Mine, too.'

'Of course, we must be grateful.'

Hedi nodded. She studied the woman again because she seemed to be deep in thought.

Sure enough, a moment later the woman said, 'Listen, Hedi, when you came in here, did you bring any valuables with you?'

'Just my watch, that's all.'

'I had a watch too, and my rings and crucifix.' The woman's dark eyes narrowed. 'I watched the soldiers bury them in a box to dig up for later.'

'Truly?' Hedi looked at her doubtfully. She had those kind

of dreams all the time, of being reunited with things. 'Why would they bury them in a box?'

'They weren't supposed to take them from us in the first place. I suppose they saw it as their pension money. But now that the SS officers are locked up overnight, they can't come and retrieve them, can they? It's up to us to retrieve our own possessions.'

It made sense. 'I would very much like to have my watch back,' Hedi said, scratching her neck. 'It was a gift from my parents.'

'And I would very much like to have my wedding ring back on my finger.'

'So... do you think you can remember where they buried it?'

'I know the exact spot. They marked it with a stone. We'll need a spade, I suppose. Although they didn't dig the hole very deep because they kept on adding to the haul.'

This was becoming most exciting and unexpected. 'But what if they catch us stealing?'

'Stealing? Idiot! How can we steal our own things?' the woman asked with unarguable logic. 'Now you're in on the plan, I need you to help me, because you're young and strong.'

'I am young, that's true,' Hedi agreed. 'Where are we going to get a spade from?'

'Do I have to think of everything?' the woman grumbled.

'Oh. I know! I shall use my bowl and spoon to dig.'

'See? You're not as stupid as you look.'

That was depressing. She used to be quite clever once, at least in some subjects. She had a merit certificate for playing the violin. She was on the point of telling the woman about it, and then she changed her mind. She didn't care what the woman thought of her, or if she did, only a little bit.

They went outside and she followed the woman around the side of the hut.

'Here it is,' the woman pointed. 'Start digging.'

The soil was sandy and dry. It kept slipping back into the hole. It hurt Hedi's knees to kneel. She was wondering if it was something the woman had dreamed up, like the British being in the power of the Nazis, when her bowl hit something, metal on metal. She looked up at her in amazement.

'Keep digging!' the woman urged. 'It's got to be clear of sand. You don't want your watch ruined, do you, because it's got sand in it?'

'I have had enough of you, you treat me like a slave,' Hedi grumbled, digging a trench around the box.

'It's for your own good. There, you can stop now. Open the lid, you deserve to.'

Hedi blew the sand from the lid and opened the box. *Treasure!* Sure enough, it was full of valuables – pearls, watches, bangles, brightly coloured beads. 'Wonderful,' she said, her voice trembling.

The woman crouched next to her. 'Find me my gold cross and my rings.'

'What do they look like? Here's a crucifix. There may be more.'

'Give me all that you find. Yes, all of them! I need to see which ones are mine. Don't look at me like that! I'm not going to steal them, am I?'

Suddenly, Hedi didn't mind about the woman's tone because she had seen her own precious watch entangled with the others, with its blue leather strap and square chrome dial. Her spirits lifted and she felt a rush of affection for it. Looking at the dial was like looking at the familiar face of someone she loved. Quickly, she fastened it onto her wrist. It slid around, face down, way too loose, even on the smallest hole, so she pushed it up her forearm, delightfully happy, and rummaged through the box for the woman's rings. The gold wedding rings had made their way to the bottom and she picked them out, stacking them on her own fingers, waggling them playfully, watching them glint.

'Stop acting the fool,' the woman said impatiently, 'and get on with it, before anyone sees us.'

There were a lot of rings in the box: a depressing amount – too many. Hedi let them drop off her fingers into the woman's cupped hands. 'I don't know how you will be able to tell which is yours,' she said doubtfully.

'I'll know, don't worry about that.'

'There are more at the bottom.' Hedi picked them up, one by one, and dropped them into the woman's lap. As she was rummaging around, a particular watch caught her eye. It was gold with a tan-leather strap, and it was very familiar to her. It belonged to her father. Her stomach tightened as she untangled it and she laid it flat on the palm of her hand. It felt warm, as if her father had only just that moment taken it off.

If she turned it over, face down, she would see the inscription on the back that commemorated twenty years of teaching at his school.

'What's wrong with you now?' the woman asked impatiently, looking up from her task of sorting.

'This is my father's watch,' Hedi said. She turned it over and read his name and the inscription. 'He was here.'

The woman thought about it and snorted. 'Listen to yourself! Why would he be in the women's compound? He must have given it your mother for her to wear. It looks valuable.'

Hedi frowned. 'You're right. That makes sense. He must have given it to my mother.' A fresh realisation came to her. 'She might have been in the hut with us all this time!'

'Impossible! Don't you think she would have seen you at roll call? A woman would know her own child.'

'I look nothing like she remembered,' Hedi said stubbornly. Otherwise she would have to consider this alternative – her mother was lost in the tangled waste heaps of the dead.

She wound the watch up. 'What time do you have?' she asked the woman.

'How should I know? Maybe ten, eleven o'clock?'

'Let's say ten thirty, then.' After adjusting the winder, she fastened her father's watch on her wrist. Even at its smallest it was too big, so she pushed it up until it was above the sharp bones of her elbow.

The woman was looking at her steadily.

'What?' Hedi demanded. 'Forget it. You can take over the search for your rings,' she said to the woman.

'No need. I've found them.' The woman slid the rings onto her thumb and carried the rest of the jewellery back to the box in the lap of her shirt. She emptied it in and put the lid on the box again, scooping the sandy soil over it once more. She dusted the soil from her hands and fell forward weakly on all fours. 'Ow! Help me up, will you?' she pleaded.

Hedi helped the woman to her feet and they faced each other in the secret shadows of the hut. 'My mother is here,' Hedi said stubbornly. 'I can feel it.'

'How long is it since you saw her?'

'Maybe a year ago.'

The woman laughed grimly. 'She didn't have a chance. Look at us, Hedi! After just a few months we're all bones and teeth.'

'You don't know everything,' Hedi told her, as if denying the impossible would banish her fears.

The woman scratched her scabs. 'That's true. You want me to come and help you look for her?'

'You don't even know what she looks like,' Hedi said. 'But yes, come with me.'

They went back into the hut. Hedi had never ventured beyond the first stack of planks before. They were territorial, that way. Deeper in, she trudged through the gloom and filth, looking at every person stacked above another person in the dim

light: the fit and the dying. 'Mama!' she called helplessly. 'Are
you here?'

'Shut up!' one of the 'fit' shouted back. 'We're trying to
sleep!'

'I'm your mama,' someone called out weakly.

It didn't sound like her at all, but Hedi checked the
woman's face closely, just to be sure. She felt a sudden surge of
panic. *Could this sick woman truly be her?*

The wiry black hair which stood up straight from her forehead looked familiar, as if the woman had been taken by
surprise. She was lying on a low plank, slick with sweat, her skin
yellow, her mouth open, the breath rasping in her throat like a
gentle snore. Hedi knelt next to her and pressed her lips against
her feverish forehead. 'Mama! I bet you didn't think I'd find
you,' she whispered, keeping her voice light. 'Guess what, I've
got something to show you. It's Papa's watch.' She unfastened
the watch from her upper arm and pressed it against the
woman's ear so she could hear it tick. 'Can you hear it?'

'This is her?' interrupted the woman with no name.

'Maybe.' Hedi frowned and looked down at the woman.
The snoring had stopped and she was silent.

'Quickly, Hedi, talk to her,' the woman nudged her
urgently, 'while her soul can still hear you.'

'Mama, I love you,' Hedi said desperately, and the words came
from deep in her heart. The brown eyes opened for a moment, softened, and glazed. 'Mama?' Grief overcame her, grief for this dead
woman who was not her mother after all. Her mother had grey eyes,
like her own. Her sobbing was ugly, uncontrollable. She pressed her
fists against her heart. *I can't stand the pain,* she thought.

The woman with no name was praying the Lord's prayer
meaningfully over Hedi's tears, the least facetious she'd ever
been. 'Thy kingdom come... Thy Will be done on Earth...'

When she finished, she pulled the blanket over the dead

woman's face and helped Hedi to her feet. Her eyes betrayed nothing.

Hedi wiped her cheeks, speaking angrily between sobs, 'I don't know why I'm crying! That's not even her!' She ran her hand across her nose. 'You have wasted your prayer on the wrong person! Stupid woman! Why would she say she was my mama?'

'Hedi, a prayer is never wasted. She claimed you, believing you were her lost child. You gave her the courage to leave her suffering behind.'

Hedi pressed her fingers against her eyes, bereft and full of pain. She wanted to die herself, to put an end to her hollow suffering. 'I should have known it wasn't her. My mother would have said my name.'

'That is a very important point you have made, that we are called by our names.'

You're not.

They went back to their own territory and Hedi climbed miserably onto her bunk. She was helpless to stop her tears, sorrowing for the dead woman. She didn't understand it. She had never grieved for her parents, not even on the day they were taken away. She had clung on to hope. But now she was mourning bitterly for some stranger. Exhausted, she closed her sore eyes and pressed the watch against her ear for consolation. The reassuring rhythm was her father's heartbeat.

When Hedi woke up, it was still daylight. She felt exhausted, resigned.

She held her watch in front of her face. She realised she could see her reflection in the chrome casing.

Without their small cushions of fat, her nondescript grey eyes had sunk deep into her head. If they dropped in any deeper, she thought, they would be lost inside her skull where they would rattle around for the rest of her life like pinballs.

Blue hollows shaded her cheekbones like fresh bruises. Her mouth was thin, like that of some old crone, and her lips were pale and disapproving in their meanness. Frowning, she bit them to get the blood flowing. *Uch*, she was ugly.

She fastened the watch back on her arm again, wishing now that she hadn't looked at herself. She had no hope of a man loving her now. She had fondly imagined that after this was over, she and the woman would keep in touch, and some day in the future, she would invite the woman to her wedding. She assumed by then the woman might have remembered her name, or at least thought up a new one. After all, she couldn't remain 'the woman with no name' forever.

The woman with no name was lying on her back next to her, staring at her own hand intently, like a hypnotist. Her wedding band had brought her husband close to her.

'Listen,' Hedi said to her, thinking she could learn something, 'this husband of yours, Karl. You kissed him, and you married him,' she said, thinking it over.

'Not all on the same evening,' the woman said.

'No, I realise that. And you had the nosebleed.'

'Yes, and because of the nosebleed, Karl gave me his handkerchief. That's when I knew we were in love.'

'Truly? That's interesting. What if he hadn't had a handkerchief? Would you have left him?'

'What sort of question is that? I had my own handkerchief. Who doesn't have their own handkerchief?'

'But—'

'But the point is, he gave me his, you see? He was looking after me.'

Hedi scratched behind her ear and popped a louse against her skull with her thumbnail. The story seemed most unsatisfactory. *The deciding factor was a handkerchief? Don't make me laugh!* Good looks, that was what she wanted in a husband, the kind of looks that made your heart sing, someone like the soldier with the red hair who had the face of an angel and the cool eyes of an ice-melt river. That way, she wouldn't care what he talked about or if he had a handkerchief, she would just enjoy him like some beautiful possession that smelled of soap. It seemed simple, put like that. 'So now, your Karl, what did he call you when you were in love, do you remember? Darling, sweetie?'

The woman lowered her hand and smiled dreamily. 'He called me Ursula,' she said, her voice softening.

Hedi sat up so suddenly she hit her head on the plank above her. 'Ow. That's your name, then! Ursula!'

For a moment, the woman looked at her uncertainly. She scratched her forehead, leaving three white marks on her skin that slowly filled with blood. 'Ursula,' she said, trying the word out, as if she was unsure she was pronouncing it properly. 'Ursula?' Then she nodded slowly. 'You know, you're right. That's who I was. I was Ursula.'

'It's who you are still!'

The woman, Ursula, seemed to think this over for a minute, then she turned her mouth down and shook her head. She laid herself down very carefully and gently, as if all her fragile bones had been newly broken, and she stared at the plank above her head.

Hedi waited for her to say something more, but she was unblinking for so long that she began to worry she was dead, that the shock of remembering her name had killed her.

But she wasn't dead because she suddenly turned away and faced the wall.

Hedi stared at the back of her head for a moment, rejected. Was that all the thanks she got for finding out her name?

She waited for her to turn back, and in the meantime, she watched the lice moving in Ursula's tangled hair. She felt responsible for Ursula's sudden stupor. *Forget you've got a name*, she wanted to say. *You were right all along, it's not important.*

To comfort herself, she looked at her watch. It was the only proof she had of the life she'd had before this one. She looked at her father's watch. It gave her hope of a life after it.

These watches were her history. *These watches, I never thought I'd see them again. This is the watch my parents gave me for my birthday. This is the watch that my father was given by his place of employment.* She imagined telling her future husband the story.

Telling her children about it.

22

THEA

PRESENT DAY

'But you didn't.' Thea stretched, clasping her hands behind her head as she looked up at the last gilded clouds of sunset fading from the darkening sky. 'You didn't tell Maggie about it.'

The trees behind the hotel were turning violet. She rubbed the back of her neck under her hair, where the spar of the deckchair pressed into it, as she thought over Hedi's last remark.

'No, that is correct,' Hedi said. 'I didn't tell her.'

In the twilight, it was hard for Thea to make out the details of her grandmother's face. 'I've been thinking, we should tell Maggie that you're staying with me. She might be trying to get hold of you.'

'She won't be,' Hedi said firmly, swatting the idea away.

'You know something? You're very similar. You're as stubborn as each other.'

The breeze was rippling the water, shattering reflections that shimmered and danced like tinsel. The twinkling reflections were joined by a bright new light. Thea gazed up at the hotel. It was coming from one of the bedrooms.

A man was standing by the window; a woman joined him and he put his arm around her shoulders, pulling her close. Side by side, heads inclined towards each other, they stood looking at the same magical river. Thea felt a pang of envy, and deep regret.

'Can they see us?' Hedi whispered, as if they were hiding.

Thea moved her chair closer to Hedi's. Picking up the blanket, she spread it over their laps – she felt suddenly in need of comfort. 'They must be able to see the lights of the cottage. Maybe they're on their honeymoon,' Thea said wistfully and she held up her glass. The wine coloured everything a rosy, festive red. She swirled it around, and it was cold on her lips, chilled now by the evening air.

Across the river, the woman in the hotel room closed the curtains. The light dimmed. The tableau was over. There was something sad and final about it, Thea thought, as if they'd been shut out of something precious. She felt a sudden longing. *I wish... I wish...*

Hedi chuckled softly to herself. 'For a moment, I had the strongest feeling I was looking at us, at me and Harry. You know that feeling?'

'What do you mean?'

'Of being outside time? As if the passing years have no relevance and the past is still present?'

'I'm not sure. Kind of.'

'I suppose it was looking at that couple. I felt that Harry and I were still there, on our honeymoon,' Hedi said.

'Did you honeymoon someplace like that?'

'Not someplace *like* that, *there.*'

'Truly? Are you serious?' Thea asked in disbelief. *Truly* wasn't a word she would usually use; she'd absorbed it from Hedi's stories. It was the nature of stories, she supposed, that they became a part of your own experience in the listening of them. *For better or worse.* Hedi had been right about that. She reached down for her glass, unsettled. 'You honeymooned in the George III Hotel? How come?'

'Because Harry was brought up in Bear Cave, and this is also where we got married,' Hedi said. 'I thought you knew that. Isn't that the reason we're here?'

'No!' Thea raised her voice in surprise. 'How could I – you never said... huh,' she reasoned, 'I suppose I must have recognised the name when I stopped here, on some level.' She thought about it. 'Did I come here as a child?'

'Not as a child. As a baby.'

'Of course, yes: as a baby. It would have been before the... estrangement.'

'Ess – strange – ment,' Hedi said, dragging the word out. 'That's it exactly; it was before Maggie and I became strangers.'

'I suppose I recognised Bear Cave without realising its significance. She must have talked about it when I was small. It's the only explanation.' An owl hooted in the distance. The sound travelled plaintively across the water. 'We *definitely* ought to go to the hotel for supper. Let's go tomorrow night, I'll book us a table.'

'No, let's not do that yet,' Hedi said quickly.

'Why not?'

'Because it's not the right time.'

'Okay. Whenever you're ready,' Thea said, realising she'd been insensitive. She'd imagined Hedi would enjoy reminiscing about happy memories for a change, but her grief was still raw and being in her honeymoon hotel would obviously intensify her loss. 'Are you cold? Do you want to go back to The Hideaway?'

'I'm not cold, it's just that – a goose has walked over my grave.' Hedi sat forward and cupped her chin in her hands as she looked intently across at the closed curtains in the bedroom of the hotel. She sighed. 'I never imagined it would be like this. I never imagined coming back, nor talking freely.' Hedi brushed a lock of white hair from her forehead. 'Come, let's head back to the house. I will show my father's watch to you.'

Gathering up the blanket, Thea got to her feet and followed her grandmother through the black, dew-silvered grass.

Back indoors, Thea drew the curtains.

Hedi fetched the suitcase from her room and put it on the table and smoothed her hands affectionately over the old leather. The burnished glow tanned her face gold.

'Everything's in here,' she said, glancing at Thea, 'my souvenirs. My emotions, also.'

Thea nodded and automatically felt for the skin-warmed gold charm dangling in her cleavage. She hadn't said much to Hedi about this gift because she couldn't put into words how deeply, tearfully grateful she was to be given it. She and Maggie had moved around so often that they'd kept their possessions to a minimum. Being unworldly and unmaterialistic, untethered, as her mother put it, had become a way of life and they were proud of being free spirits. Better to feel superior than deprived, right?

But she was reassured by the way Hedi's face softened when she noticed the gesture.

Hedi opened the suitcase. With a smile, she took the watch out, closed the case and handed it to Thea with a salesman's flourish. 'Please. Go ahead. Take a look.'

Thea turned it over to read the inscription:

To Paul Fischer
The Best Teacher Inspires.

She smiled. 'That's lovely.'

'Yes.' Hedi smiled modestly and inclined her head. 'He was a good man, everyone said so. He taught English.' She filled the kettle, switched it on and turned back to Thea. 'Your father,' she began rather hesitantly, clasping her hands behind her back. 'Do you mind if I ask you about him?'

Yes, I do. For a moment, Thea's breath caught in her throat, and she flushed. 'No, go for it,' she said lightly, putting the watch back on top of the suitcase. She should have realised this was coming sooner or later, with all the talk about fathers. 'What do you want to know?'

'You've met him?'

Thea gave a wry laugh. 'I've met him once. We had lunch.' Thea hesitated and threaded a strand of hair behind her ear. 'Did you meet him? Did Maggie bring him home?'

'No. Harry wanted her to, once we knew she was expecting. He wanted to talk to him, man to man, to discuss his responsibilities, but Maggie said it was none of our business.' Hedi met Thea's eyes sympathetically. 'You know, if it's uncomfortable for you to talk about it, you don't have to say anything more. I will perfectly understand.'

'It's okay,' Thea said honestly, realising that suddenly, it was. 'He was nothing like I'd expected. We had lunch and it was really awkward. He was married with two sons when he met her. After a few months she wanted him to make a commitment and he asked her to wait until his boys left for uni and he would ask his wife for a divorce. Maggie walked out on him there and then, and that was that, as far as he was concerned. He said he hadn't known that she was pregnant.'

'What kind of man did he seem, to you?'

'Wary, suspicious.' She forced a laugh. 'He wanted me to do a DNA test. He was anxious to know what I wanted from him, whether it was a one-off financial contribution or ongoing support. You'd think, if that's the first thing that someone has to ask...' She puffed out a self-deprecating laugh. 'Basically, it was humiliating. He asked how Maggie was. I told him she was happy and living in New York. That I was happy, and I had thought it would be nice for us to meet. No ulterior motives. But it wasn't. We shook hands, and it was like shaking hands after an interview for a job that you both know you haven't got.'

'He was older than she was?'

'Yes. He must have been twice her age when she met him.' Thea buzzed the charm back and forth along the links of the gold chain. 'I'd always thought that Maggie was a free spirit who brought me up as a single parent because she didn't want to commit. But it wasn't that. She just fell for the wrong guy.'

'Our perfect girl,' Hedi sighed. 'It was as if we'd never known her.'

There it was again, that phrase. It smacked of naivete. 'You didn't,' Thea said. 'Nobody's perfect.'

Hedi's expression froze for a moment, as if she was considering this possibility for the first time, 'No. Of course,' she said stiffly. 'You are entirely correct.'

Thea squeezed her temples. She glanced at the watch lying on top of the suitcase – her great-grandfather's watch, she reminded herself. It gave her a longing for home, that geographically undefinable place of the heart. 'I think I'll go to bed now,' she said.

'Have I upset you?' Hedi asked anxiously, catching her arm. 'Please forgive me.'

'Really, I'm fine. It's not you.' *It's not you, it's that couple standing in the window of the hotel that we both identified with so strongly.* 'I just feel suddenly tired, that's all. I'll be fine in the morning. Good night,' she said, kissing Hedi's cheek.

'Good night.'

23

HEDI

'A donkey ride?' Thea said in surprise over breakfast. 'Seriously?'

'Of course. We're near the seaside. We have to do things properly. What's wrong? What's that expression on your face? You don't like donkeys?'

'We're too old for donkey rides,' Thea protested, buttering her toast. 'Donkeys are fine, for kids.'

'Nonsense! Adults the whole world over travel on donkeys. Ever since Jesus.' Hedi was relieved to see Thea smile.

Her granddaughter put her butter knife down. Her hair was tied loosely back from her face and in the sunlight coming through the window it shone like a copper halo. 'If it will make you happy, I'll do it,' she said.

If it will make you happy. Hedi leant forward, her arms on the table. 'Tell me what would make you happy.'

Thea looked surprised. 'I *am* happy.'

Hedi frowned at her. *Was she being truthful?* That was the problem; she couldn't tell. Living with Harry for seventy-odd years, she'd got to read every nuance of his moods and expressions, so that she knew him as intimately as she knew her own self. However, other people's behaviour was something that had to be learnt over time. She had never seen Thea carelessly happy. Of course, circumstances hadn't allowed for it. Their first meeting had been at Harry's funeral and their next meeting had been with the social worker; not the most pleasant of memories. Added to that, every night since they'd arrived, Hedi had been telling her granddaughter about Belsen. When had she given her a chance to be happy? She suddenly realised that Thea was grinning at her.

'You're so funny when you're thinking, Hedi,' she said fondly.

'Am I?' Hedi was surprised and pleased to be thought of as funny.

Thea stood up. 'Come on. Let's do the dishes, and then we'll go to Barmouth and find ourselves a donkey.'

They crossed on the ferry and once they reached the other side, they trudged through the sand, swinging their shoes in their hands. It was a beautiful day. Blue sea met the blue sky, encircling yellow sandbanks with white foam. Gulls screeched above their heads, and in the distance they could hear the music from the fairground. Once or twice, Hedi stopped to look towards the horizon, giving her heart a rest from its exertions and her lungs a chance to fill with air again.

'Thea, listen, you were six months old when you first came on these donkeys with me,' she said. 'And you giggled! You had the most infectious giggle! Whenever we got on a bus or a train, you could see passengers debating whether to move away to some more distant seat, and by the end of the journey they would be taking it in turns to hold you.' She remembered Thea's glee, the weight of her, and the weight of responsibility, the smell of the donkeys, their reassuring sturdiness, the jingling of their bridles and that mysterious holy cross of coarse, dark hair on their backs.

'Oh well, if I enjoyed it that much, I'll stop worrying.'

'You shared your biscuit with ours. He was very gentle with you. Donkeys are extremely intelligent creatures. Easy to work with, except for those times that they know better than their owners. You can never get a donkey to change his mind on a subject once he's made it up.'

'My grandmother, the donkey whisperer,' Thea said, laughing. 'Who knew?'

The man in charge of the donkeys was happy to have two adults wanting a ride. Hedi repeated the story about baby Thea and the biscuit.

'Ginger Nuts,' the man said. 'They can hear a packet of Ginger Nuts rustle from half a mile away.'

'What did I tell you?' Hedi said. 'Very intelligent.'

With one foot in the stirrup, Thea climbed up, her red hair flying in the breeze, and looked at Hedi over her shoulder. 'Race you,' she said.

Hedi laughed, because the donkeys walked at their own pace, pondering their own mysteries as they wandered up and down their stretch of beach. She liked the movement, the feel of their manes, their placid warmth beneath her hands.

Ahead of them the unceasing blue sea rolled and undulated, and she was suddenly breathless with the beauty of the day. Filled with an intense love of life, she was about to share her enjoyment with Thea when her donkey stopped dead and let out a startling, two-toned bray.

Holidaymakers turned to look as the donkey began dumping a dry, neat mountain of manure on the sand: *thump, thump thump.*

Hedi felt the dignified thing to do was to pretend she hadn't noticed a thing. She continued to stare into the distance.

Thump, thump. What had this creature been eating? *Thump, thump, thump.*

A teenaged boy ambled over with a spade and a bag and began shovelling. Hedi pretended not to notice him, either. After a few moments, she glanced at Thea, wondering if she knew what was happening. *Ach,* she could tell by her face that she knew, all right.

Thea, too, was facing towards the sea, mouth tight shut, tears of laughter rolling down her cheeks.

'What's so funny?' Hedi asked crossly.

'You are!' Thea stuck her nose in the air and mimicked Hedi's expression, a mixture of haughtiness and disgust.

Hedi felt the imitation of her bordered on being offensive, but at the same time, the situation did have its funny side, and she started to laugh, too.

'That bray, and all those inconvenient thuds!' Thea said, wiping her eyes. 'Oh, Hedi!'

And suddenly, just like that, Hedi didn't care that she was the object of her granddaughter's amusement. She had made her happy, and that was the main thing. *That's what happiness looks like,* she thought.

24

HEDI

'Ursula? Are you awake?'

Ursula didn't reply and she didn't move. In fact, she didn't seem to have moved all night. She was shutting Hedi out, which wasn't fair, because without Hedi to dig the hole for her, she would never have got her rings back. Hedi felt that she deserved some credit for that, at least. It had obviously been a mistake, reminding Ursula of who she had been. Hedi deeply regretted it. The woman had been perfectly happy before, when she had no name. A little insane, of course, but at least she had been anonymous in her misery, which is all a person wants.

From day-to-day, very little changed in the camp. The initial burst of optimism had given way to a new sense of resignation and despondency over the conditions and the enormity of the task of dealing with them.

Now that she no longer had Magda to lie next to and look after, Hedi decided to try to regain Ursula's favour.

She spent some time helpfully picking the lice from her hair, crushing them between her nails. Ursula didn't even thank her. It was frustrating.

. . .

A few days later, there was a tap at the door. 'Attention!'

The copper-haired soldier stood there, his black outline cut out of the bright daylight.

Hedi turned away. Since she'd seen her own face in her chrome watch case, she felt resentful towards him, as if he'd misled her that she was beautiful, lied to her for his own evil reasons.

'Just to let you know,' he announced from the doorway, 'we are going to give this hut a clean.'

There was little reaction from anyone.

'Why? Who cares?' the woman in the top bunk asked.

Hedi stared across at him disinterestedly. Why would they worry about having the hut cleaned? Food, that was the thing, *sauerkraut*, something to delight the taste buds, anything less boring than stew.

As if misinterpreting their silence the soldier said, 'Don't worry, we've got some decent men for the job. And after that,' he continued, 'the hut will be deloused.'

Now that was something to celebrate! Being deloused, Hedi thought, that was an entirely different matter. Lice were a plague, a torment.

Perhaps disappointed by the lack of reaction, the soldier turned to leave.

'Hey!' Hedi called out to him.

'Yes? What is it?' he said over his shoulder.

'How is Magda, do you know?'

He turned around and came over to her, and in the light, all the detail of his features became clear again. His face was very serious. Up close, he had a shaving cut on his jaw with pinpoints of blood on it like a string of rubies.

'You don't have to keep calling me "hey", you know,' he said with a smile.

Hedi had never seen eyes like his before, eyes as deep as a trout stream, brown flecks in it like pebbles, eyes you could bathe in. She looked away quickly. It was too painful to tolerate his gaze along with her other pains. 'Sorry.'

'Don't apologise. My name's Harold Lewis. Harry.'

Hedi flashed him a look and lowered her head, cringing in shame. She didn't want him to pollute his clear green eyes with her scrawny image.

'What's your name?' he prompted.

'Hedi Fischer,' she muttered.

'Your sister is doing well, Hedi. I can pass on a message to her if you like.'

Hedi was stricken with panic. She buried her fingers in her hair and scratched vigorously. Of course she had a message for Magda, but where to start? Her mind was blank.

Harry Lewis said, 'Tell you what, I'll bring you paper and a pen, and you can write her a note. When you've done it, I'll give it to her myself.'

'Yes. Exactly that,' she said, confused for no good reason. *Please go away and leave me be.*

His expression altered a little, as if she'd said it out loud. He lowered his voice. 'Just hang on a little longer, Hedi. The war is going to be over soon. Adolf's topped himself.'

'What do you mean?'

'Hitler. He's taken his own life.'

Hedi stared at him. It took a moment to sink in. 'How do you know that?'

'It was on the news. Him and his girl, they did it together last night.'

Hedi repeated the phrase in her head. *Him and his girl.* That was all this obscene war boiled down to, in the end: a madman and his lover.

'Good riddance to him, that's what I say,' he added softly. He gave a faint smile. 'It means you'll be able to go home soon, Hedi.'

'Yes. I'll be able to go home.' The realisation burst on her like a miracle. She would return to all the evidence of her family's lives: the photographs, the books, the radio, the clothes, all their joint possessions. The house would be a shrine, a testimony to the family they once were and to the love they once shared. She was so happy that she laughed out loud. 'Thank you!'

Harry nodded briskly. He left without another word and opened the door. Light streamed in.

Hedi closed her eyes, feeling content. It seemed to her that the light continued to hover over her for a while, as if he'd left part of himself behind with her.

Harry returned with some sheets of lined notepaper and a pen for her to write her note on. 'Here you are. I'll collect it later.'

Hedi nodded. She was amazed he'd remembered.

He didn't move. He seemed to be waiting for her to reply.

She nodded again, lost for words, and finally he turned away.

What was the matter with her? She either spoke too much, or not enough. *He must think I'm a dolt.*

Well, never mind, she told herself, lying on her side to write the letter. She had plenty to say to Magda. It was to be a chatty, upbeat letter, the kind she would write to a pen pal. The important thing was to show faith that everything was all right.

She imagined Magda being surprised and overjoyed when she read it.

For a moment, Hedi's mind slipped back to the memory of the fierce heat brought on by Magda's fever. But a clean bed and warm milk would cure a person of anything. She could remember the way her mother's fresh nightdresses smelled when she was ill, nightdresses which seemed to have a healing power of their own. Her mother must have thought so too, otherwise why not just put her in one of her own clean nightgowns?

She tapped her teeth with the pen and after a moment's thought, she began to write.

Dearest Magda,

I hope you are getting fit and well now. The French women hope to go home before long, and the next nationality to go will be the Belgians. I long to see you soon, and I have managed to avoid typhus or any other disease to which some of our camp mates have succumbed. I have been very lucky to remain in good health throughout my stay.

I hope you think of me as much as I think of you. I have grown up a lot and I'm not the child I was when we said goodbye. When the war is over we will look back on this trial...

Hedi chewed the end of her pen, unsure how to end the sentence. She continued:

... knowing that we survived the worst that life could throw at us, safe in the knowledge that nothing will ever be this bad again.

Your affectionate sister,

Hedi

She read it through carefully and signed the letter, folded it up and wrote Magda's name on it in block capitals.

. . .

No matter what, Ursula remained completely unresponsive. Hedi felt the resentment building up in her. She'd had enough. It all sickened her. She tried to keep it hidden at first. She attempted to be reasonable. 'Listen! I have completely forgotten your name,' she told Ursula, 'so don't worry about that.'

The woman didn't move. She didn't reply. She had retreated from the world as surely as a dead thing.

Hedi began to get angry and she pulled Ursula's tangled hair in frustration, slyly and experimentally at first, and then she began yanking it more brutally. She banged Ursula's head against the plank. She just wanted a reaction. 'You! Woman! Talk to me!' she bellowed into Ursula's ear so that she couldn't avoid hearing.

Nothing.

Hedi desperately wanted her to die. It was almost a disappointment that she was still alive. 'If you're going to go, just get on with it,' she said.

Later, her mood changed again. Driven by the pain of loneliness, she punched the woman's inert shoulder, knuckles on bone.

'Idiot! You know you're going to die, don't you?' she asked furiously. 'You know how stupid that is? How wasteful? Do you ever think of anyone except for yourself?'

Punch.

Her voice rose to a pitiful wail. 'Don't you ever think of *me*?'

That was the question, all right. It desolated her.

She sucked her bruised knuckles. She hadn't heard back from Magda. There was no one left in the world to care about her.

Her father had been arrested for his politics and her mother for defending him, even though she herself had no interest in politics whatsoever. Her mother was content to leave politics firstly to her father, who knew everything, and secondly, to those in charge of the country, who, she reluctantly conceded, knew nearly as much as he did. If the wrong party got in, well, so what? People would get bored soon enough and vote for a change, wasn't that always the way?

Hedi could perfectly well imagine her mother offering this philosophy in all innocence to anyone who asked. She was naive, that way. Of anyone, her mother was the last person you would imagine to be a political prisoner. She was a happy *hausfrau*. Her last words to Hedi – as she quickly fastened her floral headscarf under her softly padded chin – had been: 'Put the supper on. We won't be long.'

Huh.

Hedi knew better. She had seen the expression on her father's face when he heard the knock on the door. You could tell a great deal from the way a door was knocked.

For a moment, he had looked around the room with the joyful gratitude of a man memorising a sunset. His gaze settled on his wife, and just briefly, his eyes flooded with sorrow.

When Hedi saw that look, she ran to him in a panic, and he took her face in his warm hands and pressed his nose against hers and waggled his eyebrows at her in that quirky way he had, because he possessed a good sense of humour. He was known for it *ektually*, for his wit and his quick mind. And then he kissed her forehead, let her go, and he opened the door to two men in uniform.

'And that was that,' Hedi explained to Ursula's bony spine. 'No fond hug or loving promises, just a waggle of the eyebrows for our last goodbye. As if it was a joke.' Except for the warning look she saw pass between him and her mother, she would have believed that's what he truly thought. 'My mother grabbed her coat so that she could reason with them.' *Put the supper on. We won't be long.*

'Shut up!' a tetchy voice called out from a tier above, interrupting her. 'We're trying to die in peace here.'

Hedi leaned back to see who it was.

The woman was looking down from the very top tier of the planks. Her sunken cheeks looked like holes in her skull. Her teeth were too large in her jaw, like a wolf's muzzle.

'I'm sorry I've held you up from dying,' Hedi said coldly.

The woman sneered. 'Stop going on and on about yourself. You're boring me! You think your story is any worse than anyone else's?'

'It's the only one I've got,' Hedi said with dignity.

'Your name is Hedi, isn't it?'

'So?'

'I'm Renate. Forget that crazy woman next to you. She doesn't want to live. Me, I'm still hopeful.'

'Good for you.' Hedi didn't feel like being sociable. She retreated to the bottom of her plank and lay sulking on her back with her arms folded, but it was uncomfortable to hold the pose too long, even to make a point. She wanted to sob, but her body had forgotten how to make tears, which was pitiful.

Sometime after midday, she was dozing when she heard the loudspeaker car broadcasting a message in French across the camp.

In response, there was a cheer from the back of the hut. Hedi listened in astonishment as the group of French women started singing the 'Marseillaise', their voices growing louder, reedier as they formed a feeble, tottering line through the hut, heading towards the door, arms pumping, legs kicking, wobbling into each other.

'They are preparing for evacuation and repatriation,' Renate told her.

Whatever the reason, truly, the French women were very joyful to watch, and Hedi started humming their anthem along with them and she got off the plank and began to mimic their marching dance. Some of the women who had the strength to do it began to clap the women as they left.

'*Bon chance!*' Renate called from the top bunk. 'The war is over!'

As Hedi clapped them out, she kept one eye on Ursula, fully expecting her to spring up at any moment and tag along at the end of the hobbling, dancing line, swearing she was French. It was just the kind of trick she would get up to. But Ursula didn't even raise her head.

It didn't dampen Hedi's good mood for long. She sighed with satisfaction. She was enjoying the novel feeling of progress when a British officer came in with some Hungarian soldiers.

'We are about to commence delousing operations,' he said cheerfully. 'We're going to get this place dusted. Ready with the DDT guns, George?'

'Ready, Tommy!'

All British soldiers were Tommy, and all Hungarians were George. This amused Hedi no end. *How childish!* Wouldn't it be hilarious, she thought, if a British soldier called George and a Hungarian called Tommy came across one another one day! Imagine the confusion!

The dust guns were brought in attached to cables and then the whole hut was lost in a fog. The delousing team was thorough, dusting women, beds, and every stagnant corner of the hut with great good humour before they were satisfied that it was a job well done. They rolled Ursula over to powder under her mattress, and then they rolled her back again to do her other side. Hedi approved of their thoroughness, feeling as in charge as a proud housewife, a role she intended to embrace diligently in the near future.

Next morning, Hedi lay on her plank and watched one of the medical team check whether Ursula was dead yet. She wasn't.

Who cared, anyway? Not her. She had given up on her. In

the end, they were all only responsible for themselves. That was the way it was in here.

All she wanted to do was go home, clean the house and find a job. That was her dream. It seemed within reach, at last.

They were soon to be moved to a renovated hut, awaiting repatriation. An American Quaker would then take her to her hometown of Celle. But so as not to soil their new accommodation, first the internees were going to be put through the human laundry, to be cleaned up.

Most of the people in their hut were deeply concerned about this. The human laundry was in Camp One. Rumour had it that agonising screams had been heard coming from the laundry block. It had a bad reputation because it was staffed by Wehrmacht nurses. Well, what could one expect, except for screams? Those who'd arrived at Belsen from Auschwitz knew what the screams meant; they were terrified by this fresh horror that they were being subjected to, despite the war being officially over. Showers meant gas.

Women, those who could still walk, began to leave the camp in droves.

Hedi decided to see for herself. She had been given hope for the future, and if there was no future, she might as well know now so she could stop planning for it.

She tagged along at the back of a line of feeble, infirm women. The screams coming from inside the building block were real enough, but the apathetic internees in the line didn't seemed to be worried about their fate. All that mattered was doing as they were told.

Even Hedi baulked as she saw the nurses waiting for them, their faces grim. They were strong, well fed, capable of tearing a living skeleton apart with their bare hands like a cooked chicken.

She hoped that if the worst was exactly what had been rumoured, a friendly and possibly grovelling conversation might convince them that she had only joined the line by accident; she would ask whether she could help them in any way? She didn't look so bad now, even if she was a little thin; she would tell them she was, like the late Führer, a vegetarian.

'Take your garment off and lie down on the table,' a nurse commanded her. When Hedi didn't respond, the nurse grabbed her and began to unbutton her striped shirt.

'Stop,' Hedi pleaded, holding the garment together. 'Leave me some pride! I'll do it myself.'

'Hey! You're German! Where do you come from?'

'Celle.'

'Just down the road! How did you get mixed up with these Dutch women?'

'They're Dutch? I didn't know. I just do what I'm told,' Hedi said.

'Ha! Good girl. I have to warn you,' the nurse confided, 'what we are about to do is not pleasant, but these sores you have, it's important, you see, to clean them so you can heal.'

A nurse at the adjacent table was vigorously scrubbing a whimpering, inert woman as if she was a filthy floor.

'That's fine, I don't care about pain. I'm looking forward to being clean. Will you hold my watches for me?' she asked, sliding them off her arm.

The water was steaming hot and the scrubbing brush was brutal, like being scraped by pins. It was agony. Hedi kept her eyes shut and removed her mind from the pain as best she could. It wouldn't go on forever and being scrubbed, she told herself, wasn't going to kill her.

The nicest bit came afterwards, when she was being soaped gently like a baby from head to foot. She was tearful with gratitude at being touched in such a kind way. The nurse washed her hair until it foamed with suds, and then she rinsed her thoroughly, patted her dry and combed her hair with the efficient tenderness of a mother.

The pleasure of being clean, a pleasure that she only appreciated once it was over, was a surprise and a revelation. It was as if with the filth she had also shed a layer of ugliness. It was an astonishing luxury.

'All done! It's over,' the nurse said, wrapping her up in a blanket.

'Can I have my shirt back, please?' Hedi didn't ask about the watches. If the nurse had taken them as payment for her thorough job, so be it.

'Oh, we can do better than that,' the nurse said. 'You're going to have a new set of clothes. We have a whole department store for you to choose from! You want to look nice for when you return to Celle, don't you? There is transport waiting for you outside. Here, don't forget your watches.'

It was like a dream, Hedi thought, quickly checking her reflection in the back of the watch. Hello, skin! Already her combed hair was drying into curls. 'This department store,' she began. 'What exactly—'

'Go! You'll soon find out,' the nurse said with a smile, turning her attention to the next internee.

She was dusted with DDT before she left and a Red Cross nurse, a delicate British woman with mousey hair and light grey eyes, took over. 'We are now off to our very own Harrods to get you some fresh clothes,' she said cheerfully. 'Do you know Harrods?'

'I'm sorry, no.'

'It's a wonderful store in London. It has a motto: *Omnia Omnibus Ubique*. All things for all people, everywhere.'

Hedi was confused. 'I don't understand.'

'Don't worry about it. It's just a joke. I haven't been here long.' The woman's eyes reddened and she pressed her lips together.

At a guess, she was only a couple of years older than Hedi, and Hedi nodded, puzzling about this joke that she didn't understand. But she understood the woman's reason for telling it. It was so that she could pretend this was all perfectly normal.

Hedi felt the burden of shame come over her again. She wanted to apologise for the way things were here, for the vile smell, for the evil that had been forced on this woman as part of her job. The woman was obviously tender-hearted, with a delicate, freckled face, and Hedi had no doubt that this experience would imprint itself through her life like a watermark.

'I like the joke,' she said kindly, to reassure her. 'Harrods, in London...' She couldn't remember the motto.

The nurse nodded gratefully. 'It's just a silly joke of ours,' she said.

The clothing store was up some steps at the top of the building. As they went through the door it was like entering a large warehouse full of treasure. It was packed with women internees rummaging through the piles enthusiastically, like shopping on market day. They were throwing garments to the side and snatching up others, and there were clothes everywhere, on rails, on tables and hanging over chairs. Chaos! There were boxes and boxes full of shoes. A mirror was propped up against the wall reflecting all this magnificence. Hedi held her blanket tight around her throat in astonishment.

She was rooted to the spot, overcome. It was too much. Suddenly she just wanted to go back to the dark familiarity of the hut, and she turned towards the door.

The Red Cross woman touched her hand with her cool fingers, understanding immediately. 'You might want to start with underwear,' she prompted shyly. 'You can choose two sets.'

'You're right,' Hedi whispered. Underwear, that was the place to start. More than anything, she longed to wear something colourful. Her life had been grey for a long time now and the clothes around her dazzled in their abundance and beauty.

She joined in the search for something suitable; it was a big task as there were whole mounds of items to sort through. She started giggling as she held a very strange, huge garment up in a salmon-pink colour, marvelling at the bloomers, with their gathered legs and a little frill of lace.

The Red Cross woman smiled back. But Hedi immediately grew serious again because shopping was a serious business when you hadn't done it for a long time. Everything she picked up that looked the right size was too big when she held it against her body. Okay then, something smaller, and although the smaller sizes of underwear looked impossibly small, they fitted her perfectly. The bra, in particular, suggested the hope of Hedi one day having a figure again, and she smiled shyly at herself in the mirror. *Hello! Where have you been hiding all this time?*

Now for a dress: more than anything she had a raging hunger for a red dress. Nothing else would do right at this moment. Of the few red dresses that she untangled from the jumble, she found one with pockets and a tie belt, and sleeves that finished just above the elbow. The dress was so bright that the colour gave her a ready-made blush.

'Oh, I say,' the British woman said, clapping her hands together in approval.

'This is me, don't you think?' Hedi appealed, although she had never worn red before.

'I should say so! And a coat, you'll be wanting a coat.'

'Yes, a coat, of course, something practical.' Hedi was light-headed with pride and a wary, untrustable happiness, as if she'd fallen in love. It was like being born again. She couldn't stop looking to check how she looked. She'd become an entirely different person altogether. It was a very strange feeling, like the excitement of meeting someone from the distant past who she was extremely fond of and hadn't ever expected to see again.

She picked out a couple of coats, but the ones she imagined would fit her were too big. The sleeves hung down and completely covered her hands. Now suddenly even her arms had shrunk! She waggled the empty sleeves at the British woman like elephants' trunks, and they laughed together because really, it was very comical to see.

'It absolutely swamps you,' the British woman said. 'Wait a minute.' She collected a fresh selection of overcoats and Hedi tried each one on very seriously, turning critically to check how they looked from the back and the side. Who would have thought she would be so fussy all of a sudden? Only a month ago, she had fought for a dead woman's lice-riddled shirt newer than her own. And now look at her! Wearing the perfectly respectable type of coat her mother would have approved of.

Fastened over the frivolous red dress, the coat looked very smart, just the thing now that she was older and wiser. She thought about her broad-minded intellectual father who would have died older and wiser, having learnt before his death that there was a heavy price to be paid for freedom of expression. Live and learn, she thought, her heart sinking with sorrow for him and his lost beliefs.

Next, with her coat over her shoulders, she looked at shoes.

Strangely, they were all mixed up in boxes, all different sizes and styles. 'Why are these not tied together?' she asked.

'I *know*,' the woman said sympathetically. 'Don't ask me! But if you find one you like, I'll help you find its partner,' she offered.

Hedi considered her ideal shoe, taking the luxury of choice seriously. 'I would like a small heel, but nothing too high, of course. Black I think, rather than brown, and a strap, not a lace-up,' she said, looking through the box for something sensible – but not too sensible.

It was easier to judge whether the shoes would fit her; she was looking for a small size. She suddenly unearthed a sparkly gold shoe with 'Starlight Ballroom' written in gold along the instep and she laughed with delight as she balanced it on her palm. 'What on earth is this jewel doing amongst all these dull ones?'

'Sweet, isn't it?'

Of course, it was entirely unsuitable, and not sensible at all, but she tucked it under her arm, unwilling to let it go without at least finding its partner and trying the pair on together, just for the fun of it. It only took a few minutes of searching; she sat down to tighten the ankle straps and crossed one leg casually over the other to admire the effect.

Hedi looked up and saw that the British woman was watching her with a strange half-smile, her chin trembling.

'You should have them,' the British woman said, as if it was that simple.

'Yes, I should have them,' Hedi repeated, testing the idea.

'Go and look at yourself in the mirror.'

Walking towards the mirror, Hedi felt tall and elegant, and her reflection showed she *was* tall and elegant in the gold shoes and the red dress, with the formal dark coat slung nonchalantly over her shoulders and her dark hair curling around her thin face. She suddenly imagined the terrible things that might happen to them if the shoes were hers. 'What if they get stolen and...?' she began,

'You'll be on your way home, soon, won't you?'

'Yes.'

'You're German, aren't you?'

The enemy. Hedi dared herself to meet the British woman's washed-out eyes. 'That's right.'

'This war hasn't been kind to any of us, has it?' the woman said softly. She rubbed her temples with her fingertips, twisting her tired eyes momentarily out of shape. 'This is going to sound trivial, but er... we had a consignment today and the medics are going absolutely spare about it. They're still trying to get antibiotics and anything that will make a difference, really. Instead, boxes and boxes of lipsticks turned up.' She gave a little awkward laugh. 'I don't suppose you'd like one to match your dress?'

Hedi was puzzled. She wasn't sure that she'd understood the woman properly. 'You don't suppose I'd like a lipstick?'

'It's trivial, I know, but we've got a quantity of them.'

'A lipstick.' The unexpected word seemed like a miracle. 'Actually, I would like a lipstick very much.'

'Oh! In that case, I'll fetch one for you. I'm so pleased,' the Red Cross woman said, her eyes bright with pleasure. 'I wasn't sure if you'd think it was frivolous of me to mention it. Don't move. You can stay and admire yourself a little longer.'

Moments later she was back, as promised, with several lipsticks.

'I've never worn lipstick before,' Hedi confessed, sliding one up to its full extent and inhaling its delicate fragrance. Applying it carefully in the mirror, she pressed her lips together the way her mother used to do. It scented her breath. 'What do you think?' She turned to the Red Cross woman for approval.

Again, the woman's pale eyes were pink with tears. 'What a transformation,' she said.

And it was. 'Thank you so much,' Hedi whispered with gratitude.

'How many would you like?'

This sounded like a trick question because Hedi had, stupidly, only asked for one. But she and the woman seemed to be on a good footing with their bursts of laughter, the second lot of laughter they'd shared that day because she had also made the nurse laugh by trying on the huge coats and flapping around the sleeves like elephants' trunks. 'If possible, two or three. Not all for me, of course,' she added quickly, 'but for my sister, and also for a woman who I upset by reminding her about who she used to be.' She was fully prepared to claim this as a comical comment if the nurse was offended.

'Righty-ho,' the woman said obligingly. She opened a large box and gave her four. 'Have fun with them,' she said.

When she smiled, she didn't look nearly so plain as Hedi

had first thought. 'Here,' Hedi said, handing her one of the lipsticks back. 'This is for you.' The woman had a boxful right next to her, but she could hardly take one for herself – this however was a gift.

The nurse hesitated. 'I'm afraid it's against regulations to wear...' she began, but then she looked across the busy warehouse and changed her mind. 'Thanks.' She took the lipstick and held it up between her thumb and forefinger. 'I'll be needing this soon.' She gave a shy smile. 'I'm going home.'

'You're going home,' Hedi repeated those beautiful words. 'You're leaving this department store.'

'Harrods.'

'That's it, Harrods. I was trying to remember. Thank you, from my heart.' Hedi felt suddenly tearful.

'Oh, I can't take any credit,' the woman said. 'It's the first time since I've been here that I've felt of any use.'

'What's your name?' Hedi asked.

'Hilary.'

'Hilary. Hilary, I'll never forget you,' she said fervently.

Just then, somebody called Hilary's name sharply, and she shook Hedi's hand in a brief goodbye and hurried away.

Hedi lost sight of her in the bustling crowd of internees sorting through the clothing. *Hilary*, she repeated to herself. She felt that something momentously big had happened.

Part of the clean, new-look Hedi was utterly revolted at the idea of returning to the hut in her lovely clothes, but her desire to be admired triumphed over it. It wasn't for completely selfish motives, either. She had the lipsticks, and one of them was for Ursula.

Ursula hadn't moved. She was lying on the plank, curled up with her face hidden under a blanket.

Hedi approached her. She could taste the DDT powder in

her throat. 'Listen, you,' she said to the woman. If there was one thing she had learned from all this it was not to dare use the woman's name. 'The human laundry is just a bathhouse, nothing sinister, just a place where they give you a good scrub with soap and hot water. I've just had one myself. Turn over and look at me! I promise you, you won't recognise me.'

It was no use. Ursula had sunk so deep into herself that she was beyond reach.

Hedi raised her voice in the hope that she could hear her in the depths of her unconscious. 'When you are clean, they take you to a British department store. I can't remember the name, but it has a Latin motto anyhow, and you choose your own underwear and coats and dresses and shoes, and you can try them on and find out if they fit. I've got gold shoes.'

Poking her head over the top bunk, Renate, the woman with teeth like a wolf, said, 'Hey! Girl! What's that you say?'

Hedi looked up warily. 'I was telling her I've got gold shoes,' she repeated. She held out one foot. 'See?'

'Gold shoes! Where did you get those?'

'From the Red Cross.'

The woman wriggled a little further over the plank, resting her weight on her elbows, her wild hair softening her fierce features with shadow. 'What's that on your face?' she asked suspiciously.

Hedi had been clicking together the three lipsticks in her new coat pocket, and now she removed her hand quickly. 'Where on my face? Oh! You mean the lipstick?'

'What do you think I mean? Your nose? How many have you got?'

'Just the one nose,' Hedi replied innocently, turning up the collar of her coat and feeling the wool caress her cheek. Despite her jauntiness, she was wondering if this was going to end badly, when suddenly with a guttural cry the woman toppled head first off the bunk.

Instinctively, Hedi jumped out of the way but at the last moment she caught hold of the woman's flailing arm.

'Idiot!' Renate screamed. 'Let my hand go! You want to marry me now?'

Hedi instantly released her hand and it flopped onto the woman's own face like a dead starfish.

'Imbecile!' she raged. 'Dropping my own hand on me!'

'Don't blame me,' Hedi said indignantly, 'I'm not in charge of your hand, am I?'

'You've killed me,' the woman accused her. 'Ow! Help me up, will you?'

Hedi helped her up. It was like lifting a bundle of sticks, if sticks could tremble.

The woman grabbed hold of Ursula's plank to steady herself and returned her fascinated attention to Hedi's feet. 'Gold shoes,' she marvelled. 'Are the British giving them out to everyone?' she asked hopefully.

'You can choose anything you like once you've had the beauty treatment,' Hedi said confidently. 'Absolutely anything!'

The woman scratched her cheek absently, picking off a scab, but the same hunger that Hedi felt for the red dress burned in the woman's eyes.

Suddenly, gratified by her reaction, it wasn't enough for Hedi to show off what she'd acquired; she was eager to share out her happiness. 'Listen,' she said to Renate, 'I have a gift for you. Hold out your hand and close your eyes.'

'A gift?'

The woman screwed her eyes up tight. She was trembling so hard that the lipstick jittered around on her palm.

'Hold it tight, now,' Hedi warned, and she curled the woman's fingers around it to keep it safe. 'Now you can look.'

'What is it?' Renate asked tremulously, peeping into her fist. She opened her fingers very cautiously, as if afraid that what she was holding might suddenly escape and fly away. Seeing what was cupped in her hand, she dotted the lipstick case with butterfly kisses, her eyes dancing with pleasure. 'A gift,' she said breathlessly, uncapping it. She closed her eyes and pouted like a film star as she applied it. 'Tell me! How do I look?'

It was surprising what a difference red lips made to her. 'Like a woman,' Hedi said.

Renate nodded her approval. 'And you, too. I can see you're not a kid any more. You are kind, to give me a lipstick.'

'I was going to give it to Ursula,' Hedi said truthfully, 'but you know... well, obviously... you can see how it is with her. She's gone.' She shrugged and glanced at the comatose woman.

Hedi's words had an unforeseen effect – for the first time in days, Ursula made a noise. It startled them both.

It was faint and discordant, like the distant creak of a long-unused gate, a rusty protest of indignation. Fearing that Ursula was going to demand the lipstick back, Renate clambered back up to her bunk out of reach.

'My lipstick,' Ursula croaked hoarsely through cracked lips. It sounded like a long-dead voice from the grave. She turned onto her stomach and looked at Hedi, bleary-eyed and accusing.

Hedi stared at her in astonishment. 'I thought you were dead!'

Ursula snorted.

It was a bad idea in her condition because the effort of being sarcastic combined with a bone-dry mouth made her choke.

Hedi fetched her some water from the bucket, and Ursula recovered enough to hold her hand out for the lipstick.

Once she had it in her hand, she took the cap off so that she could admire the pure red brightness of it. In the shadow of the bunks, it glowed like a flame. She sniffed it and said hoarsely. 'The scent of glamour.'

Hedi smiled happily.

That lipstick, it smelled of romance.

25

THEA
PRESENT DAY

Thea was scooped up comfortably in the striped deckchair, staring at the stars, listening to the ebb and flow of the black water against the jetty, and the ebb and flow of Hedi's voice. Her words merged with the lapping water and the hollow of the night. Thea's hands had been cupped around her glass for so long that her wine was beginning to warm.

Next to her, Hedi began to chuckle deep in her throat. 'Soon, every woman in the camp had red lips! And it didn't matter that they were still wearing their striped shirts, and their hair hadn't grown back, they were walking tall again with a flirty swing of the hips and a different air about them. The mood in the camp changed after that, and as we got our femininity back and our figures returned, the next thing we all wanted was a man.'

'That's progress.' Thea laughed.

'It was a turning point,' Hedi said. 'To this day, when I need to get through a bad time, I wait for Hilary in some shape or form.' She reached for her glass. As she bent forward, the moonlight gleamed through her white hair, giving her a ghostly appearance. 'You understand what I'm saying, don't you?'

I'm tipsy, Thea thought cheerfully, feeling confident about the fact. *Didn't expect audience participation.* 'Kind of,' she conceded. 'You're saying Hilary was sort of an angel.' She stretched out her bare legs which gleamed pale in the moonlight. She was barefoot. She wiggled her toes, wondering what she'd done with her trainers. A memory came back to her, of her and Hedi launching them on the water, watching them race away like little boats.

'Exactly!' *Eksectly.* Hedi sat back again, raising her glass up high. She was silent for a moment. Then she said, 'You are my Hilary, now.'

Thea watched a car's headlights cut through the darkness on a distant road in the hills. It looked as if it was flying.

Hedi put her glass down again and reached out to her.

Thea felt her hand lying soft and safe in Hedi's warm grasp. It was a good feeling: not just loving, but comforting, somehow.

Hedi continued happily, 'The important thing about angels is to recognise them when you see them.'

The following morning, Thea woke up with a thumping headache, hung-over and out of sorts. She went into the kitchen and had a look round for her trainers. She swallowed a couple of painkillers and put the kettle on, trying to be quiet so as not to disturb Hedi.

That's it. I'm not having wine tonight.

She looked at herself closely in the mirror. She looked as shabby as she felt. Hair wild, eyes bleary, lips pale. Her breath clouded her image to a welcome soft-focus blur. She wondered how Hedi was feeling. Everything was quiet inside her room. They'd been up late. If it weren't for her hangover, she wouldn't have got out of bed herself yet.

Thea made a coffee and went to sit outside on the step to

drink it, half hoping to find her shoes on it. She thought about the previous night. Hedi and Maggie were so alike, it was amazing they didn't get on. They both had huge energy for enjoyment; they literally enjoyed themselves – it wasn't a phrase that Thea had thought about much before, but she understood it now. This thirty-year rift between them was part of the same dynamic. If you're going to be estranged from someone, you can't be half-hearted about it, you've got to go all out and put your heart and soul into it and hate them passionately for the rest of your life.

She wondered if she was the same. A watered-down version, maybe, but the genetic link was still strong enough to have an effect.

So what? It was all very well to be insightful about other people – they were so simple to read while she herself was so complicated.

The idea made her smile.

The wind was a cool breath on her face. It stroked the vast pelt of grass, silvering the blades, shimmying the trees.

She imagined the young Hedi wearing her gold shoes and her lipstick and her red dress: born again. Unsurprisingly, young Hedi was quite similar to elderly Hedi.

Her headache was fading, and she wondered whether she should make Hedi a coffee. It was ten o'clock. Hedi seemed unaffected by wine, but Thea had always been bad at detecting drunkenness in others when she was drunk herself. Friends had to actually fall over in front of her, and even then she was inclined to give them the benefit of the doubt.

She went back inside, boiled the kettle, and made two more cups, stirring the coffee in vigorously so that the spoon chimed against the china.

She popped two more painkillers out of the pack, just in case, and went to Hedi's bedroom door and listened intently for signs of life. The low-level anxiety brought on by the hangover suddenly intensified. Then she tapped on the door. 'Morning, Hedi!' Thea said, more cheerfully than she felt, 'I've made you a coffee.' Silence. Her own tone sounded fake and too loud as the words echoed in her head.

Thea went inside. The bedroom was empty, the bed was made and the curtains were open. The dark woods behind the cottage leaked a core of sunlight, like a lantern.

She went back into the kitchen, put the mug down and tried to get her head straight. She remembered locking the door and saying good night and then – nothing.

She went back outside, squinting against the daylight. At the bottom of the meadow she saw a long stick come into view. Something was dangling on it like a speared fish, and Hedi materialised gradually up the slope from the river.

She seemed unbelievably cheerful as she got nearer, brandishing her find. 'Look what I have rescued for you!' she called out.

Thea watched her trainer fly through the air towards her. It squelched as it landed in the grass a few feet away, and she grinned. 'Good shot!'

'It was caught in some debris by the bank. The other one is floating under the jetty,' Hedi said breathlessly, patting her chest. 'As you see, this is for the left foot, and therefore, I declare myself the winner.' Hedi retrieved the shoe, propped it up against the wall and left it to dry in the sun. She was in high spirits. 'You can get the other one while I make breakfast. Bacon sandwiches? My turn to cook – you're looking a little feeble this morning. After that, I think we should go for a walk along Bear Cave Falls,' she said. 'I want to show you the lakes. Harry used to fish there.'

26

HEDI

BELSEN, MAY 1944

'Of course, unlike with me and Karl, nothing is ever going to come of your fascination with Harry,' Ursula said to Hedi, looking up from her letter from her husband. She and the women had already exchanged addresses and there seemed little more to say now, which was Ursula's reason for reading them her mail. 'Harry's a Tommy, and as soon as the camp is cleared he'll be going home.'

'I know that.' Hedi was lying on her plank with her navy coat in her arms. One of the American Quakers was giving her a lift back home to Celle that afternoon, and she was saying her goodbyes. She had been debating whether to say goodbye to Harry before leaving the camp. It was only good manners, after all, but Ursula said it was a bad idea. 'I'd forgotten how bossy you are, Ursula,' Hedi grumbled. 'You were better company when you were dying. At least you were quiet.'

'In my opinion, Hedi, you should say goodbye to him,' Renate said. She was sitting on the top bunk, swinging her legs so she could admire her new shoes. They were silver dancing shoes, a size too big for her, and they had fallen off her feet a couple of times, but she was certain that when she went home and ate proper food they would fit her perfectly.

They had all been through the human laundry now, but they had come back to the hut because in Camp Two they had been split up. They didn't want to be apart, even though, at best, they only tolerated each other.

The camp's Postal Service was working efficiently and as a result, Ursula had found out that Karl had been captured as a prisoner of war. He had thought always and only of her, he wrote. Sensing the other women losing interest, Ursula quickly finished reading the letter to them: '...*I have spent the last couple of months making you a gift out of a spent shell case. Your ever-loving Karl.* There we are. Nice, isn't it?'

Hedi and Renate exchanged doubtful glances. What kind of gift was a spent shell case? But as they were both meant to be impressed, they made no comment.

Renate had received a note from her married daughter, so she too was content, but Hedi had received no reply from Magda, who was still in the hospital block.

She climbed down from the bunk and checked the time on both her watches. She didn't have long. 'Renate is right,' she decided. 'I should say goodbye to Harry.'

She picked up her bag containing her possessions, her lipstick, her tin bowl and spoon, the spare clothes that Hilary has given her. As she reached the door, Ursula called out, 'Good luck!'

'Yes! Good luck, Hedi!' Renate said.

It was good, Hedi thought, to be back outside in the early summer warmth, once more going to the Panzer Training school with a mission, her coat flying out behind her. Before she walked past the burial pits, she buttoned it up out of respect, at the same time fervently hoping that there might be another film crew waiting for someone glamorous to show up, in which case, she was perfectly ready to unbutton it again.

But for now, the place was deserted, and the lone birch sapling was her only witness. Hedi bowed her head and said a prayer for her mother, buried there.

She headed towards the hospital thinking about Ursula. Her recovery was a weight off her mind. After accidentally sending the woman into despair she had now made her happy again with nothing but a lipstick, and that was good. They were in a state of neutrality once more.

Hedi was approaching the hospital block when she saw a familiar figure in khaki leaning against a tree, his hair as bright as sunset. She could always pick Harry out immediately from any group of soldiers, as if there was a force that pulled her to him. A wisp of smoke curled from his cigarette and blurred the leafy branches above his head. He looked deep in thought.

She tossed her dark hair away from her face, feeling confident. She smiled in anticipation. *Won't he be surprised to see me like this!*

A string of unlit coloured lights dangled from a branch, tap-tap-tapping against the white tree trunk.

She was planning to creep up on him playfully: *guess who?* But there was something so self-contained in the way he was standing that she hesitated, watching him cautiously from a little way off.

He turned towards her eagerly, as if he'd been expecting her. He grinned and she waited for him to express his astonishment at her transformation.

'Hello, Harry,' she said, tossing her hair back.

'Hullo, Hedi,' he said cheerfully, stubbing out his cigarette on the sole of his boot. 'I was just thinking about you.'

'You were?'

'Yes.' He set the string of lights swinging from the birch branch like a pendulum. 'We're organising a dance for the weekend.'

Hedi was standing close to him under the shade of the

tree. She looked at his lovely face. The afternoon sunlight paddled on his shoulders like blossom. His face glowed with good health, and freckles dotted the bridge of his nose. She glanced briefly into his green eyes and quickly looked away again.

'A dance? That's nice,' she said vaguely. She wondered who it was for. There were plenty of women around the camp apart from the internees. There were Queen Alexandra nurses, the Red Cross, Quakers, journalists...

'Do you like dancing?' Harry asked her.

She laughed. 'Of course I do!'

'Good! Will you come with me?'

Now she stared at him in surprise, hesitating just long enough for his expression to change. 'Harry, I can't, I—'

'I know. No fraternising,' he said, giving her a wry smile. Awkwardly, he scratched the back of his neck under his collar. 'But I've been thinking about it and the thing is, Hedi...' He stopped suddenly and frowned, looking her up and down in a puzzled way. 'You know,' he said, 'there's something different about you today, somehow.'

Finally, he'd noticed! She felt the excitement building up in her. His uncertainty was bringing her confidence back. *You look different somehow?* What a thing to say! And how like a man!

Snippets of the amused conversations her mother and her friends had had about their husbands came back to her, dealt out between them in the afternoons like playing cards. Now she understood.

'I'm wearing new clothes and lipstick,' she explained.

'Yes! That's it. I knew it was something. You look nice.'

'Thank you.' They were standing very close now under the shade of the tree. She could feel the warm smoky breath of his words as he spoke. She looked from his mouth, which was saying one thing, into his eyes, which were saying something deeper.

In her gold shoes, she was almost as tall as he was. Impulsively she kissed him, her lips tight and hard on his.

His mouth was soft and warm in response, and his eyes widened, a flash of green as they stared into hers. Then he closed them with a hum of pleasure, his eyelashes resting on his cheeks, and she closed her eyes too, and let her mouth relax and become sensitive on his. His saliva tasted cool and smoky with cigarettes.

In the darkness of her eyelids she became pure sensation. A pulse pounded in her temples, she felt the ground softening under her feet, her body melting as she pressed herself against him, tasting his flickering tongue. She thought wildly: *Yes! This is what life is all about!*

Harry broke off the kiss and buried his face in her hair, his breath roaring in her ear.

She stood back from him a little to catch her breath, her hand on his chest. They looked at each other in surprise.

She saw him sharply for the first time, the pores on his face, the glint of stubble, the smell of soap on his throat, the sweat from his exertions.

She thought anxiously: *I hope I don't have a nosebleed.* His beautiful mouth was reddened with her lipstick. She wiped it with the pad of her thumb, which he kissed. His green eyes regained their focus, and he said hoarsely, 'Hedi?'

'Harry, I'm leaving the camp. I've come to say goodbye,' she said. 'I'm going home.'

Harry was still holding her lipstick-smeared thumb against his reddened mouth. He was very still. He looked puzzled. Then he frowned. 'When?'

'This afternoon.'

He let her go and forced a rueful grin. 'So that's a goodbye kiss.'

Hedi had hurt him, she realised that. It had been an awful mistake to kiss him.

She ran her tongue along her lower lip where she could still taste him. The kiss had been truly astonishing. She had felt suddenly the revelation of what love was. It made sense to her for the first time. The great mystery, she thought now, was how much of a secret people managed to keep it: how well adults hid it from the world and went about their normal business as if nothing had changed. But it was like the difference between an approaching shadow and the person who casts the shadow. 'I'm sorry,' she said.

'How are you getting there?'

'One of the Quakers is driving me. Bernard.'

'Ah. You've got it sorted. Best of luck, Hedi.'

'Thank you for everything,' she said formally as they shook hands.

A couple of soldiers, Bill and Shaw, were coming over to the tree carrying paper lanterns. Harry's gaze slid to them and back to Hedi. He raised his eyebrows at her.

The gesture, the way he did it, reminded her of her father and she felt her heart break.

Bernard, the American Quaker, was waiting for her in the yard in a Red Cross vehicle. He gave her a big smile and invited her to sit in the front passenger seat. He had volunteered to take her and another internee home to Celle, and Hedi was the first to be dropped off.

He drove in silence as she directed him, looking at her familiar surroundings as they skirted Lüneburg Heath. Acres of skeletal, burnt trees striped the road in sunlight. Hedi felt nervous. She was reassured when she saw the castle still standing in her bomb-damaged town, dazzling white against the red rooftops of the houses.

She guided the driver through the familiar streets with a

growing sense of alarm until suddenly she was unaccountably lost. They had reached an enormous building site.

'Forgive me,' she said, confused. 'We've taken a wrong turn somehow.'

He pulled into the kerb and let the vehicle idle. 'That's okay,' he said amiably. 'Take your time to get your bearings. I guess it's been a while.'

'Yes,' she said in dismay. 'I was mistaken. This is it.' Where her house had been there was now rubble. The whole row of houses had been bombed, demolished, reduced to dust and debris. She felt herself fragment, disintegrate. 'This is where I lived. How can this be?'

An old man was trudging towards them. Suddenly she recognised him. It was their neighbour, Dr Schmidt, a well-to-do man who was only around her father's age. His clothes were hanging off him, and his greying beard hid his collar, but his presence gave her hope. He was the kind of man who always knew what to do.

'I know that man, he's a neighbour of ours. Thanks for the lift,' she said, 'I'm getting out.'

Bernard put the vehicle into gear. 'I'll come by in thirty minutes to see you're okay. If you're not here, I'll assume it's all good.'

Hedi nodded, holding back tears.

She opened the door and as she got out, her morose companion in the back climbed over into the front seat without a word.

They drove away and she walked towards the old man who was now kicking furiously at a length of wood blocking his path.

'Dr Schmidt!'

He cried out in confusion at seeing her, as if he'd been lost in a world of his own thoughts. 'Hedi Fischer? Is that you? What are you doing here?'

She was holding back her distress with great effort. 'I didn't realise...' she waved her hands at the ruins of the houses, reduced to planks, bricks and plaster, the red roof tiles half-buried like relics in the dust. 'I wanted to come home.'

'Home?' Frank Schmidt turned the corners of his mouth down in mockery and contempt and the grey hairs on his chin spiked like a hedgehog. 'What's wrong with you? You think your folks are on holiday somewhere? Trust me, your father was beaten to death and your mother went up the chimney.' He turned to look at the remnants of his house. 'Look at it!' He snorted fiercely into the back of his throat and spat the phlegm into the ruins. 'They're dead – my family, your family, the lot of them.' He turned his watery brown eyes to Hedi. 'All dead and finished with.' His eyes gleamed with malice. 'Better for you if you were dead, too.'

His harsh words stung with cruelty. 'Too bad for me I'm not, then,' she said, tossing her hair away from her face.

'Me,' Frank Schmidt confided, 'I tried to drown myself in the pond. In my textbooks it's described as a pleasant way to go, but do you know how hard it is to drown yourself?' In the face of Hedi's shocked silence, his voice roared in the emptiness. 'Come! Answer me!'

Hedi was very afraid. She shook her head.

'No, you don't,' he said resentfully. 'Take it from me, it's not an ending that the body gives in to easily. I assisted my wife and my girls by holding them under. That's the last thing I did for them. But who was left to help me?' he asked piteously. He kicked a lump of plaster and it shattered under his boot.

Hedi's heart was thudding in her chest. With every thud, the blood pulsed behind her eyes. Her vision blurred. She wanted to run, but she couldn't move. Something very bad was happening, she could feel it like a poison gas, and she was letting it happen without a fight.

Her neighbour's expression was dark and knowing as he watched her.

She was frightened of him.

She wondered suddenly, was it Dr Schmidt who'd had her father arrested? Whoever had reported him as a *politikal*, Hedi knew it had been someone who knew them. Someone respectable and self-important, the class of person her father described as the 'dangerous self-righteous', someone who despised him because he thought differently.

Dr Schmidt gestured towards the ruins of his house. 'Anyhow. I've come to find my pistol. It's buried in there. You can use it once I'm finished with it,' he added graciously, 'as a favour.' He turned and gazed at the rubble. When he turned back to Hedi, his watery brown eyes glinted with cunning. 'But first, you have to help me find it.'

A gust of wind stirred the dust into life around them.

It's over. She accepted that now. The desperate futility of living weighed her down. She nodded and covered her face with her hands. But she didn't cry. She was relieved. It was like sinking into a soft bed after a long day's exertions. All that she had been through... it had all been hard, too hard, and for what? She'd survived arrest, incarceration, starvation, typhus, typhoid, but it turned out to be one long joke that had led nowhere.

That was her home. Nowhere. How large was the hole on which their solid house had stood! How solid and safe it had seemed when they'd lived there! But they had been fooled. It had offered them no protection. It was crushed like an eggshell.

Frank Schmidt was clambering precariously up the rubble of his own property, shifting wood, plaster, and bricks with his bare hands. He was strong. His mission energised him.

Hedi took her coat off and hung it on an apple tree branch. She rolled up the sleeves of her red dress carefully.

'Good girl,' Frank said approvingly, looking back at her. 'See this patch of green wallpaper with the bird and the trellis? This is my study. Around this area is where my pistol is.'

'I understand,' she said, scrambling up to join him. Her foot slipped into a hole and she fell onto her knees in a puff of dust that made her eyes gritty. She coughed it out of her lungs and reached out for him. 'Give me a hand, will you?'

'Up you come,' he said, pulling her to her feet. His palms were rough and scraped. His mood had changed and she was reassured. He was once more the smiling, good-humoured neighbour she recognised. She was grateful, but she knew he was very soon going to be dead and her eyes widened with horror.

'What is it?' he asked. 'Tell me!'

'When we find the pistol, let me use it first,' she pleaded, grabbing his arm. 'I can't bear to see you...' She couldn't bring herself to finish the sentence. Over these past months the land-scape had been the pale hills of the dead.

'Bah, don't worry about that now, we've got to find it yet,' he said logically, unfastening her fingers from his coat sleeve one by one. 'Concentrate! It's in a mahogany box inlaid with mother-of-pearl. It belonged to my mother and I liked to have it on my desk hereabouts. The pistol is loaded. I had it ready for when the Russians came.' Galvanised, he began digging like a terrier, throwing planks and bricks to one side in a frenzy. He unearthed an intact wooden drawer. He stopped what he was doing and flicked through the papers. 'Bills,' he said ruefully. 'Wouldn't you know they'd survive,' he added, flinging the whole lot away from him. They scattered in the breeze like a flock of white doves.

Hedi could see the corner of the mahogany box with its mother-of-pearl inlay right there, excavated from the rubble between his feet. Its sudden appearance had an inevitability about it. It was unmissable. She had seen it, and now he would see it. The way the box was angled, it seemed to have taken on a teasing quality. *Peekaboo!*

'Ah!' Frank said happily. 'Look! Here it is! No wonder I

couldn't find it, I'm standing on it. Didn't I tell you this is where it was?'

He rocked the box until it came loose from the debris and then he pulled it free and wiped the lid clean with his sleeve. 'Here, hold it for me,' he said. 'It's locked, but I've got the key in my wallet.'

Hedi held the box while he looked for his key. She hoped he wouldn't find it, but at the same time, irrationally, she didn't want him to be disappointed.

'Stop shaking, girl! Hold it still while I open it.' He inserted the little key, and there was a click of the latch. He slipped the key carefully back into his wallet. 'Give it to me,' he ordered.

'Dr Schmidt,' she hugged the box to her chest, 'I can be your family if you want,' she offered desperately.

He stared at her for a moment, and then he chuckled as if she'd said something amusing. He wrenched the box out of her hands, balanced it on one knee and opened it. It had a blue velvet lining. 'Hello, my old friend,' he said warmly to the pistol. He took it out and put the box down. It slid down the white dust like a sleigh in the snow. Frank checked the pistol, shut it again and looked at Hedi calmly, holding it out to her. 'You first,' he said politely.

'I can't!' Hedi trembled on the brink of panic. 'I'm not ready!'

He relaxed his arm. He looked surprised and annoyed. 'Why not? What are you waiting for?'

Hedi had always been nervous of Dr Schmidt, although her father had respected his views. If only he could hear him now, she thought, he would think differently.

'Answer me, girl!'

'To be rescued,' she said truthfully.

'But isn't that exactly what I'm doing?' He sounded like an impatient schoolteacher talking to a bad student. 'Rescuing you?'

'I suppose so,' she conceded, and shut her eyes. It was difficult to get her thoughts straight. This was too abrupt an ending. She had been taught that it was important to be obedient, to do what she was told, but the problem was, just recently she had learned to think for herself. Hedi touched each of her watches like they were talismans, and had a sudden, tremendous realisation.

The American Quaker, Bernard, would be coming back any minute in the Red Cross van. In fact... yes, as she raised her head she could already hear the motor in the distance. She held her hair back from her face and squinted to protect her eyes against the dust. From where she was standing high on the mound of Dr Schmidt's house, she could see the van coming along the road.

'Here is my ride,' she said triumphantly as the vehicle slowed down.

Dr Schmidt turned to look. He seemed to be fading from the earth already, with his dusty coat and white beard.

Hedi could see the American Quaker's face plainly through the windscreen. He was looking for her as he cruised towards them. He hadn't seen her.

'I'd better go.' The debris shifted under her feet as she stumbled down the ruins. 'Hey!' she yelled at him, sliding on her back. She watched the van drive straight past. 'Come back! Come back!' As she scrambled to her feet, the vehicle dwindled in the distance, until only the red symbol remained visible. 'No!' she screamed after it, anguish tearing through her throat.

The gunshot made her jump.

Immobile with shock, her ears ringing, Hedi carried on staring down the street. She was afraid to move, scared of what she'd see. Then presently her coat came into focus, hanging on the apple tree, waving in the breeze. She brushed the dust from her dress as best she could before retrieving it, picked up her bag and making sure she didn't look back, she started to walk.

27

HARRY

Harry stormed into the yard, cooling off after having a shouting match with the matron at the British General Hospital. The hospital had been set up in the camp by Queen Alexandra's army nurses with a rigid and inflexible regimen, and a way of doing things that they refused to deviate from. As a result, they were highly critical of the internee nurses, and, as they saw it, the general laxity of discipline amongst the medical staff. The atmosphere, to say the least, had become pretty unpleasant, and he'd made it clear who was to blame.

He took a few deep breaths. *Leave her to it*, he told himself. His role in Belsen was over now. He'd played his part. He was ready to go home, with as much alcohol as he could smuggle out with him.

He was about to go back inside the hospital when he saw the Red Cross vehicle pull into the yard, and he went over to speak to the driver.

'You saw Hedi home safely?' he asked Bernard.

The Quaker rubbed his jaw and whistled a low, two-toned note of despair. 'Home? There was precious little of it left. Her street has been bombed to oblivion.'

Harry frowned. 'So where did she go?'

'She met up with a neighbour, this old guy she knew. I guess she went with him somewhere.'

'Did you talk to him?'

'No, why would I? I don't speak German. In any case, there was a weird feeling in the air. I told her I'd take her back to the camp if she wanted, but there was no sign of her when I got back and someone took a shot at me, so I didn't hang around. She seemed fine when I left her.'

'But her house had been bombed.'

'Yeah.' Bernard shrugged. 'Tough times.'

'Right.' Harry took his cap off and raked his fingers through his hair. 'Have you still got her address?'

Bernard took a notebook out of his pocket and flicked through it. 'Here.' He tore the page out and handed it to Harry. 'I can give you rough directions to get there, if you like?'

Harry glanced at the address. The hospital could wait. 'I'll find her,' he said.

Harry commandeered an ambulance with keys in the ignition, left the camp and drove towards Celle. He'd had the idea of asking for directions en route but everywhere he passed was pretty deserted.

As he entered the town, he saw a white castle that looked like something out of a fairy tale. *How did that survive unscathed?* He glanced at the address again, cursing his own stupidity – he should have brought Bernard along with him.

Still, now Harry had got this far, he was reluctant to turn around.

His mind jumped back to the matron again: the superior, contemptuous, haughty tone she used, pointing out various misdemeanours to the nurses with great relish; a bowl that wasn't clean enough, a dressing dropped on the floor. Occupied by his thoughts, he almost missed the slender figure of a girl in a red dress walking in the shadow of the trees, her bag over her shoulder, her coat in her arms.

He pulled up and jumped out. Hedi was very pale and she stared at him with strange, dead eyes, her eyelashes and hair, all of her, powdered with white dust.

Harry put his hand on her forehead. She was cold and breathing hard. He took her wrist and checked her racing pulse. 'Put your coat on,' he said. He helped her into it and put his tunic around her shoulders. He opened the passenger door and helped her into the seat. He found a grey blanket from the back and tucked it around her.

He'd never known her to be this quiet. He remembered her excitement when she'd said she was going home. Now she was a different woman and her silence alarmed him. He felt there was something he should do, not just as a medical officer but as a friend. He sat with her and listened to her breathing gradually become more regular. *Oh, Hedi*, he thought.

'I've lost everything,' she whispered.

'You've got me.' He was a poor substitute for her home and family, he knew that.

For a moment, she didn't respond. Then she leaned towards him and rested against him.

More than anything, he wanted to protect her. He put his arm around her shoulders, and waited, watching the trees sway and the shadows flickering across the road.

He didn't know if they could make it work together, but he would give it his best shot. He thought about Bernard hearing gunfire and kept the thought to himself.

28

HEDI
PRESENT DAY

Hedi was out of breath from the effort of walking. She clutched her ribs. 'I didn't talk to Harry about Dr Schmidt until a long time later,' she said. 'And even then, I didn't tell him how death had tempted me.'

They were following a narrow, leafy, winding road, stopping frequently by the stream in shade fragranced with moss. The lane was steep. Thea's trainers weren't yet dry and they had developed a squeak. She was worried that the walk was too much for Hedi. 'Maybe we've seen enough water for now?' she said.

'No, we're not there yet,' Hedi said.

'Not where?'

'I told you! The place where Harry fished. I want you to see it,' she insisted. 'If you don't see it, how can you show it to your children?'

'Children?'

'You're going to have children,' Hedi stated brusquely, in the same tone that she'd say, 'eat up.'

'Okay, well, I'll show it to them on Google Earth.'

Hedi folded her arms crossly. 'You're being facetious.'

'Sorry. It's a longer walk than I realised and you're—'

'Old?'

'I was going to say out of breath, but you are old actually, now you mention it.'

'Is that so?'

'I should have driven.' If Thea had driven, they would have been there and back by now. But the frequent stops, resting on mossy logs or stone walls under a canopy of branches had a meditative quality. It was like a pilgrimage. 'So Harry came to look for you,' she said, to show she'd been paying attention. She felt a weird feeling between her shoulders. Then she heard her ringtone. *My phone.*

This time last month she wouldn't have been able to live without it. Thea unhooked her bag from her shoulders and felt around inside it. The screen glowed artificially bright in the green glade.

ADAM.

Her heart lurched. 'It's um... the art teacher from my school. I'd better take it.'

She pressed the answer button and sat down on a tree trunk again, aware of Hedi's enquiring gaze.

'Adam!' she said cheerfully, for Hedi's benefit.

'Hi, Thea. How's your holiday?'

She loved his voice. Not *just* his voice, because there were other reasons she'd loved him, but his voice, too.

Hedi gestured for her to move up a little, and when she didn't move, she squashed between Thea and a rotten branch, as eager and expectant as a puppy.

'Fine! All good!' Thea said. *Why are you calling me?* she wanted to ask. *It's over! Haven't you got the message yet?*

Hedi nudged her sharply with her elbow. 'Give that phone to me.'

'What? No! Let go! Sorry, Adam. Not you. It's no one.'

Hedi thrust her face in hers indignantly and glared at her.

'Actually, I'm with my grandmother. Yes, I know I told you that. Turns out, she's still going strong after all. She's sitting right next to me. We're on a walk.'

'Let me talk to him,' Hedi said.

Thea held her phone out of reach. 'You don't even know him.'

'That's why I need to talk to him. Give it to me.'

Great. 'Adam, she wants to talk to you.' *Behave,* she mouthed.

Hedi ignored her. 'Good afternoon, I'm Hedi, the "no one" she told you about. My father was also a teacher, as a matter of fact. It's an honourable profession. "The Best Teacher Inspires." Now listen, Adam, because this is important. Under that...' she narrowed her eyes and looked at Thea critically, '...that immovable exterior, Thea is a kind and sensitive soul. Oh, you know that already? Well then. It is obvious that she loves you and I think if you come here we can—'

What? Thea grabbed the phone from her and cut off the call, burning with anger. 'Thanks a lot, Hedi! That was personal! My private life has nothing to do with you!' She got to her feet, grabbed her bag and strode ahead up the lane, churned up with embarrassment and adrenaline.

Seriously! The cheek of it, intruding on a phone call like that. And then inviting Adam here! Any normal person would have wandered off a little way and pretended to examine some wildflowers or something, let the person have some privacy to take a call, but not Hedi, oh no, she had to get involved in a conversation that had nothing whatsoever to do with her. 'It's obvious she loves you?' Where did she get that from? She'd never even mentioned him to her. *Bloody woman!*

'And these trainers are still wet, by the way,' she muttered resentfully.

A few hundred yards further on, the lane ahead of her opened up, and she could see why the walk had been so arduous. The lane cut between two large lakes cupped beneath a mountain, mirroring it in the still waters. Breathing hard, she climbed up to a rocky outcrop to look out for Hedi.

Far below the estuary was meeting the sea, dividing the village of Fairbourne on one side and Barmouth on the other. She could see the ferry, a dot of white cutting the water with its wake. She felt a surge of pure happiness, only tempered by the fact there was still no sign of Hedi.

She checked the time on her phone. She'd give her five more minutes.

Although that initial wave of anger had worn off, she still didn't feel particularly warmly towards her grandmother at this moment. The point was, if she'd wanted to tell Adam she loved him, she would have. She didn't need her grandmother saying it for her. She thought of calling him to apologise. But that would open up a dialogue.

Now that Thea's indignation was stirred up again, she decided to give it a few more minutes before retracing her steps to look for Hedi. She gazed at the mountain, golden brown in the sunshine. A small boathouse cast its shadow square upon the water. It was extremely beautiful. She could imagine Harry fishing here with Hedi sitting beside him.

She liked the fact that Harry had gone back to look for her that day in Celle.

Where on earth had she got to?

With an exasperated sigh, she went back to the lane and began following the shady river down, expecting to see Hedi at any moment. But when there was no sign of her, she started to get worried.

Maybe she'd given up and gone home. *This is exactly the reason mobile phones were invented.*

She hoped she hadn't hurt her feelings. *But why should I*

feel bad? She tried to remember what she'd said. *My private life has got nothing to do with you.* It didn't, did it? There was nothing wrong with saying that. Was there?

She was still trying to justify it when she caught a glimpse of the familiar tartan dressing gown through the trees.

Hedi was staring at the rushing water, her bowed head wilting on her narrow shoulders.

'Hedi!'

Her grandmother couldn't hear her over the noise of the river.

'Hedi!'

Hedi turned her face to her. She was very pale.

Thea hurried over and knelt on the damp leaves next to her. She rested her hands on Hedi's knee and looked into Hedi's red-rimmed eyes. 'I'm sorry. I didn't mean to upset you. You okay?'

'I made you angry,' Hedi said regretfully.

Thea paused a moment. 'Yeah, you did.' No use denying it. 'Our first row. All families have rows, don't they?' she said, trying to cheer her up.

'That is so.'

'I got as far as the lakes. There's a wonderful view from up there.'

Hedi nodded.

'Do you want to go on or go back?'

'Go on,' she said in a small voice.

'Okay. Have some water, first. It's been a long walk.'

'Further than I remembered when I was young.' As Hedi took the bottle, her hands trembled. She looked wistfully at Thea.

'We'll eat our sandwiches when we get there. We deserve them,' Thea said. She drank half of her own bottle of water, packed it away, and angled her elbow towards her grandmother.

Hedi took it and, arm in arm, they got back on the lane and walked slowly up to Cregennan Lakes.

'Ah,' Hedi sighed when she looked at the view. 'It's just as I remember. Thea, I would like to lie on the grass next to you. If I do that, would you assist me in getting back up again?'

'Sure.'

Hedi lay flat on the grass, clasping her hands on her belly, and she stared up at the cloudy sky.

Thea watched her for a moment, and then lay down next to her. The clouds were silver and grey against the blueness, constantly moving and reshaping, the world was turning slowly beneath them.

Adam's phone call had unsettled her. It had broken the illusion of this being Thea's cosy, insular life. *It was nice while it lasted.* There were practicalities that both she and Adam were going to have to face pretty soon. She wasn't looking forward to it. 'I think you should tell Maggie your story,' she told her grandmother.

'Never! Don't you betray me!' Hedi said sharply. 'All that I have told you, I have told you in confidence.'

Thea sat up, baffled by her reaction. 'Hedi, she has a right to know! I don't get it,' she said in frustration. 'You're not exactly close now, are you? What have you got to lose by telling her? Seriously, I've had just about enough of our family's secrets.'

Hedi gave a low, bitter laugh. 'Ha! Secrets? You can talk! You listen to my ramblings with open ears and blank eyes, and you give nothing away of yourself. You keep yourself and your feelings hidden and buried.' Hedi put an imaginary key in a lock and turned it with a click of her tongue.

'That's unfair! It's just... I don't judge.'

'You've judged me though, haven't you?'

'No!' Thea was angry at the injustice of Hedi's words. 'How can you say that? Nothing that you've told me has made me think less of you, or of Harry. You've survived something many people didn't. If anything, I admire you for it.'

'Pah!' Hedi flicked her hand dismissively. 'I'm not talking about the past. I'm talking about now. You have your own secret, don't you? This man, Adam. He's a secret you don't trust me with. You've judged me not to be trustworthy.'

Thea felt her anger dampened down by anxiety. She tossed her hair away from her face. 'I didn't realise we were operating on a barter system.'

'You're sarcastic now? It hurts me that you think I won't understand. Why, because I'm old?'

Thea shook her head. 'No, of course not. I don't want to talk about it because it's over. Adam and I, we want different things. He said something to me, and I realised, when he said it, he didn't – *doesn't* – know me at all. He's lived a regular life, he wants what his parents have: a marriage, children, a home to bring them up in. That's not me, is it? I don't know how to do that.'

'Of course you don't, nobody does! You pick it up as you go along.'

'And they make a mess of it. Look at Maggie, and her constant search for something to fill the emptiness. It's never going to be filled. It's better to accept that fact and live with it.'

Hedi's eyes filled with tears. In the sunlight, her tears negotiated the deep lines on her face. She opened her arms and Thea, rigid with self-control, let herself be held. She could feel the crêpe-like skin of her grandmother's cheek, and she listened to the soft German words of comfort in her ear, the rhythmic patting of Hedi's hand between her shoulder blades as if she was a baby.

The gesture made her unbearably sad. Maybe it was the beauty of the place, but she was sad for Hedi, too, for the girl who had grown old and was cramming everything into one last summer holiday.

29

THEA

The following day Thea and Hedi were on the ferry from Fairbourne to Barmouth; it had been Hedi's idea. She was clutching the nylon bag containing their towels and sunscreen, her white hair blowing in the breeze. She seemed to be affected by strange whims more than most people and today she wanted to spend time by the seaside. She was excited by the idea and talked non-stop on the short trip across on the ferry.

'Listen to me, when we get there, first of all, we need to find a shop,' she said, tapping Thea's knee for attention, 'to buy the proper equipment.'

Thea raised her sunglasses to her forehead. 'What kind of equipment?'

'Wait and see.'

Equipment? That sounded ominous. 'We can hire wind-breaks and deckchairs for the day, we don't need to buy them.'

'Windbreak?' Hedi frowned and gave her a piercing look. 'Why would we need a windbreak? There's no wind. It's a beautiful day. You think it's going to be windy?'

The captain was smiling as he steered the boat across the

bay. 'You don't have to worry about any wind,' he said. 'This fair weather is settled for a few days.'

'There, you see?' Hedi said, folding her arms and looking smug. 'Thank you, Captain.'

The captain tipped his hat. He was tanned, in his sixties. He looked like a man who was enjoying life. Thea wondered enviously what it must be like to do this day after day as an actual job, coming and going, taking passengers across in the fresh sea air. She wondered how he earned a living in winter when the holidaymakers stayed away.

She felt her spirits sink. She was getting worried about her plans for the future. Not just her plans; *their* plans.

Time was passing and she and Hedi couldn't stay here indefinitely, as if they were on a permanent holiday.

She knew she should talk it over with Hedi, but she could tell the idea of going back to London and getting the flat furnished again wasn't going to go down very well. There was Hedi's emotional state to factor in, too. She had stopped insisting she was going to join Harry, as if their nightly conversations satisfied her by bringing him close to her for a little while. But when the holiday came to an end, what would happen then?

Thea would miss all this. At night, listening to Hedi's voice against the lapping of the water, Thea had begun to understand more about her family, and also more about herself and the foundations of her own behaviour. She knew her vulnerabilities but maybe she had a core of strength that she hadn't realised she possessed. If she did, she'd inherited it from Hedi, she was sure of it. Hedi was a good example of survival – and what Thea had learned from Hedi's story was that, sometimes, in the worst times, survival was nothing more than a matter of trudging through the darkness until the sun rose again.

These few weeks they'd spent together meant so much to Thea. How many people had the opportunity to really get to know each other? Even families that had been close all their lives didn't have this total immersion in family history; most grandparents didn't have the energy to talk night after night, and most grandchildren didn't have the time or the inclination to listen. But as the days passed, she and Hedi seemed to be existing in some kind of happy bubble where real life didn't intrude – or at least, they were acting as if it didn't.

But the truth was, everything had to come to an end some-time, and surely Hedi was aware of that. It was just a holiday; Thea had made that clear from the start.

'Thea, don't bite your nails,' Hedi said briskly, holding on to the side of the boat as it rocked. Then she looked concerned. 'What's wrong? You are worrying about something, I can tell.'

Say something.

But the boat was pulling up by the harbour's stone steps, and the captain cut the engine. He was reaching for the mooring ring, and it was a sunny day, 'settled' as the captain put it, and Thea didn't want to spoil it. *I'll tell her tonight*, she thought, knowing that delaying the conversation was the coward's way out.

'Don't worry about the equipment I need, I'm keeping it a secret because I just want to surprise you,' Hedi explained.

Despite herself, Thea laughed. 'You're good at that,' she said.

Half an hour later, they were in the supermarket laden with the 'equipment' for a day at the beach: two plastic buckets containing sandwiches and apple juice, two red metal spades with wooden handles, and a packet of paper flags.

Hedi had taken a great deal of care in her choice of spade. She quickly dismissed the plastic ones as being a waste of money. 'Look at this,' she said, bending one in her hands, 'truly, they are too flimsy to even last the day. We need something strong and sturdy. Wait! Look!' She had seen the red spades on a top shelf and went to fetch someone to get them down for her.

The sales assistant had told her they were not suitable for children as the metal was quite sharp, and Hedi had agreed with enthusiasm. 'But as you can see, we are no longer children,' she said, 'and you can trust us to use them diligently. Isn't that so, Thea?'

'Yes, we will use them diligently,' Thea repeated, feeling idiotic.

'Fair enough,' the sales assistant had conceded.

Thea wouldn't have been surprised if he'd argued, because Hedi was giving off the barely contained vibe of an excitable girl.

As they walked to the beach, Hedi did a little skip and then wondered aloud why skipping hadn't become an acceptable means of propulsion.

'It's faster than walking, but takes less energy than a run,' she said, demonstrating. 'Come on! Try it!'

Thea skipped alongside Hedi, the bag with the towels bouncing against her hip, the cartons of apple juice rattling inside the bucket.

Strangely enough, it was true. Ignoring the looks they were getting from passers-by, they skipped across the road to the beach and sat down on the stone steps to take off their shoes. Thea was only half aware of Hedi's breathing as she noticed that the tide was out; she gazed at the distant deep-blue sea as its lavish frill of lacy waves settled on the yellow sand.

Then she looked at her grandmother with concern. Every breath that Hedi took seemed to emit a high-pitched whine. 'Are you okay?'

'Of course I'm okay,' Hedi said, picking up her shoes. 'I may be old, but I'm happy as Larry!' *Heppy as Lerry.*

'Your chest sounds—'

'Like old bagpipes, I know that,' Hedi said, waving her hand dismissively. 'Harry liked bagpipes, *ektually*, for marching. He had a passion for a march. Now, this is the plan,' she said, scanning the area, 'we need to find the perfect spot, a little distance away from people and close to the water's edge, but not so close that we get our towels wet. Avoid like the plague anyone playing ball games! Inevitably, take it from me, the ball will be attracted to us like fate and we won't get a moment's peace.'

The warm velvety sand was soft on the surface and cool where their feet sank into it. 'How about here?'

Hedi grabbed hold of Thea's arm. 'No, are you crazy? Look, those people have a dog, he will want attention, they do that, you know. Follow me!'

They zigzagged their way along the beach until they reached the damp sand salt-marked white from the tide, and Hedi planted her spade firmly in the ground, claiming their territory. She looked around, her hands on her hips. 'This is it,' she declared grandly. 'You may unfurl the towels.'

Towels unfurled, Thea lay down on hers, resting back on her elbows, feeling the warmth of the sun on her bare limbs, utterly relaxed. Her worries faded again. It was hard to stay worried with Hedi around. She wondered if she was in denial, if they would just go on living like this indefinitely, taking each day as it came until – she wasn't quite sure what the *until* was. She didn't want to think about it too hard.

In any case, Hedi's breathing was back to normal again. She was hugging her knees, smiling distantly as she stared out at the sea.

Thea lay back on the towel and closed her eyes. She listened to the thunder of the waves and the whispering of the foam, and then she slept.

When Thea awoke, she was thirsty and disorientated, squinting at Hedi's blurred outline against the blue sky. A little girl was talking to them about a sleeping princess in a castle.

Thea sat up. Her mouth was parched. She looked around. She was surrounded by a circle of sandcastles, each flying its own bright paper flag, with staircases and seashell casement windows and a driftwood drawbridge lying across the drained moat.

'She's awake,' the little girl said.

'So she is.'

Not only were Hedi and the little girl looking down at her, but the girl's parents were, too. They were amused and expectant, as if they were watching performance art.

'Hi,' Thea said, pushing back her sweat-damp hair.

'Sorry, did we wake you?' the mother asked brightly.

Well, duh. How long had she been asleep?

'Enjoy your day,' the mother said, taking her daughter's hand, and the father chuckled. The little girl waved as they walked on up the beach, leaving a trail of footprints behind them.

'Well?' Hedi asked, watching the little family walk up the beach. 'What do you think?'

'Masterful,' Thea said. She stood up carefully to avoid messing up Hedi's architecture. 'What did we do with the apple juice?'

'I mean about the family,' Hedi said. 'We were a little family, once.' Her voice was tight and regretful, her fingers interlaced, her knuckles pressed against her chin. She said it with longing, as though she was still yearning for that elusive past that had slipped away.

Slipped?

No, Thea thought, slipped wasn't the right word. Thrown away. They could have all grown up together and lived a regular life with comfortable family traditions instead of the rootless nomadic one Maggie had embraced.

It was cruel, the way Maggie had cut her off from Hedi and Harry. *Estrangement?* That sanitised word didn't begin to describe it. Still, since Maggie had moved to New York, Thea missed her more than she cared to admit.

Thea knew what was going on. Hedi, refusing to back down, was still feeling the grief of that loss after all these years, giving Thea a taste of her lost childhood, the carefree, joyful freedom of holidays and fairs and donkeys and lakes.

She got to her feet and stepped out from the ramparts of the castle and her heart went out to her grandmother. 'I love you, Hedi,' she said, full of pity for her. It came out forcefully, almost aggressively.

Hedi looked at her with surprise and her eyes blurred with tears. 'And I love you.' For a few moments they rocked in each other's sun-warmed arms.

30

HEDI
PRESENT DAY

Back at The Hideaway that evening, Hedi sat by the wood burner although it wasn't lit. She felt as if she needed more time to think, but really, there was nothing to think about. She had been stupid and stubborn for a long time. She had to put aside her pride.

Thea too was quiet. She poured them each a glass of water from the tap and dropped in a slice of lemon. 'Here you are. We're probably a bit dehydrated,' she said.

'Ah! Probably, yes. Dehydrated, that may be so.' Hedi took the cold glass and groped for a phrase in her mind that for a moment was a little out of reach. That was it! *Tying up loose ends.* It was important to leave this world neatly, with nothing remaining for others to clear up. She had a loose end dangling – for a moment she thought of the string of coloured lights swinging from the birch tree when she and Harry had that first kiss – and better to tie it up now, why not?

Hedi sipped the water, and the lemon slice nudged her lips. She rested the cold glass on her knee. 'Thea,' she began. 'I would like to request to borrow your phone?'

Thea looked surprised. 'Yes, of course. You'll have to walk down to the meadow, though, to get a signal.'

'I know.'

'Hedi... everything's all right, isn't it?'

Hedi thought about the question. She watched Thea twist a strand of copper hair around her finger. She had made her granddaughter anxious.

After the many years she'd lived in this country, she understood that this open question was the polite and roundabout way of getting information without asking for it. She knew that Thea was courteous enough to accept a *yes, I'm fine* as an answer. *Yes, I'm fine* could mean anything you wanted it to mean, including *no, things are dreadful but I'm not telling you that*. 'Yes,' she said obligingly. And then she added, 'I have realised I must speak to Maggie after all. You see, I have been thinking about it since you mentioned it and I agree with you, after seeing the family on the beach, she should know that I am here in Bear Cave spending time with you. Don't worry, I am prepared for her to rebuff me. She is very busy, after all.'

She saw Thea relax.

'Shall we take a glass of wine down there? Fortify ourselves?' Thea suggested.

Wine! The word gave Hedi a lift. But she shook her head. 'No, I think it is the kind of conversation that needs clear thinking on my part. I am prone to being sharp with people, you may have noticed, but I will exercise self-discipline for the duration of the call.'

Thea smiled. 'Well then, I'll have a glass waiting for you. Do you want me to come with you?' she offered.

'No, there's no need. But if you could find Maggie's number for me?'

'Sure.' Thea took her phone out of her bag and pressed the little buttons until the screen lit up her calm face with a blue glow.

Hedi held the phone, feeling nervous. It was a long time since she had felt nervous about anything. It was one of the benefits of old age; there was very little left in the world that one had to do for the first time. The final performance was always the best, the most polished, the most assured.

'Okay, so, when you're ready to call her, press this red icon with the handset on it. It will turn green and start ringing.'

'She may not be in,' Hedi said hopefully, patting her white hair.

'You could leave a message and ask her to call you.'

Hedi held the phone carefully, mindful of not touching any of the other buttons. It was difficult because there were a lot of them and they were very small and her fingers were very crooked.

Thea opened the door for her. 'Good luck,' she said.

'You think I need luck?' Hedi asked from the doorway. Without waiting for a reply, she made her way down the meadow to the water's edge.

Thea sat at the table and thought about the day they had spent together.

Towards the late afternoon, after paddling, they had watched the scallop-edged tide come in over the yellow sand. It surged and filled the moat around the sandcastles and then it breached the walls and collapsed the forward turrets and rushed around their ankles, cold and thrilling. They'd squealed and danced and gathered up the towels and stood back to watch the tide ebb and flow, smoothing away all traces.

She wondered how the conversation between Hedi and Maggie was going. The minutes passed, and she read the label on the unopened wine bottle again and waited for Hedi to return.

When Hedi came back, she burst through the door and

wordlessly thrust the phone back at Thea. Her face was flushed. She sat down on the bamboo sofa, clasping her hands tightly in her lap as if she could barely hold it together.

Thea sat next to her. 'So?'

Hedi hesitated for a moment. 'I told her about how her father and I met in Belsen. I said I was holidaying with you in Bear Cave. I apologised for not telling her these things before now.'

Thea waited for her to go on. 'Was she – what did she say?'

'She said, "Thank you for the information."'

Thea frowned. 'That's it? Nothing else? She made no other comment? What did she say about us being here together?'

'Nothing. For the most part, the conversation was wholly one-sided.'

They stared at each other in silence.

'You're glad you've told her, though, aren't you?'

Hedi's face was impassive. 'What's done is done. Open the wine! Tonight, we come to a good bit! I shall tell you about the dance at Belsen, the one that Harry invited me to. The night he proposed to me.'

31

HEDI

BELSEN, MAY 1945

It was a strange feeling, turning up in the square that was now bright and glamorous beneath strings of lights and fluttering bunting. The RAF band was playing. Hedi felt cold and removed.

She felt no particular excitement or enthusiasm for the dance, just a sense of resignation. After Harry had brought her back to Belsen, Ursula and Renate had greeted her in silence. She didn't want to talk about what had happened. It was easy enough for them to see it hadn't gone as planned.

Hedi stood with her arms crossed and watched the internees brighten as they approached, cheered by the lights and the music. Many of them were still skin and bone, weak from their ordeals, blotched by scabs, mouths lipstick-red.

The British soldiers hosting the dance were mingling with the internees, as carefree as beings from another planet: jovial, exuberant, ready to have a good time with their customary energy and goodwill. Soon, everybody except Hedi was dancing. She was standing at the side of the dance floor, feeling as if she was watching the scene through a thick pane of glass. The oddest couples danced past her: thin fragile girls twirled off their feet by strong uniformed men who, it seemed, had nothing more on their minds than enjoying themselves.

Self-consciously, she crossed her arms over her chest. She wasn't in a good frame of mind. The romantic music seemed insulting. She was on the brink of angry tears, tears of self-pity. She wanted the music to stop. *Don't you understand how awful it's been for us?*

She'd had enough. She was going back to the hut.

Just then, she saw Bill dodging his way through the dancing couples towards her.

'Hullo,' he said. 'Harry's on his way. What would you like to drink?'

'Beer, please.'

'Attagirl,' Bill said with a grin. 'Follow me.'

Hedi followed him to the bar. She wasn't sure why she'd asked for a beer. She didn't drink it. She'd had sips of it at Christmastime, and to be honest the taste disgusted her, but she hadn't been sure what else to ask for. However, it was too late now. Bill was handing her a small glass of beer.

'Cheers,' he said, chinking his glass against hers.

'Cheers.' She drank it quickly because it was disgusting, put her glass down, and stifled a beery burp with the back of her hand. She blinked at the alarming effect it had on her. She already felt a little dizzy from it.

'Better out than in,' Bill said, laughing.

She tried to translate the phrase in her head and wondered at Bill's good humour in the face of her rudeness. She had noticed with interest over the time they'd been here that the British soldiers lacked any obvious discipline, in comparison with her country's own military, for whom discipline was paramount. And yet, the Tommies worked hard and got things done just the same, which was interesting. She wondered what her father would have made of it.

'Here he comes!' Bill said, looking across the square.

Hedi felt her breath catch in her throat as she saw Harry. His smile and the fresh-faced newness he had about him made him look untouched by war. He was walking slowly because he had a frail, dark-haired internee hanging on his arm.

The frail woman was smiling and waving at Hedi enthusiastically in a familiar manner. She didn't care for it at all.

Then as they got close, the woman said, 'Hedi, it's me!'

'Magda?' She couldn't believe it. 'You look...' There was no complimentary way to finish the sentence, and so she didn't.

'And you too, sister,' Magda said softly. She took Hedi's hands, running her thumbs over Hedi's knuckles. 'Harry said you would be here and I wanted to surprise you. You look wonderful.'

'So do you,' Hedi lied passionately. 'The last time I saw you...' she shook her head. 'Let's just say you didn't look so well.'

'You took care of me,' Magda said, 'and that's why I'm alive today. You were watching out for me.'

'I've missed you,' Hedi said, close to tears.

Magda smiled. 'I've missed you too, more than I can say.' She looked at her intently, her dark eyes gleaming. 'The music is a little loud for my ears. Come with me. We have much to talk about. Will you excuse us for a moment, Harry? Give me your arm, Hedi.'

Away from the glamour of the coloured lights, Magda was serious again, her cheeks hollowed by shadows. 'Listen, I have news for you. My little sister is alive and living in Sweden.'

'Oh! She is?' For a moment, Hedi hesitated, hiding her disappointment. She could guess what was coming next. 'That's wonderful! I expect you'll want to join her.'

'Yes, that is the plan. The Swedes are keeping families together and because of that I'm being evacuated.'

'How nice for you that you will be together again.' Only moments ago they had been reunited, and now she was losing Magda almost immediately. Hedi looked at the coloured bunting flapping in the breeze and waited for the feeling of loss to wash over her and pass by. It always did pass by, she'd found, after that first agonising wave.

Magda stroked her cheek sympathetically, as if she could read her thoughts. 'How about you, Hedi? Have you had news of your family?'

'News? Yes, you could say that.' Hedi bit her lower lip. 'My father is dead and my mother is in Camp One. When I leave, she will remain there without me.'

'Ah.' Magda understood and her eyes rimmed with tears. 'I'm so sorry.'

Hedi's eyes narrowed as she thought of Dr Schmidt digging in the ruins of his study for his pistol. The memory made her hollow inside. Her thoughts ricocheted in a different direction. 'Anyway. That's the way it is. Don't be sorry for me. I'm not the only one who's lost people, I know that. Ursula saw her parents being shot.'

'Who is Ursula?'

'She's the crazy woman with no name who lay on the other side of me, the one with the screeching laugh. You must recall her?'

'No, I'm sorry, I have no recollection of that.'

'Anyhow, I helped her remember it. Her name, I mean. Ursula.'

Magda gave a sweet, encouraging smile. 'You've helped a lot of people, Hedi. And now I will help you. You must come to Sweden with me. The three of us will start our lives all over again, together, as a family, a close family. They are keeping families together. Harry believes we are sisters, you know that, don't you?'

Hedi nodded.

Magda was still smiling. 'Do you remember the first time we met each other? You remember what I asked you?'

'Yes. To be your sister.'

'And you said, "I suppose I could give it a try."'

Hedi laughed despite herself. 'Did I?'

'And you *are* my sister now. So,' Magda continued eagerly, 'we're staying together as a family. It will be a new adventure for us, a new life.'

Hedi glanced towards the dance floor. Harry was standing alone while they spoke, as self-contained as always. As she looked at him, his gaze skimmed hers. He took his cigarettes out and eased one gently out of the packet. As he tried to light it, the yellow flame of his match danced and quivered around the tip.

Magda looked over at him too. She was silent for a moment, as if she was reading Hedi's thoughts. 'He's being posted back to England soon,' she said.

'Is he?' He hadn't mentioned it to her. Although Hedi knew it had to happen sometime, it wasn't something they'd spoken about. It was an eventuality that had lain dormant. In Belsen, troops came and went, their movements governed by other people's schedules.

Momentarily, Harry's gentle eyes met hers through a haze of cigarette smoke. It was like getting a glimpse into another world, a green paradise, a haven.

Hedi turned back to Magda. 'When are you going to Sweden?'

'As soon as transport has been arranged for us.'

'So soon? I will have to think about it carefully before I give you an answer.'

Magda looked frustrated. 'Hedi, be sensible! What is there to think about? Do you have anyone else to make a home with?'

Home. She shook her head. Belsen was her home now. 'No.' Well, that was the truth of it.

'Then your decision is easy, isn't that so?' Magda said with a kindly smile.

'Yes, I suppose it is.' Hedi didn't want to be forced into it, not even by Magda. She couldn't contemplate being told what to do, not right now. Glancing at the band, at the reflections of light on the instruments, she was caught up in the exuberance of the music. 'Listen to this tune! I love it! Please excuse me, Magda, I must dance to this with Harry.'

'Of course,' Magda said. 'I'm going back to rest now. I am still very weak. It's been good to see you.'

Hedi kissed her on the cheek. 'And you, too.'

Once Magda had left, she looked for Harry. He was walking towards her. He gave her a crooked smile. 'Care to dance?'

Hedi nodded, suddenly wanting more than anything to feel carefree and have fun.

Harry had a jaunty dancing style, all angles, elbows and bounce, and she took on some of his energy to begin with, and his chivalry too, because he kept a few modest inches of space between their bodies.

It was a warm summer night and as the band played she became very aware of the warmth of his hand holding hers. She thought about the kiss they'd shared. And then she became aware of her own body in her dress, the sweat under her arms, the way the fabric was moving against her skin. It felt like his hands touching her body, lightly, teasing her. She felt that she was coming to life again.

The RAF band was reading the mood on the dance floor and the next song they played was slow and romantic. There was still the impenetrable barrier of cool space between her and Harry. She pushed herself against him impulsively, putting him off balance, and he responded by grabbing her and holding her tightly as they staggered back two, three, four steps. They laughed, got their bearings, and she could feel his breath, hot in her hair.

That's better, Hedi thought, now she was in his arms. *Now we've broken the ice.*

But to her surprise, he was trembling. Her gaze travelled up past his collar to his slender neck, along the curve of his Adam's apple, resting for a moment on the red gleam of stubble under his jaw. She tilted her head to take him all in, anxiously, eagerly. His eyes were distant, his face set, and he was staring over her shoulder.

She realised with a jolt of pity and a rush of love that Harry wasn't untouched by war. His steady good humour was part of the uniform that he wore. Moments earlier, she had been dreaming of his hard body beneath his clothing, but now she was thinking about the gentle man beneath the skin.

'Do you want to stop dancing?' she asked him.

'No, let's not,' he murmured. 'Let's stay like this forever.'

'All right.' Hedi rested her head on his chest as they swayed to the music and she listened to the steady beat of his heart. He needed her, she realised, in the same way she needed him. They belonged together in a private way that they had the measure of.

Around them, the couples were still dancing, all their troubles forgotten or at least pushed into the background for now.

With her mouth against his soft throat she said, 'Magda says you're going back to England soon.'

'Yes. There's not so much to do here now. The QA nurses are running things efficiently enough. We're not needed here any more.'

'She has asked me to go to Sweden with her.'

He rubbed his jaw and his eyes met hers. 'It will be good place for her to convalesce, get her strength back. And families are better off being together.'

Hedi considered this. 'You think I should go?'

He looked at her quizzically. 'Do you *want* to go?'

'Not really,' she admitted.

'Then don't, Hedi,' he said lightly. 'Forget Sweden. Come home with me. Let's get married.'

She smiled. It was a joke, obviously, but a nice one. *Let's get married*. But the words filled her with a sweet calmness and she wanted it to be true. 'Yes,' she said, matching her tone to his. 'Let's do that.' Unlike going to Sweden, saying yes was easy.

The easy decisions are the right ones, she told herself.

They looked at each and laughed, surprising each other. It was like being given the huge, wonderful gift of anticipation, a future where there had been none.

Harry took her face in his warm hands. He moved in for a kiss when the band changed tempo and began to play a tune she'd never heard before.

The soldiers around them roared approval and Harry grabbed her hand and another Tommy caught her other hand and all the guests and soldiers linked up to form one very large circle that took up the whole of the dance floor. To Hedi's surprise, the Tommies began to sing, with exaggerated actions:

> *You put your left leg in, you put your left leg out,*
> *In out, in out, you shake it all about,*
> *You do the hokey cokey and you turn around,*
> *Knees bent, arms stretched, rah, rah, rah!*

As if copying the actions wasn't funny enough in itself, they all rushed to the centre of the circle, swinging their entwined hands high.

> *Oooooooooohhhhh! The hokey cokey!*
> *Oooooooooooohhhhh! The hokey cokey!*
> *Ooooooooooooohhhhh! The hokey cokey!*
> *That's what it's all about!*

Giggling, Hedi thought it was the best fun ever and as the song continued she and most of the internees got terribly confused and collapsed in tears of laughter as they rushed forward either too soon or too late: *Ooooohhhhh!* But that didn't stop the soldiers who carried on heartily singing at the tops of their voices:

> *You put your whole self in,*
> *You put your whole self out,*
> *In out, in out, you shake it all about,*
> *You do the hokey cokey and you turn around,*
> *That's what it's all about!*

32

THEA
PRESENT DAY

Once that earworm got into your head, it was hard to get rid of. *You put your left leg in, your left leg out...*

The following morning Thea was washing up the breakfast dishes and thinking about Harry's proposal at the dance, a happy thought, and Maggie's reaction to Hedi's story, which was weird. *Thank you for the information?* Who says that to their mother?

She raised her foam-gloved hands out of the water, staring at the iridescent bubbles in the sunlight, feeling them tickling as they popped. She wondered if she should apologise to Hedi for talking her into the phone call. She hadn't thought it through. What exactly was the appropriate response to hearing a mother reveal a secret she had kept for most of her life? What could Maggie have said right at that moment, other than, *thank you for the information?* 'Poor you? I'm so sorry for your pain?' The revelation had come out of the blue and neither of those phrases would cut it.

Thea had, somewhere in fantasy land, expected an epiphany that would reunite her mother and grandmother in a new Disneyesque relationship of mutual understanding. She'd hoped the truth would be a bond for the three of them.

You put your whole self in...

She was also going to have to work out how to convince the social workers that Hedi had come to terms with her grief and was happy to live independently. Assuming she was, of course. And also, they had to furnish the flat.

She heard a sound behind her.

'Thea?' Hedi asked anxiously from the doorway, 'may I ask why are you staring at your hands in that manner?'

Thea plunged her hands back into the hot water and groped around in the foam for the last couple of teaspoons. 'I was thinking.'

'Thinking? About something serious, it is clear.'

'I was thinking about our plans, you know, for after our holiday is over.'

Hedi considered the statement, and then she nodded and tucked her hands in the pockets of Harry's dressing gown. 'I suppose it is time we thought about that. What are your plans?'

Thea reached for the towel to dry her hands. 'School starts in September, so I'll be doing the usual things I always do, ringing parents, chasing fees, organising afternoon clubs. Then it will be autumn and Halloween, and after half term, carol concerts and the nativity play...' She let the sentence dangle. *See how busy I am?* 'Have you thought about what you'd like to do when we go back?'

Hedi looked at her steadily and shrugged. 'You know what my plans are.'

'Okay,' Thea said awkwardly, turning to face her. 'But in the meantime, I'm due back at work in ten days. I thought maybe we could go shopping for new furniture, start with the basics.'

Hedi seemed about to argue, but then she shook her head and smiled suddenly. 'Is that what's troubling you? Don't look so worried! You are imagining that, like Scheherazade, I shall go on telling you my story night after night to keep you here.' She tilted her head in a query, her dark eyes mischievous.

Thea laughed. 'And won't you?'

'It's been fun, hasn't it? For you, too?' Hedi asked.

'Oh, yes, the best! I've loved spending time with you, us being together, getting to know each other. It feels good, you know, to belong – not just to you but to Bear Cave. I've always felt somehow that I didn't have a real home, that I was always a visitor, skimming the surface of places, rootless. But now I know where I come from. I'm not explaining it very well, am I?'

For a moment, Hedi didn't reply. Then she said softly, 'You have explained it perfectly well enough. This holiday has meant a great deal to me.' She took the tea towel from Thea's hands and began to dry the dishes with elaborate attention. 'Look, don't worry. I too, have been thinking about the future. The holiday will come to an end, and I never asked you when because I didn't want to think about it. It has been perfect. The best of times.'

She busied herself putting the cereal bowls in the cupboard and the cutlery in the drawer. She hung the towel up, turned back to Thea and clapped her hands. 'Of course, we have to go back. We still have a few more days to enjoy ourselves! Now I will tell you my plans. I shall move into a retirement home. I have a place in mind, The Birches. Harry and I had friends who moved there. It's very pleasant. The residents have pastimes and committees and sherry with meals.'

'Really?'

'Or wine. Whatever you like,' Hedi said waving her hand airily.

'Where is it?'

'London. Near the Royal Free Hospital.'

'That's not far from me at all! We'll be able to visit each

other and meet for coffee. The *Birches*, too.' She smiled. 'Appropriate.'

'*Eksectly*. That is important. It's why I chose it.'

The relief was enormous, and Thea felt suddenly optimistic. She wished she'd brought up the subject before now, instead of lying awake at night worrying about it. Obviously, after all she'd been through in her life, Hedi was perfectly capable of making her own plans and decisions. The Birches. Wine in the evening. It sounded perfect.

Hedi seemed happy they'd got things straight, and she filled the kettle, humming to herself. She made the coffee, and as she handed a cup to Thea she said, 'I have something to show you today, in the village, which will be of interest to you.'

'That's intriguing.'

'It is a shortcut to an explanation, I suppose, about why, despite being deeply in love with Harry, and accepting his proposal, I made the decision to go to Sweden with Magda.'

33

HARRY

BELSEN, MAY 1945

When Harry was summoned to see his commanding officer he guessed it was about one of two things – either his bust-up with the matron, or he'd been reported for fraternising with a German internee.

Harry tapped the door and the CO called him in from the other side of the desk and asked him to sit down. He leaned across and put a fatherly hand on Harry's shoulder. He looked very uncomfortable and Harry had a sudden urge to shake him off.

The CO cleared his throat. 'It is my sad duty to inform you that your brother, Arthur, has been killed in France.'

'What?' Harry jumped to his feet aggressively. 'You're lying! That can't be right. The war in Europe is over!'

The CO withdrew himself out of arm's reach and stared out of the window, turning his back on the soldier's anger.

Harry knew what he was doing. He was giving him time to get his thoughts straight. He got himself under control and said, 'How? How did it happen?'

The CO came back to his desk and sat down. 'He was clearing landmines. It might be of some consolation to you to know that he died peacefully in the service of his country. His pals were with him to the end.'

Harry didn't respond. He had said that kind of thing himself, so he didn't attach any truth to it. He'd seen death up close on the battlefields, slow painful deaths and quick violent ones. He'd seen the dirty deaths in the camp. It never looked romantic or anything other than what it was.

He stood up, saluted and went to the mess to get drunk.

Sitting in the mellow amber light of the spirit bottles behind the bar, he put his feet on a table and raised the glass in his hand before drowning his sorrows.

God give my parents the strength to bear Arthur's death, was his last sober thought.

Harry had been keen to join the army and take this last bite of adventure, knowing it was the kind of adventure that would be denied him as a general practitioner back home in Bear Cave. His future had been mapped out for him since he was a school-boy, but sometimes, let's face it, a man didn't want to follow a map. Maps were for guidance. Sometimes a man just wanted to find his own way through life.

He had seen the admiration and envy in his father's eyes – his father had been too young to fight in the First World War, and he was too old for this one. Harry was living it for him.

But none of them had banked on Arthur signing up, too.

Arthur was seventeen, just a boy when Harry saw him on his last leave.

He'd been looking at himself closely in his father's shaving mirror with his usual optimism, stroking his jaw and pinching the fluff on it, as fine as a pussy willow bud.

'It's coming along, isn't it?'

Harry laughed. 'I've seen more hairs on Aunty Mary's chin!

Trust me, when you have to shave every day, the novelty soon wears off.'

He stared into his drink and for a moment it was like staring at something wonderfully familiar – there was a dead insect in the whisky at the bottom of the glass. It reminded him of an amber brooch that his mother wore, and for a moment he was comforted by the sensation of home. He fished the insect out with his finger and put it on the arm of his chair. He shook his head.

Losing Arthur was going to break their hearts.

He knocked back his drink and looked up from his empty glass. His old mate, Bill, had come through the door, and he called him over. 'Bill! Billy, my old pal! Come and have a drink and top me up while you're at it. Have a whisky. I'll tell you something, the Germans know how to keep a well-stocked bar, I'll give them that.'

He watched Bill pour the whiskies before coming to sit in a leather chair. It leaked a sigh of air as he sat in it.

The whisky had numbed Harry to a hollowed-out state of emptiness. That was the whole point of drinking, wasn't it? It was the perfect anaesthetic. It had done its job and he didn't feel anything particular at all. He prodded the loss of Arthur like a bad tooth, to test the pain, and regretted it. 'Bill, I went to the woods with my girl after the dance,' he said. The words stuck together in his mouth like toffee.

'Hedi,' Bill said knowingly, swirling his drink around in his glass.

'That's right.' Harry sat up straighter. 'I love her, too.'

'Do you, now?'

'I do now. I've asked her to marry me.'

Bill shook his head tolerantly. 'You're drunk, pal.'

Harry frowned. He felt he should take offence at the observation, even though he agreed with it. He tried to get out of the chair and his whisky splashed onto his hand and trickled into his sleeve. 'Steady!' he cautioned himself. 'Bill. Help me up, will you. I'm going to see her, going to celebrate our engagement.'

'Wait till tomorrow,' Bill advised. 'I've just come from Camp One and they're in a heck of a party mood over there – it's their last day there before they move to Camp Three. I had a woman come up behind me and pinch my bum. She wasn't subtle about it, either.'

Harry sniggered. 'Lucky you.'

'Not really,' Bill said ruefully. 'I felt like a rabbit being snatched by a hawk.' He blinked and rubbed his hands vigorously over his face, as if he was cleaning off the strains of the day. 'They're still wearing those lipsticks that the Red Cross brought in. Even the sick are holding on to them like grim death.'

Harry tapped his glass against his teeth thoughtfully. 'Hedi wears lipstick. I can taste it on her. She tastes like flowers.'

'Taste a lot of flowers, do you?'

'Can't. Hay fever. Might give it another try, though. That's right. I've asked her to marry me.'

Bill was looking at him steadily. 'Yeah, you said.'

There was something in the way he said it that penetrated Harry's alcoholic fog. '"Yeah, you said"? What's that mean?'

'Leave it, Harry. Let's just have a quiet drink. Let's drink to Arthur.'

'Not yet,' Harry persisted. 'What did you mean?'

'All I'm saying is, tomorrow's another day.'

'So what? I'll feel the same tomorrow, and the day after that,' Harry said stubbornly, and then he saw it again, the faintest sceptical shrug of Bill's dark eyebrows. He felt the anger roll up in him unexpectedly, like a bank of mist over the hills, and in a sudden rage he threw his glass at him, whisky showering amber rain, the glass bouncing off Bill's shoulder and hitting the ground, smashing in an explosion of crystal shards.

In the bar, all conversation stopped. The air hummed with silence.

Bill got to his feet and the glass crunched under his boots as he towered over Harry. 'She's German,' he said coldly. 'How can you forgive her? How will your parents forgive her?'

Harry raised his fists, braced for a fight, but Bill turned round and walked out.

The hum of conversation buzzed around the mess again.

Harry slumped back in his chair. Bill's glass was still on the table, half full. Harry reached out and fastened his fingers around it. *Mustn't waste it*, he thought.

34

HEDI

BELSEN, MAY 1945

Hedi was meeting Harry in the early evening, by the gate to the woods.

She saw him from a distance, a familiar figure in khaki leaning on the gate of a field.

As she approached him, he looked weighed down by his worries. She saw the defeated hunch of his shoulders.

She realised he wasn't aware of her presence in the way he usually was. Fear chilled her. That attraction, their connection, the way they were attuned to each other, it was broken, like a wire had been cut. She called his name and when he turned around, she knew they were dead and useless.

He was crying silently, his tired eyes sore and swollen with grief. It was a shock to see him like that.

'What is it, Harry?' she asked in alarm.

'My brother Arthur's been killed.' He stubbed out his cigarette on the sole of his boot and looked at her bleakly. 'This bloody war,' he said, and he laid his arms on top of the gate and buried his face in them. His grief settled on him like a cloud.

Hedi put her arms around his waist to give him her warmth. His uniform smelled of wool. He turned at her touch and curled into her, resting his cool face in the curve of her neck. They stood together like that, swaying slightly, lost in sorrow, with the smell of soap and fresh grass.

She raised her head to look at him. She watched a tear rolling down his cheek. Pressing her own cheek against his, she shared the heat of it and blotted it away. His sorrow tenderised her heart. To comfort him she kissed his burning tears, tasting the salt of them on her lips.

His breath shuddered against her neck, and presently he took his own weight on himself again and looked closely at her. 'Hedi,' he said hopelessly, his eyebrows meeting in a frown. 'How do you bear it?'

She wanted to give him an answer, the right answer, a helpful and uplifting one, but in the end, with her heart breaking, she told him the truth. 'I don't know. Somehow you just do.'

35

HEDI
PRESENT DAY

Hedi took Thea to the church next to Martin's shop and held open the gate.

It was very peaceful, open, echoing with birdsong, timeless, grey headstones embedded in sweet green grass, bright with flowers.

While Hedi looked at the graves, Thea googled The Birches retirement home out of curiosity. She couldn't find a result and she tried variations on the theme without success: *Birches, Birches Retirement Home, Silver Birches*, until Hedi called her over to show her Harry's parents' grave.

'Your great-grandparents,' she said. 'I was very fond of them.' She rested her hand on the headstone.

'What I didn't tell you was, after the dance,' Hedi continued, 'and Harry's thrilling proposal of marriage, he and I went for a walk in the woods, to be alone.' She looked at Thea and arched her eyebrows. 'I say alone; we were not quite alone because around us in the dark was the occasional glow of a cigarette end, burning red, pinpointing other couples finding privacy. I will not embarrass you by describing what happened next, Thea. You are a woman, you can imagine it, and as I am your grandmother, it would not be seemly for me to go into detail. Suffice it to say, being close to Harry in that way, lying together afterwards in the cool of the night on a bed of leaves and damp moss was better than I could ever have dreamed of. It revealed to me the wonderful consolation of life.' Her voice trembled with emotion.

She took Thea by the arm and led her to the shady porch of the church.

A wooden plaque commemorated the dead of the two world wars. There were, Thea saw, a depressing number of names on it for such a small village. Hedi rocked forward on the balls of her feet, her hands clasped behind her back.

Hedi ran her finger over the lettering. 'There he is,' she said softly, 'Harry's brother, Arthur. He would have been your great-uncle.'

'He was only eighteen.'

'That is correct.' Hedi sighed. She moved a small pile of newsletters from the stone bench to make room for them to sit down. When she was settled, she sat very straight and cupped her hands over her knees like a child. The light was shining through the thick glass of the arched, leaded window. Diamonds of light fell on her, dazzling as glitter, showing every line and wrinkle on her creased face. 'But I have left out a bit of my story.' She hesitated, as if she wasn't sure how to continue. 'You see, I knew what Arthur's death meant. I could never be accepted by Harry's family now.'

36

HEDI

BELSEN, MAY 1945

Ursula and Renate were going home. They had invited Hedi along with them to say goodbye to their old hut. It was bitter-sweet. The place had been their home for over a year and they stood together, reminiscing, leaning against the empty wooden bunks.

'So this is goodbye,' Ursula said, checking her watch and tapping her foot in her sensible shoes.

'Don't say that.'

'Why not? It had to happen sometime. We have the rest of our lives to get on with.'

'Get on with? You make it sound as if it's going to be hard work,' Hedi complained.

'It will be. We will have to build new lives from the mud and debris of the old ones. Who knows, it may turn out better than we ever imagined.'

'Or worse,' Renate said.

'Of course, there is always that possibility. When are you going to Sweden, Hedi?'

Sweden. She hated the word. 'Any day now.'

'Very sensible. You had no future with Harry.'

'Why Sweden?' Renate asked.

Ursula answered for Hedi. 'Her sister is going and they try to keep families together.'

'Even ersatz ones?'

'Don't tease her, Renate,' Ursula said sharply. 'You'll be treated well, Hedi. The Swedes seem fair-minded, although a little too serious for my liking, you know, the ones I've met.'

'Truly? They're serious? But they have fun, don't they?' Hedi asked anxiously.

'I expect so, on occasion. At least, they have a reputation for drinking a lot. You know, Hedi,' Ursula said, patting her cheek with uncharacteristic gentleness, 'if you like, you can come and live with Karl and me. You and I know each other quite well now, don't you think? And we've been through a lot together. It will be a shock for you, going to Sweden as a refugee and living in a different country with a different language.'

'A refugee?' Hedi said, taking in the fact for the first time. 'I'll be a refugee?'

'What did you think,' Renate asked with an incredulous laugh, 'that you'd be treated as an honoured guest?'

'Of course not.' But neither had she thought she'd be a refugee. Hedi looked around the empty hut in sudden panic. 'I don't want to leave! I just want to stay here, in this hut with you two. It's where I belong,' she said fretfully. 'I'm sad to go. Does it show how pathetic I am, that I want to stay here?' She was close to tears.

'It's not the hut that's making you sad,' Renate said.

'It's the end of *everything*,' Hedi said, letting the tears fall. She was so unhappy. She decided she'd say yes to Ursula's offer. She wanted the older woman to say she couldn't bear for them to be parted because she'd become like a daughter to her.

But Ursula didn't repeat the suggestion. Maybe she already regretted the offer. The truth was, at times, most times, they drove each other crazy and there was no saying what Karl would think about the arrangement.

Ursula said firmly, as if she was following Hedi's train of thought. 'Magda will take good care of you, you know that. You will have a good life with a suitable husband and a family of your very own. All this will pass and be forgotten.'

Hedi didn't believe her.

Renate began to speak, but Ursula spoke over her, 'Take it from me, Hedi, I am right.'

'Yes, I forgot that about you, that you are always right,' Hedi grumbled and Renate laughed.

Ursula put her arm around Hedi's shoulders. 'Come here. Listen to me. We have survived. We should be proud of that.'

Hedi didn't feel particularly proud of it. She wondered what that meant for the ones that didn't survive. Were they meant, in the afterlife, to feel ashamed? It seemed in her experience to be a matter of chance whether a person lived or died. Take Lena. She had made the best of it, living on her wits and bartering her body for chocolate and a mattress, but she'd died in the filth on the floor like the most wretched and compliant of inmates.

'Goodbye, hut,' Ursula said.

There was nothing left to do but follow them out for the last time. Hedi lingered behind in the doorway. She looked at the planks and the grimy window. Her tears had passed and she felt resigned. She was leaving for an uncertain future. But what alternative was there except to carry on? There was nothing she could do about anything.

She would never forget that feeling of helplessness. It was branded into her very soul, for good or bad.

37

HARRY

BELSEN, MAY 21ST

Harry tried not to think of Hedi. He threw himself into his last few jobs before they left the camp for good.

As each of the huts in Camp One was cleared for the final time, they were burnt to the ground. As they burned, the huts gave off a thick plume of acrid black smoke that lingered densely over the camp. It smelled of evil.

On 21 May there was a final ceremony planned for the last hut in Camp One, which was taking place amidst much pomp and fanfare. It had been decided by Harry's superiors that the destruction of the very last hut should be commemorated in some fine and fitting way. There were to be speeches, and it was compulsory for all military personnel to attend. To ensure this, they were given time off specially for the occasion.

'Once the speeches have finished, we're going to turn on the flamethrowers, my boy,' the colonel in charge explained, in words that smelled of brandy.

He'd sought Harry out personally, seeming to be under the impression that carrying out this gesture of revenge would help Harry out of his depression.

'Yes, sir.' Harry had stared at him blankly, sick to his soul. Life was empty, futile. War was futile. There would be other dictators, new Hitlers – these human threats were as numerous as lice.

He felt a weariness deep in his soul. His nights were long and sleepless. His brain kept him awake, jabbering to him, introducing him to a succession of faces he recognised, too many to count, some intact and some blown apart, of all the people he had failed to save. His conscience reminded him of how the deaths in the camp had continued relentlessly after their arrival. It berated him over his upbeat letters home which had encouraged Arthur by giving him a false impression of what the trenches were really like.

Defeated, he lay awake going over sections of his student medical book to distract himself, remembering each malaise in alphabetical order, testing himself.

Harry and Bill had been tasked with organising the construction of a display stand in front of the last hut, on which they pinned a poster of Hitler, flanked by swastikas and Iron Cross flags.

It was felt to generally be symbolic to have this closing ceremony with the tableau of the enemy, and the colonel wanted it recorded for posterity.

Harry did as he was ordered. When they'd finished, he stared at the images with loathing. The poster of Hitler was flapping in the breeze.

'I'm not sure this is a good idea,' Bill said, scratching the back of his neck and standing back critically from the platform that they had constructed. He stared up at the poster. 'It's too victorious, don't you agree?'

'I wish it was Hitler himself. I'd have gladly burned him up with a flamethrower,' Harry said bitterly. He looked at the display with a jaundiced eye. He was wondering whether Hedi would turn up to witness the fanfare.

The colonel expected that the remaining internees would be jubilant, delighted to celebrate this wholehearted destruction; he imagined they would have some kind of party with loud hurrahs, and hats would be thrown into the air. He was keen for as many internees as possible to attend.

Harry wasn't sure it was going to turn out like that. Maybe the crowd of onlookers would live up to his expectations. Maybe they wouldn't. There was no knowing. He'd prided himself on being a good judge of character once. Now he knew that character was not fixed. It was malleable and it depended on circumstances. Being civilised wasn't inherent in any man. It was a luxury of the fortunate.

He wanted the ceremony to be over with. He wanted the pain to pass. He wanted to go home, throw himself into his old life again, live decently for Arthur's sake. In time he would forget Hedi, the smooth feel of her sun-tanned skin, her bright, intelligent eyes, the flush of colour along her cheekbones. Most of all he wanted to forget the unfocused look of despair he'd seen in her eyes when he'd told her about his brother by the gate to the field.

She'd told him their relationship was impossible now.

He should have realised that himself, probably from the start. *No fraternising.* Rules were there for a reason.

But he loved her because of that first evening they drove into the horror camp. Safe from the battlefields, he had found a new hell: the nightmarish smell and the silence of the hopeless, starving crowd of skeletal zombies stumbling towards the car on the brink of death had horrified him.

Stifling a scream, he had felt his sanity leave him.

But then her eyes met his, and she'd torn off the birch branch and thrown it to him, giving him a hero's welcome in this godless place.

He had seen God shining through her eyes that evening. It had given him strength.

'Hedi,' he said hoarsely, and he choked back a sob.

'Take it easy, old pal,' Bill said, alarmed. 'Hang on. We won't be here much longer. We're nearly done.'

At four o'clock that afternoon, Harry was standing in a guard of honour. The new garrison commander was making a speech about how the British had never sullied the Union flag by flying it at Belsen.

Harry wasn't listening. He was scanning the crowd for Hedi.

His heart leaped as he saw her in her gold shoes, her dark hair lavish and unruly. She was with a smartly dressed woman, the woman who had forgotten her name. The woman was looking at him with dark hooded eyes, but Hedi hadn't seen him. He willed her to look at him.

All her attention was directed towards the poster of Hitler, and the swastikas. He carried on staring at her, expecting her to feel the intense pull of his gaze, but as a few minutes went by he had a sudden burst of insight – it wasn't that she hadn't seen him, it was that she was deliberately ignoring him.

She was standing stiffly, immobile, and he could tell by the tension in her shoulders what an effort it was taking her not to look at him. He felt a grim exultation at their shared pain, their last emotional connection.

The Union flag was raised. It fluttered listlessly in their direction as the 113rd Light Anti-aircraft Regiment fired a salute to the dead. The onlookers flinched at the noise.

Then the colonels got into the Bren Carrier and aimed the flamethrowers at the last hut still standing in Camp One. There was a throaty roar of heat. It ignited instantly, enveloped in flames. The onlookers were silent and the only noise was the deafening *rat tat tat* destruction of the collapsing timbers enveloped in the flames, like sticks dragging along railings. Out of the raging flames spewed black smoke. It was eye-wateringly thick and choking and blowing straight at them. He blinked his stinging eyes and lost sight of Hedi.

Hitler's image and the swastikas flared brightly for a moment, and died, reduced to flakes of black ash that floated on the air.

Under the dark, toxic cloud of destruction the band played a rousing rendition of 'God save the King'.

The Union flag was lowered again.

And that was that.

38

HEDI
SWEDEN, LATE MAY 1945

Days later, Hedi and Magda were on the Red Cross train, travelling across northern Germany to the port of Lübeck. Hedi was looking out of the window at the widespread destruction. It grieved her. It was impossible to imagine these towns could ever be rebuilt.

'You're quiet, Hedi,' Magda said, nudging her. 'You haven't said a word since we left. It's not like you.'

'What do you expect me to say? It's different for you, you're going to see your sister.' Hedi rested her head against the window. The wheels rattled on the rails, bumping her head gently against the glass. The regular rhythm stuck in her mind. *Sauerkraut mit wurst, Sauerkraut mit wurst.* 'What if Eva doesn't like me?'

'Is that what you're worrying about?'

Hedi shrugged. If she started talking about what was worrying her, she would never stop. It would be an endless flow of troubles and tears.

'She will love you,' Magda said, 'in the same way that I love you, let me assure you of that.'

'You don't know that she will,' Hedi said, turning up her

collar for comfort, but it wasn't in the hope of further reassurance, it was more of an intellectual argument. Magda couldn't possibly know whether Eva would love her, or not. 'She might be jealous and resentful. You're introducing her to a replacement sister – me. You'd mislaid the first one, so, hey, it doesn't matter, I've found another one, she will do instead. Now you have a spare.'

Magda frowned and fidgeted awkwardly in her seat. She was still frail and sitting was uncomfortable for her. 'It wasn't like that at all.'

'Truly, it was. You told me I could be your sister. You didn't say you'd like to have me as a friend because you liked my character.'

'Of course I liked your character! It's more of a compliment to want you as a sister rather than a friend, surely you can see that. Being a sister is a most wonderful relationship in the world. It's a compliment!'

Hedi's breath clouded the window and she wrote her name in the condensation: *Hedi Fischer*. She stared at it gloomily.

She was no longer Hedi Fischer, because she had taken Magda's name to keep up the pretence that they were a family. She was Hedi Klein. This Red Cross mission was meant for sick people who were being quarantined in a sanatorium until they'd recovered. There was nothing wrong with her, and she was here under completely false pretences. Once they'd recovered, they would be put in a refugee camp surrounded by barbed wire. That was the bleak outlook for Hedi Klein.

Magda, for all that she was recovering, was still weak from her illness and a couple of months in a sanatorium would restore her to good health. She had everything to look forward to.

Me, what have I got to look forward to? Hedi wondered.

'I don't know what's wrong with you,' Magda said sadly. 'Nothing I do can please you.'

'So stop trying,' Hedi replied. She saw Magda's eyes fill with tears and she was instantly sorry. She grabbed her friend's hand and it lay inert and delicate in hers. 'Forgive me, please, I didn't mean it. I'm not angry because of you, it's just that I miss Harry. Don't say anything – I know that I'll get over him and that it will soon all be in the past, but right now I'm angry and sad and I can't help it for the moment. I'm not going to cry, so don't be nice about it. It suits me better to be angry with you.'

Magda cringed like a sea anemone that had curled up in defence. Hedi apologised, sorry she'd hurt her. 'I've been with two strong women, you see, who teased me mercilessly. I'd forgotten how...' Her voice tailed off.

Magda said sadly, 'I understand.' She closed her eyes.

Her understanding made Hedi annoyed all over again. Truly, it was impossible to know how Magda had survived the camp.

The rhythm of the train continued its litany of *sauerkraut mit wurst*; Hedi closed her eyes too, and pretended to sleep.

Once they reached the port of Lübeck, they disembarked from the train and joined a disorganised queue to wait their turn to be steam-bathed and fumigated by the Swedish authorities.

The steam caused panic, but eventually, order was restored, and as they queued, for all that Magda said she had forgiven Hedi, she was very quiet. She nursed her bruised feelings, one thin shoulder raised protectively against her cheek, averting her face to hide her tears.

Hedi hated herself. She had ruined Magda's enjoyment and anticipation. She had said the wrong thing. In her new life in Sweden, she was going to think hard about every word before she spoke it. She would examine it carefully like fake currency before handing an opinion over.

She told Magda about her resolution to change her ways.

'You say a lot of hurtful things,' Magda pointed out.

'I know, I'm an animal,' Hedi replied regretfully.

'You're a bull in a china shop.'

'A bull, yes. Whereas you, you're more like a mouse. It is very easy for a bull to hurt a mouse by accident.'

'Or deliberately, if it so chooses.'

'Yes, that's true.' Hedi was suddenly desperate to change the subject. She looked at the relief workers in charge of the queue. 'One thing I've noticed about these Swedes, they don't smile much, have you noticed?'

'Maybe it's out of respect. They know what we've been through.'

'The Tommies knew what we'd been through. After all, they were in there with us, but nevertheless, they were very easy-going, don't you think? I miss that.'

Magda made a non-committal noise that might have been agreement or disagreement.

'It's just an observation,' Hedi said.

Scrubbed, cleaned and fumigated, they were on the ferry across to Helsinborg.

Hedi watched her homeland shrink in the distance. She could always go back, she told herself. This had been her own choice, to come with Magda. Nobody had forced her.

She held her hair away from her face, tasted the salty air on her lips. She stared at the waves and felt the throb of the engines vibrate through her feet.

She thought of Harry at the ceremony for the burning of the last hut. She had seen him before he'd seen her and the first thing she had noticed was how old and tired he'd got in the space of a few days. And yet he was all superficial brightness, too, from his bright red hair to the buttons of his tunic and the gleam of his belt, right down to – she stifled a lustful groan – *to his boots*, she told herself firmly.

Magda had recovered her good humour and she was excited at the thought of being reunited with Eva.

'What does she look like?' Hedi asked.

'She's fair and very chatty. She likes dolls. She wants to be a nurse. She did this funny thing once and pulled the leg off her doll so she could mend it. It was attached by a hook with a rubber band and as she pulled it the rubber band snapped, and my father pretended to take it to the hospital and he spent all evening in his study trying to replace the rubber band with a new one with my mother's crocheting hook. It was so funny!'

'So funny!' Hedi repeated, laughing, and she went back to looking at the sea.

39

HARRY

BEAR CAVE, AUGUST 1945

After Belsen, Harry returned quietly to Bear Cave. He got out at the railway station and held the door open for an elderly man who was getting on the train.

Structurally, at least, Bear Cave had emerged from the war unscathed, but it all looked strange to him. A cool breeze was drifting over from the estuary. It smelled briny, and a noisy crow flew overhead, throwing its shadow on yellow irises that flared bright by the bullrushes. Sheep grumbled incessantly on the hillside like the officers' in the mess after a briefing.

Harry walked into the house with his kitbag over his shoulder and found his mother in the kitchen, peeling potatoes.

She looked at him in astonishment. 'Harry? Is it you?' she asked, as if she couldn't believe the evidence of her own eyes, and then she dropped the potato and the knife and burst into tears. 'I was thinking of you just now,' she said, 'and here you are.'

She was flushed and healthy from country air. Her hair was in a net, and she pulled it off quickly and fluffed her red curls. She had lost a little weight because of the rationing, he noticed.

'Have you eaten?' she asked him.

'No,' he said, and he realised how hungry he was.

She made him a cold roast pork sandwich and added salad from the garden and tomatoes from the greenhouse. The smell of those tomatoes took him straight back to innocence. He wanted to talk about Arthur but at the same time, he didn't want to upset her.

'Your father is going to be surprised,' she said, taking off her apron. 'He's proud of you, you know. The way he talks about you... We saw a film in the cinema that Richard Dimbleby made at Belsen, and even if they played the situation up a little, it was still the most dreadful thing to see.'

Harry stopped chewing and looked up at her. 'They didn't have to play it up,' he said.

She saw his expression and she came and stood behind him, stroking his hair. 'My poor boy,' she said softly. 'No, I can see that. It must have been awful for you.'

'I fell in love with a German girl in the camp,' he said. He had meant it to come out matter-of-factly, but his voice juddered as if he couldn't get enough air in his lungs to say the words.

Her hand moved from his head and she came to sit at the table opposite him. Her face was still as she tried to absorb this information. 'A guard?' she asked cautiously.

'No, an internee. Her father was an intellectual. He thought Nazism was ridiculous.'

'He was jailed for that?'

'He was murdered for that.'

She poured herself a cup of tea out of the brown teapot and topped up Harry's cup, adding milk, undertaking each mundane action with a consideration that it didn't warrant. She picked up her teaspoon, put it back on the saucer again with a clatter and got to the point. 'Harry, I know you,' she said.

'You've known me all my life,' he said drily.

'If it was of no consequence, you wouldn't have mentioned it.'

Harry was silent.

His mother's steady green eyes rested on him and she gave a faint smile. 'You told me you fell in love with her,' she said, resting her warm hand over his. 'So, I'm asking you this. Why isn't she here with you? Where is she?'

Where was she?

That was the question.

The Red Cross team in Belsen had no record of a Hedi Fischer being transported, not to Sweden or to anywhere else.

By November, Harry was back in London, working in St Thomas's Hospital. He had just finished his rounds when a strong desire for a strawberry milkshake came over him. Actually, desire wasn't the word. It hit him like a craving. He could see it now, pale pink in the glass, with two striped paper straws emerging from the bubbles resting against the rim. He could smell it, that sweet, fake strawberry milkshake smell.

He hurried up to the canteen and asked if they could make him one.

'I'm afraid not,' the server said, 'but there's a milk bar down the road. Turn right out of the main entrance and you can't miss it.'

Harry wrapped up against the cold, bemused. It started to sleet as he hurried to the milk bar. It was Ovaltine weather but he wanted a milkshake. He had to have it. It was imperative.

The milk bar was thin and narrow, empty of customers. One wall was lined with some kind of brown reflective material to give the illusion of space. A wireless was on in the background, and a newscaster was reporting something or other in sober tones. Harry sat on the middle stool and caught the eye of the waitress behind the counter. Middle-aged, with sandy hair, she was so short she could barely see over it. 'What will you have?'

'A strawberry milkshake, please,' he said. 'A large one.'

The making of the strawberry milkshake involved a lot of mechanical noise from some large milkshake contraption that the woman operated, but the drink, when she put it in front of him, was just as he'd imagined, frothy and pale pink. The smell was heavenly.

He drank it quickly, half listening to the radio commentator talking, when to his astonishment he heard a familiar voice saying in German-accented English, 'I am indeed grateful to the Swedish people for their diligent hospitality.'

'And do you intend to make your home in Sweden now?'

The wireless was suddenly silent; Harry listened to dead air. 'Could you turn the volume up, please?' he asked the waitress sharply.

But it wasn't the volume that was at fault. Hedi was still working out her reply.

'I really have nowhere else to go,' she replied over the airwaves.

'Yes, you do!' Harry said to the radio.

'Who—' began the waitress.

'Be quiet!' Harry said, banging his fist on the counter.

It was over. The interviewer concluded the report on the plight of German refugees, brought to listeners from Uppsala, Sweden.

'Uppsala,' Harry said. 'That's where she is.' He laughed aloud, and tipped the waitress, apologising for his behaviour. 'I've found her!'

40

THEA

PRESENT DAY

'How weird is that?' Thea said to Hedi from the stone bench in the church porch in Bear Cave, 'that Harry got that craving for a strawberry milkshake.'

'Indeed.' Hedi nodded, resting her hands on her lap.

'I mean it seems to be, kind of...' Thea wasn't really sure what it seemed to be. *Wouldn't it be helpful*, she thought, *if our lives were always signposted as clearly as that, taking all the guesswork out of them?* 'What happened after that?'

'Harry came to Uppsala. And he brought me back with him, and we were married here, in this very church.'

'Wow! And then you honeymooned in the George III Hotel.'

'*Eksectly!*'

'We really should go there before we leave. I'd love to see it.'

Hedi got to her feet and Thea followed her out to the churchyard.

An elderly woman was putting flowers on a grave. She straightened cautiously and looked at them with interest. 'Old age,' she explained. 'I'm ninety-seven, you know. I'm going to keep going until I'm a hundred. I want a telegram from the Queen.'

'Good plan,' Thea said encouragingly, hoping the woman's positive attitude would rub off on Hedi.

'I know you,' Hedi said. 'You used to live at the end of the row of white cottages.'

'I still do. I know you too. Not the face, but the voice. You married Harry Lewis.'

Hedi laughed with delight. 'That is correct.'

'How is he?'

'He died this year.'

'Only this year? You're lucky, having him this good long time. I lost Jim in 1975. And is this your granddaughter?'

'Thea.'

'Well! Look at you! You've got your grandfather's hair and no mistake. And his mother's, too. I remember when this one,' she tapped Hedi on the shoulder, 'came to Bear Cave with Harry that first time. Harry's mother wanted us to rally round and give them a warm welcome at the station. I can't say it was easy, I'll admit, because we were very fond of Arthur. But you looked so frightened, Hedi, when you got off that train, and Harry was so protective that our hearts went out to you.'

'Myra!' Hedi said suddenly. 'That's your name! Myra and Jim.'

'That's it! Fancy you remembering!'

'I have done a lot of remembering these past few weeks,' Hedi said.

'You know where I live, so don't be strangers,' Myra said.

'*Myra...*' Hedi marvelled as they walked back to The Hideaway.

They walked down the track in and out of sunshine striped by the woods.

'I'd like a cup of tea,' Hedi said as they passed Thea's parked car.

'Me too. Who's that?' Thea raised her sunglasses. She could see the shadowy figure of a woman sitting on the doorstep with a small silver wheelie case next to her. She recognised the case. 'It's Maggie!' she cried in disbelief.

Hearing their voices, the woman got to her feet. She was wearing a tiered denim dress. Her dark, wavy hair was flowing over her shoulders. 'Hey!' she called, waving to them.

'Oh!' Hedi clutched Thea in shock. She gave a wavering cry, a combination of joy and pain at seeing her daughter for the first time in thirty-three years.

Maggie kicked off her wedges, ran towards them, and held out her arms to Hedi.

Hedi, that stalwart who had lived through so much, fell into them, sobbing.

'I knew you hadn't gone far because the car was here,' Maggie said, 'so I thought I'd wait.'

'It's so good to see you.' Thea smiled, and took a deep breath, wanting to absorb it all. She suddenly felt intensely, happily alive. The smell of grass, the rush of the distant water, the sound of birdsong, the warmth of the sun, and a sight she never thought she'd see: her mother and grandmother clasped in each other's arms.

Maggie looked at her over Hedi's shoulder. Her eyes were bright with tears.

Early evening, the three of them were sitting on the very edge of the wooden jetty, dangling their feet in the clear, swirling water, feeling the pull of the tide. The sky was turquoise, the sun was smudged with cloud. The hotel glowed white, casting its sun-bleached reflection across the water towards them.

'And you two do this every night, you sit here drinking wine and watching the sunset?' Maggie asked, amused.

'Pretty much,' Thea said.

'And what do you do in the daytime?'

Thea and Hedi told her about the fair, the donkey rides, the walk to the lakes.

Maggie listened, amused. 'You did all the things we used to do when I was young,' she commented, tilting her head to look at her mother.

Hedi returned her gaze and lifted her chin. 'All the good things, at least,' she said.

Maggie sighed and stroked her mother's arm. 'You know, I've been thinking about my childhood a lot since Harry died. You and he were good parents.' She made the admission in a small voice, as if she half-hoped Hedi wouldn't hear.

'Pah!' Hedi said crossly, waving a dismissive hand. 'Don't say that.'

'No, I mean it,' Maggie persisted. 'I didn't appreciate stability – what you and Harry had. But I do now. You and he, you held it together, you know? You could have fallen apart under the strain of your past, but you didn't. I understand that now. You gave me a good childhood, a child's childhood.'

The breeze blew Maggie's dark hair and she held it back from her face and stared at her feet tinted green in the water. Without looking at her mother, Maggie took a shuddering breath and went on hesitantly, 'I never felt I could get close to you, Hedi. You always acted as if your life was perfect. I understand why you were like that, now, of course I do, and I know how much you must have suffered, but that day we argued, I just wanted you to understand how very unhappy I was. But you were so angry, as if I was ruining our perfect happiness and I couldn't take it any more. I'd made a mess of my life and I couldn't carry on pretending life was wonderful. It was too hard.'

Thea glanced anxiously at Hedi and saw her pinching her fingers against her mouth, as if she was locking her words in tight.

Say something, please make it right, Thea willed her. She could see the effort it had taken Maggie to come here, and the risk she was taking now in being honest.

'You wanted us to be close,' Hedi said softly at last, her voice trembling.

'Like you are with Thea. I wanted us to have that.'

Thea looked across the water at the hotel in the distance with its fluttering flags. It looked bright and unattainable, but it wasn't, not really. It was just a bridge away. *The things we learn from our parents*, she thought. *Like when you argue with someone, it's all over and you have to run for your life.* But she'd found through Hedi that it didn't have to be like that; irritations ebbed and flowed, you just had to live with them, wait them out.

Thea felt an unexpected surge of joy, as if this was something she and Hedi had discovered together. 'Me too,' she said to Maggie.

'Yeah? You and I, we used to have that closeness, didn't we?' Maggie said wistfully. 'If I hadn't moved to New York, we would still have it.'

Thea smiled at her. *It's fine*, she almost said, but sitting here on the warm wooden planks under the clear blue sky, talking openly, she said instead, 'It's true. I've missed you. I didn't want you to go. I felt kind of abandoned, which is ridiculous, really. New York's not even that far away.' She lifted her legs out of the water. A strand of green weed had caught round her pale ankle. It looked beautiful.

Maggie leaned over and nudged Thea's bare shoulder affectionately. Thea nudged her back.

'I'm so glad I came. I've missed you, too.' Maggie picked up her wine and pointed towards the ice-white hotel with her glass. 'I'm staying over there tonight. I wasn't sure how things would go between us, but just in case, I booked a family room. Let's have dinner there together, shall we? Stay the night?'

Thea leaned forward to glance at Hedi, wondering if she

was ready to go back to the place where she and Harry had spent their honeymoon. She caught her eye and raised her eyebrows in a query: *how do you feel about it?*

Hedi's grey eyes were bright with happiness. She nodded in agreement. 'Yes. Let's go tonight and celebrate.'

41

THEA

They took it in turns to use the bath under the window, but Hedi insisted on going first. 'You see, it will take me longer to get ready,' she said grandly, 'and I want to look my best.'

She bathed quickly, put on Harry's plaid dressing gown, wrapped a towel around her head and called to them, 'Come in my room now.'

As Thea went in, Hedi was studying herself closely in the mirror. 'I don't look so bad for an old lady,' she said. She turned to look at them hopefully. 'It's true, isn't it?'

'Absolutely.'

'You haven't changed,' Maggie said. 'Your hair is white, that's all.'

Hedi took the towel off and huffed her displeasure. 'Ach! Too late to do anything about that now,' she said. 'Yours is still dark, Magda.'

'Magda?' Thea said in surprise. 'I'd forgotten you were Magda.'

'Magda Hilary,' Maggie said with a laugh, rolling her eyes. 'Hedi, seriously, what were you thinking!'

Hedi smiled gently and turned to her daughter and put her

hands on Maggie's head as if giving her a blessing. 'They were the two women who shone the light of hope over me in the camp. Those names will protect you from the darkness and keep you safe.'

For a long moment, the two women looked at each other with renewed love and understanding.

'Ah. Well, in that case...'

Hedi began towelling her hair dry and Maggie said, 'Clairol. That's the reason my hair's still dark. Do you want me to blow-dry your hair?'

Hedi's face lit up. 'Yes please! And my cheeks, you have anything for them, like a panstick? I have caught the sun.'

Thea sat on the edge of the bed. 'I've got some foundation you can use. You just have to blend it a bit, with a sponge.' Seeing Hedi's alarmed expression, she said, 'I can do your make-up if you like, after Maggie's finished styling your hair.'

'Truly?'

'Yes, sure.'

While Hedi chose what to wear, Thea showered quickly, got dressed and brought a chair from the kitchen for Hedi to sit on.

Maggie blow-dried her hair smooth and had a shower while Thea applied foundation, eyeliner, eyeshadow, mascara, and finally Hedi's red lipstick, with a brush for staying power. 'Are you ready for the reveal?'

Hedi nodded. 'Yes, I'm ready.'

Thea unhooked the mirror from the back of the door and propped it in front of Hedi. 'There! What do you think?'

Hedi nodded again, and smoothed her palms down her hair, cupping them under her chin. She smiled at her reflection, and her face lifted with joy. 'Hello!' she said seductively. Then she was serious again. 'I need my watches.'

'Here they are,' Thea said, picking them up from the bedside table.

'Thank you.' Hedi laid them on the palm of her hand and looked up at Thea with a smile. 'This one of my father's, you must give to Adam. He will enjoy the inscription.'

'Hedi, I really can't—'

'Pah! It doesn't mean you have to marry him. Just give it to him is all I ask. What else should I take tonight?'

'Your handbag, your lipstick. Wash bag. Nightgown. We haven't got far to go if we forget anything,' Thea pointed out.

Their table in the restaurant was by the window. The winding estuary was spread out beneath them, calm and golden in the mellow evening light.

Thea looked at the woods on the other side. 'Look over there, you can see The Hideaway,' she said.

'Cute little place, isn't it,' Maggie said dreamily. 'How did you find it? Airbnb?'

Thea played with the stem of the wine glass. 'Just chance, really. I saw a sign saying it was to let.'

'That was lucky.'

'Yeah.'

Hedi was engrossed in reading the menu. She called the waiter over a couple of times to check on things that she wasn't sure about, and she took the same amount of time studying the wine list. She looked very poised, very elegant, with the same endearing dignity she had shown when they went to Claridge's. Then she consulted Maggie about her choice.

Thea kept out of it. She didn't mind which wine she drank, as long as it came quickly. She rested her chin on her fist and looked at them as they discussed it in depth. It was funny, they were really very similar. She wondered if they were aware of it. She guessed she took after Harry, with her red hair and green eyes, but there must also be some of them in her too. It was a nice feeling.

These few weeks with Hedi, she had learned a lot about her grandparents, and about her great-grandparents and the reception committee at the station. *You're in love with her? So where is she?*

Today she'd seen the war memorial with her great-uncle's name on it.

Harry was Hedi's true home.

She felt she was piecing things together, and that the whole amounted to something bigger than she knew.

Thea thought of Adam, and his gentleness when she'd told him about the meeting with her father.

Adam had given her space to work out their relationship. She knew she'd hurt him, and she felt sick at the thought.

I love him.

Hedi closed the wine list with a snap – she had made her decision.

Maggie talked about New York, and about nothing much at all. They were, Thea realised, happy in each other's company, enjoying each other, enjoying themselves.

Their starters arrived and the wine came, and the low lights shone on their glasses.

Hedi, too, was on sparkling form, and as they ate and drank, the sun sank slowly in the sky to the west, turning the water rose-red. 'See how romantic it is, Thea?' Hedi said, spreading her arm expansively towards the window.

Through the window, the countryside was dark. The three of them looked beautiful, reflected in the glass. There was another image there too, one she couldn't quite make out.

'A little glass of port each, to finish?'

Afterwards, they went up to their room. They gave Hedi the king-sized bed. Maggie had the single and Thea pulled out the sofa bed and collapsed on it, giggling.

They lay awake in the light of the reading lamp, talking until the early hours, buzzing with too much excitement to sleep. *Do you remember...?*

Time compressed.

'Shall I switch the light off?' Maggie asked.

'Good night!'

'Good night.'

'Good night.'

In the silence, Thea felt herself drifting off to sleep.

Sometime before dawn, Thea was woken by the sound of someone moving around. She saw Hedi silhouetted in the bathroom door for a moment, before the door shut, and then she sunk back into sleep.

Maggie woke her roughly next morning, her voice high and tight. 'Thea, Hedi's gone.'

Disorientated and struggling to wake, Thea pushed the bed cover back and mumbled, 'She'll be on the jetty.'

'No, I mean – she's...'

Thea squinted up at her mother and sat up, realising something was very wrong. 'What?'

'Come here.' Maggie was standing by the side of the bed looking down at Hedi.

During the night, Hedi had brushed her hair and reapplied her lipstick. She looked perfect – very still, very beautiful, and very happy.

Thea felt a deep sadness lodge like a block in her chest. She felt the pressure of her tears. They weren't for Hedi, they were for herself. She was going to miss her desperately.

'She's with Harry, now,' she said.

EPILOGUE

The day after Hedi's funeral in St Catherine's Church in Bear Cave, Thea and Maggie were in The Hideaway packing up their things. It didn't take long. They laid the two blue-and-white striped deckchairs on the back seat of the car and put Hedi's tan-leather suitcases on top.

They took a last walk through the long, lush grass of the meadow, down to the jetty. It was a beautiful day. The estuary shone like silver.

'I've been thinking... maybe we should buy this place?' Maggie said. 'We could come here every summer, all of us.'

Thea glanced at her, hooking a strand of copper hair behind her ear. 'Yeah? Who's the "all"?'

'Me and my man, you and Adam. Your kids.'

'*My* kids?'

'No, *yours*, plural. Don't look at me like that. Adam told me you both want a family.'

'Hah. It was why I left him. He wanted everything I didn't want.'

'Back then you didn't,' Maggie said. 'It's different now

though, isn't it? Come on, I'm your mother. I notice these things.'

Thea glanced at her. With the sunlight on her face, she looked her age. *We've grown up*, Thea thought.

Those hours in the still of the night listening to Hedi's voice drifting over the sound of the water, they were what she'd left her: not a history lesson, but the story of her and Harry's love. 'What makes you say that?'

'First of all, he came to the funeral of someone he didn't know, because you loved her. And secondly, when I saw the two of you together, I knew.'

Thea tucked her hands in the pockets of her shorts. 'Is that so.'

Maggie laughed. 'I know what you're doing. Don't come all Harry on me,' she said.

'Or else what?' Thea replied, tossing her hair over her shoulder. 'You'll push me into the estuary?'

'Might do.'

'You first!' She grabbed her mother and they mock-wrestled on the jetty. It ended in a hug. They swayed in each other's arms for a few moments, then dried their eyes and headed back to the car.

A LETTER FROM NORMA

Dear Reader,

I hope you have enjoyed the story of *The Hideaway*. If you want to keep up to date with my latest releases, just sign up at the following link. I can promise that your email address will never be shared and you can unsubscribe at any time.

www.bookouture.com/norma-curtis

This is a story about home. It's hard to define home, but you know it when you're there. It's hard to define love, as well. Even if you can tick off certain qualities, love amounts to a person's pure, real, individual self with its virtues and flaws; the whole of them. When someone keeps part of themselves secret, you can't love the whole of them because you don't really know them.

In this story, spending time in the wild peace of Bear Cave, Thea and Hedi show an open-heartedness, and a willingness to share and to listen to each other. As the bond between them grows, despite their differences, ultimately they both find their hearts' desires in entirely different ways. Some of the circumstances in this story are the worst that mankind can inflict. One thing I've become sure of during the writing and researching is that no matter where and what trials we go through, the human spirit has the capacity to shine through the deepest darkness: remaining steadfast, bright, hopeful, untarnished, and full of love.

It's always fabulous to hear from my readers – please feel free to get in touch directly on my Facebook page, or through Twitter, Instagram, Goodreads or my website. If you have a moment, and if you enjoyed *The Hideaway,* a review would be very much appreciated. I'd dearly love to hear what you thought, and positive reviews help to get our stories out to more people.

Warmest wishes,

Norma Curtis

www.normacurtisauthor.com

 facebook.com/ncurtisbooks
twitter.com/TheNormaCurtis

ACKNOWLEDGEMENTS

This is a work of imagination. To find out more about Belsen after the liberation, I recommend *After Daybreak* by Ben Shephard. The letter written by Lt Colonel Gonin was supplied by Mark Liddell for the Bergen Belsen website: www. bergenbelsen.co.uk

I've been obsessed by this story so I want to give thanks and apologies for talking about it non-stop while writing it. Elaine, Pat and William, Erika and Mike, Johnny and Louise, Edward, my son Joe and my husband Paul know the story as well as I do by now, and put up with me, and didn't once tell me to shut up, which says it all about their loveliness and tolerance.

My ace agent Judith Murdoch, on reading the first few chapters, kept me going by giving the most succinct and insightful advice, perfect in its brevity: 'Love it. Ditch the first chapter.' Sorted!

Kathryn Taussig my brilliant editor pointed out where the characterisation needed more work, and once again, thank you so much, because the story is much better for it.

Writing is a lonely business, but the bit that come after it is a collaboration, which I love. A book is nothing without a reader and readers can never really know the overwhelming gratitude writers feel when you 'get' it: booklovers, bloggers, reviewers, agents and publishers alike. You're the other half – no, let's be real – three quarters of the equation, because let's face it, it's a pointless journey without you.

Printed in Great Britain
by Amazon

84830627R00171